REUNITED WITH HIS LONG-LOST CINDERELLA

Laura Martin

MILLS & BOON

First Published in Great Britain 2019
by Mills & Boon, an imprint of HarperCollins*Publishers*
1 London Bridge Street, London, SE1 9GF

© 2019 Laura Martin

ISBN: 978-0-263-26905-5

MIX
Paper from
responsible sources
FSC˚ C007454

This book is produced from independently certified FSC™ paper
to ensure responsible forest management.
For more information visit www.harpercollins.co.uk/green.

Printed and bound in Spain
by CPI, Barcelona

Laura Martin writes historical romances with an adventurous undercurrent. When not writing she spends her time working as a doctor in Cambridgeshire, where she lives with her husband. In her spare moments Laura loves to lose herself in a book, and has been known to read from cover to cover in a single day when the story is particularly gripping. She also loves to travel—especially to visit historical sites and far-flung shores.

For Sophie—your friendship is one of the greatest gifts.

Chapter One

Surveying the ballroom, Ben found himself unable to believe he was actually there. Dressed in the finest evening wear, cravat tight around his neck and jacket tailored to precision across his broad shoulders, the son of a land steward was attending one of the most exclusive balls in London.

'I'm not sure these masks conceal our identities,' George Fitzgerald said from his position beside him.

Ben shrugged. 'I'm not sure they're meant to.'

They were standing at the perimeter of the Scotsworths' ballroom for what Ben had been informed was an annual masquerade ball. The women were dressed in flamboyant outfits and their masks were nearly all elaborately decorated. Many of the men had gone for a more subtle and less time-consuming approach of wearing their normal evening jackets and adding simple black or single-coloured masks that covered their eyes. Ben's was black, but did have a rather annoying feather protruding from one edge that every so often would flop in his face and tickle his forehead.

'Why are we here?' Fitzgerald asked shrewdly.

Since arriving in London three weeks ago they'd attended a number of balls and soirées, even once braving the unknown world of the opera, but tonight was the first night Ben had actually insisted they accept an invitation.

'To enjoy the magic of a masquerade ball,' Ben said with a straight face.

Fitzgerald laughed, clapped his friend on the shoulders and shook his head. 'Keep your secrets for now, Crawford—one day I'll find out what you've been up to these last few weeks.'

Ben grinned, but it was almost entirely forced. He hoped no one would find out quite how pathetic he'd been in the weeks since their arrival in London. When Sam Robertson, the third member of their little group, had suggested the trip back to their homeland from Australia, Ben had quickly agreed. He had told his friends that he wanted to see his family again, at least what was left of it. Eighteen years ago, he'd left his father and younger brother behind in a sleepy Essex village. For four years he hadn't heard a word from them—the post never arrived for prisoners held on the hulk ships on the Thames or during the eight-month voyage to Australia. Only once he was working as a convict worker for the late Mr Fitzgerald the elder did he receive a tattered and torn envelope.

His father had written every month and must have paid considerable sums of money to ensure his communications were loaded on to the ships heading for Australia. Ben had no doubt most of these letters had never left England and could be found disintegrating at the bottom of the Thames. But one had got through—one conscientious and kind pensioner guard had taken Ben's father's money and promised to do his best to place the letter in Ben's hand and, nearly a year later, he did just that.

Ever since Ben had kept in contact with his father from the other side of the world. Of course, he was keen to return to Essex and see the old man again and would do so as soon as his father returned from his poorly timed trip to Yorkshire. His father was an estate manager and as such at the whim of the Earl he worked for, but soon he would be back home in Essex and Ben would see him for the first time since the age of twelve. However, the other reason for his agreeing to the trip to England he wasn't even sure would appear tonight. For three weeks, he'd haunted the ballrooms of London, hoping to catch a glimpse of the girl he'd left behind all those years ago.

Francesca. She was a woman now, of course. A woman who'd probably hadn't thought of him much at all these last eighteen years. When he'd landed in England he'd made some discreet enquiries and found she'd been married and recently widowed. He was beginning to understand those in mourning didn't socialise as much as the rest of the lords and ladies and had started to despair of ever setting eyes on her, but tonight he'd heard a rumour Francesca would be in attendance to chaperon her younger sister.

So here he was, waiting eagerly for a glimpse of the woman who probably didn't even remember him.

He surveyed the ballroom again and for an instant it felt as though his heart stopped in his chest. There she was, unmistakable despite the mask and the eighteen years since he'd last seen her. Dressed in muted greys and violets, colours he was informed signalled the period of half-mourning, Lady Francesca Somersham still cut a striking figure. She was older than most of the debutantes, but having been married and widowed in the years since Ben had last seen her that was hardly surprising. Despite being almost thirty she still turned heads and Ben saw two gentlemen start in her direction as soon as they noticed her entrance into the ballroom.

This was what he'd been waiting for the past three weeks, but now she was here in the same room as him he was unsure of what he wanted next.

'Enough,' he murmured to himself. He wasn't the lowly son of a steward any more. Over the years since he'd finished his sentence Ben had worked hard and taken risks, most of which had paid off, meaning he was now a very successful Australian landowner. There was no need to skulk about watching from a distance. Today he would talk to the woman he had been dreaming about for the past eighteen years despite his best efforts to forget her.

Quickly, he weaved through the crowds, ignoring the appraising looks from the masked debutantes. Fitzgerald was correct, these flimsy masks didn't do much to conceal the face, but he was largely unknown and as such was a man of interest.

'Mr Crawford,' a pretty young woman murmured in his ear as he moved past her. 'We really must find some time to spend together.'

Ben grimaced, but quickly turned it into a smile. Since arriving in London he had made the acquaintance of a number of women, mostly widows or those with husbands happy to turn a blind eye. He'd danced with them, talked to them, but never anything more despite their sometimes quite obvious offering of themselves. Ben might have a reputation as a man the ladies could not resist, but nothing was going to jeopardise his getting close to Lady Somersham, especially not a meaningless fling.

'I await that moment with anticipation,' he said, planting a fleeting kiss on the young lady's hand, but moving on quickly, using the press of people to his advantage and weaving a path away from Mrs Templeton's inviting eyes.

Suddenly she was in front of him and for a moment Ben felt the breath being sucked out of his lungs. She was beautiful. Gone was the gangly-legged, freckle-nosed girl he'd played with throughout his childhood and in her place was a woman of poise and grace. Ben took a moment to study her hair, sleek and tamed into a complicated bun at the back of her head. When they were children Francesca's hair had always been an uncontrollable mess, frizzy and wild and more often than not flying behind her as she did something dangerous at great speed. He felt a sharp stab of desire deep inside him and fought to keep himself under control.

'Lady Somersham,' Ben said, pausing a couple of feet in front of her and bowing formally. He might have been brought up the son of a steward, but he was a great imitator and just a couple of days in London society had led to him being able to replicate the gestures and customs perfectly.

Francesca turned to him and, even though nearly every other part of her had changed, she fixed the same mischievous blue eyes on him that he remembered from childhood.

'You have me at a disadvantage,' she said after studying him for a few seconds.

'Isn't that the point of masquerade balls?' Ben asked. 'To conjure an atmosphere of mystery and allow you to creep into dark corners with an unknown admirer.'

'Perhaps to conjure an atmosphere of mystery…' Lady Somersham conceded. 'But I'm sure my mother always told me to keep away from strange men and dark corners.'

'And do you always take your mother's advice?'

There was that smile, just a hint of the impish grin he remembered from childhood.

'She likes to think I do.'

'Lady Somersham,' a deep voice boomed, causing heads to turn in their direction even half a ballroom away. This was the overweight, red-faced man who was destined to be Francesca's next husband if rumours were to be believed.

'You're not meant to tell anyone who I am, Lord Huntley,' Francesca said, turning to face the man. She smiled at him, too, but Ben could tell this was forced, a mere upturning of the corners of her mouth with no glimmer of pleasure in her eyes.

'Nonsense. Everyone knows who everyone else is. Damn ridiculous idea if you ask me, all this prancing around in masks.'

Ben noted Lord Huntley had not deigned to don a mask of his own, leaving his red-rimmed and wrinkled eyes unadorned. Surely a mask would be of benefit to this man, even if it were purely to draw one's eyes away from his generous jowls.

'I think it is rather fun,' Lady Somersham said and Ben had to wonder if she was just saying it to be perverse. Lord Huntley made him want to run in the opposite direction and he never had the awful prospect of having to one day be intimate with the man hanging over him.

'Where's your father?' Lord Huntley barked, looking around as if Lord Pottersdown might be hiding behind a pot plant or marble statue.

'I'm not sure,' Francesca said, her eyes involuntarily flicking towards the doors that led into the ballroom. The gaming tables, no doubt. These past few weeks Ben had learned a lot about Francesca's life just by listening to gossip. The ballrooms and dinner parties were rife with it and, although there was a lot of exaggeration and a few things that were clearly completely fabricated, you could glean some very interesting things if you filtered the dross out.

'Losing more of the family fortune,' Lord Huntley snorted derisively. He'd come to the same conclusion, it would seem.

Ben saw Francesca's cheeks redden under the delicate rim of the mask and for an instant got the urge to manhandle Lord Huntley outside and send him on his way for embarrassing her. Then he remembered that he wasn't her protector, he wasn't anything to her, just a man who had once been a boy she'd known. A man she might not even remember.

'Wait here,' Lord Huntley commanded. 'I'll

go fetch him. We need to pin down the agreement for this marriage.'

'I'm still in mourning…' Francesca said, but Lord Huntley had already departed, heading through the ballroom with his rotund belly leading the way. Not once had he even acknowledged Ben's presence.

'I'm sorry,' Francesca said, trying to fight the tears that were building in her eyes. 'That was incredibly rude, you shouldn't have had to see that.'

Really she was apologising for Lord Huntley, the oaf of a man who would one day soon be her husband. The thought made her feel peculiarly queasy.

Trying to focus on the man in front of her, she couldn't help but notice how he was the opposite of Lord Huntley, being tall and broad shouldered. She could tell there wasn't a single ounce of fat on him even through the thick material of his jacket. His skin didn't have that sickly grey tone to it, instead there was an unusual but healthy tan on his cheeks as if he spent a large portion of his day outdoors.

'The best way to avoid discussing your marriage to him tonight is to not be here when he returns with your father,' the masked stranger said nonchalantly. Feeling her eyes widen, Francesca tried not to splutter. Most people would politely ignore the exchange they had just witnessed, but it seemed the man in front of her wasn't about to do that. 'Come on,' he said, a gleam in his eye that Francesca found vaguely familiar.

Offering her his arm, he flashed her a rather seductive smile as she hesitated. What she should do was wait here for her father and the man who was angling to become her future husband and listen while they discussed her like a horse for sale. Not that she had any illusions that her presence would make any difference to the outcome. She had absolutely no say in whom she married or when, both her father and Lord Huntley had made that perfectly clear.

Feeling rebellious, she took the man's arm and allowed him to lead her through the ballroom away from the direction Lord Huntley had disappeared in.

'You must tell me your name,' she said, peeking up at him from under a carefully curled ringlet that framed her face. Her hair was difficult to tame, but her current maid was an expert at fighting the curly locks into submission and making her look presentable. As long as she didn't go out in the rain.

'Ben,' he offered.

'I can't call you Ben.'

He shrugged, smiled at her and said, 'That's all you're getting. This is a night of mystery after all.'

'Well, Ben,' she said, leaning in so no one would overhear her being quite so familiar with a stranger, 'now you've removed me from having to discuss my future with Lord Huntley, what do you propose?' She felt reckless, giddy. Francesca knew it was because she was near to hysteria, her emotions running high at the thought of having her whole future decided for her and a marriage to another man she did not like.

'We could go somewhere a little more private,' he suggested, that glint in his eyes again. Francesca trawled back through her memory, trying to place the man. They must have been introduced before, otherwise why was she finding him quite so peculiarly familiar? It was a sensation rather than anything else, a feeling rooted deep inside that she knew the man escorting her around the ballroom.

'I don't think that's wise,' she said. Years earlier she might have been tempted. He was a good-looking man and she was desperate for a dash of romance, of adventure. But she wasn't a giddy debutante any longer, far from it. She was a widow in her late twenties, and that meant she'd had plenty of time to realise that liaisons with strange men in dark corners never ended well for anyone, no matter how tempting it might be.

She glanced at the man beside her and saw he wasn't surprised by her answer. Francesca knew many widows had a looser sense of what was acceptable behaviour and what wasn't, with many of them engaging in discreet affairs, but she wasn't one of them. Her father had made it clear when she'd been forced to go back and live with her parents that she would keep her reputation pristine and pure so no potential suitors would be put off. It had worked, she thought glumly, she wasn't even out of her mourning period for her first husband, Lord Somersham, and she was practically betrothed to Lord Huntley.

'Then dance with me,' he said, pausing before changing direction to the dance floor.

'I'm not meant to dance,' she said, gesturing to her half-mourning clothes.

'Surely this world is more fun if you do one or two things you're not supposed to.'

She felt herself hesitate. She would love to dance, especially with this man by her side. He was strong and young and had a vitality about him that neither her late husband or Lord Huntley had ever exuded. Imagining what it would be like to be swept around the ballroom in his strong arms, she felt herself nodding.

Trying to close her mind off to all the whispers and disapproval that would be coming her way, she allowed her companion to lead her into position. Francesca loved to dance, she'd loved to dance since she was small and had often roped in anyone and everyone to be her dance partner. Governesses, maids, the grouchy old butler, even Ben Crawford, the skinny little son of the estate manager she'd spent her summers playing with.

Ben. She looked up quickly, but the idea was absurd. This man, this charming and confident and attractive man in front of her, was not Ben Crawford. The son of an estate manager wouldn't be so self-assured in a room full of lord and ladies, and of course he couldn't be here, he'd been transported to Australia all those years ago. Francesca suppressed the feelings of sadness that always threatened to overtake her when she thought about her childhood friend. Now wasn't the time.

She glanced at her companion again. He *did* have something about him though, the same cheeky smile and the same mischief in his eyes. Perhaps that was why she thought the man looked familiar. He reminded her of the friend she had lost all those years ago.

The music started and Francesca felt the pleasure diffuse through her body. She felt as though she was walking on the clouds whenever she danced, loving the instinctive way her body would move to the music. Her partner was both well practised and a natural dancer, twirling her round effortlessly and all the time managing to keep those lively eyes fixed on her and a smile on his lips.

For a second Francesca wondered what it would be like to have a man like this slip into her bed every night, to feel his hard body on top of hers and his soft lips on her skin. Instinctively she knew he would not be selfish in taking his pleasure and a blush spread across her cheeks as she imagined an unending night of passion with him.

'Now you must tell me what has put such a beautiful blush on your cheeks,' he murmured, leaning in close so his breath tickled her ear.

Francesca was unable to speak, knowing her voice would come out as a muted squeak if she opened her mouth.

'Perhaps you're thinking of moving in just

a little closer,' he whispered, pressing his hand ever so slightly harder into the small of her back. Against her better judgement Francesca allowed her body to press closer in to his, feeling the delightful swish of his legs against hers as they danced. 'Or perhaps you're imagining how it might feel if I kissed you here,' he said, raising a finger and oh-so-briefly trailing it across the skin of her neck.

Now she was imagining that.

'Or here.' His fingers had dropped to her collarbone.

Guiltily Francesca glanced around the ballroom to see if anyone had seen the entirely inappropriate touch she'd just allowed. No doubt the gossips were already judging her for dancing when she was still in half-mourning. Even though this was a masquerade ball she was under no illusion that no one knew who she was.

Thankfully the music stopped and she felt the spell break. Her companion stepped away and bowed formally, only the sparkling of his eyes hinting at the inappropriate way he'd acted during their dance.

'I hear the private terrace is a beautifully secluded spot,' he murmured in her ear as he escorted her back to the perimeter of the ballroom. 'If you go out of the ballroom, through the third door on the left and into the library, there are glass doors leading on to the private terrace there.'

He bowed again, then placed a kiss on her gloved hand before disappearing off into the crowd.

Francesca watched him go. There was no way she could join him on this private terrace, no matter how much her body wanted her to. Sighing, she turned back to look for her father and Lord Huntley. It had been a wonderful interlude with her mysterious gentlemen, but nothing more. She had to focus on coming to terms with marrying yet another man she did not particularly like.

Chapter Two

Ben watched her from a distance. It was strange seeing the girl he'd once known so well gliding across the ballroom, turning heads as she went. When Ben had been sentenced to transportation at the age of twelve, Francesca had only been ten. Of course she'd been pretty, but in a wild and unfettered sort of way. Now she was elegant and there was no hint of the girl who used to race him across the fields on horseback or dare him to boost her to the top of a hay bale.

It was unsettling, talking to her again. For eighteen years he'd been unable to rid his thoughts of her. They'd only been children when he'd been arrested for stealing jewellery from her father, children who had spent every moment they could together. He'd loved her then, in the pure and innocent way one child could love another, and he knew she had felt the same way. Even when her father had cajoled and threatened her, trying to stop her from speaking up in Ben's defence, she'd spoken out, she'd protested his innocence. It hadn't changed the outcome—no one had been willing to listen to a ten-year-old girl when her father—a viscount, no less—had told a different story, but she'd defied her father all the same. All for him.

He'd thought about her a lot over the last eighteen years, wondering how her life had turned out, wondering if she would still be living in luxury as he toiled away under the heat of the Australian sun. Once he'd finished his sentence and little by little bought up parcels of land, turning them into one of the largest farms in Australia, he thought he might move on, but still he couldn't forget about her.

Ben wasn't so naïve to think she even remembered him from all those years ago. She'd probably never thought of the young boy who she had played so closely with, but he hadn't been able to forget her. So when his friend Sam Robertson voiced his plan to come to England Ben had been eager to accompany him. He wanted to look her in the eye, to see if she was the same girl he'd known all those years ago or if she had been irretrievably changed by almost a lifetime of socialising and living by the rules of the *ton*.

Never had he expected to feel quite so unsettled at seeing her again, though. She was beautiful, but Ben had known a lot of beautiful women throughout his life and none of them seemed to have this power, this pull. Throughout their dance all he could think of was sweeping her away from the ballroom, finding some deserted room and depositing her on something soft so he could spend the night exploring her body.

That was why he'd had to leave her, to give himself time to dampen down the entirely inappropriate desire he was feeling. Of course he knew she wouldn't take him up on the offer to meet him on the private terrace, but he'd been unable to resist making the suggestion, just in case she decided to surprise him.

He didn't know what he wanted from Francesca now. All his thoughts had been on seeing her again, looking into the eyes of the girl he'd once cared for so much—he hadn't thought past that initial meeting.

Liar, the little voice in his head called out. He knew exactly what he wanted from her. He wanted to gather her in his arms and sweep her away somewhere private. Somewhere he could spend the whole night becoming acquainted with the most beautiful woman in the ballroom.

'Who was that?' George Fitzgerald asked as he found his friend at the edge of the ballroom.

'A very pretty lady,' Ben said with a grin. 'Can you do me a favour?'

'Of course.'

'She's finding it a little difficult to slip away from her companions. Could you go tell her that her father is a little worse for wear and is recovering in the library, show her the way—it's the third door on the left out of the ballroom. Do it discreetly, but not too discreetly.'

'You have a trick for everything, don't you?' Fitzgerald said, clapping his friend on the shoulder and making his way through the crowd.

Ben watched for a moment then slipped away, wanting to get to the library before Francesca. It would be private and, if they were caught alone together, no doubt a scandal would ensue, but it was unlikely that would happen. Everyone was too caught up in the revelry of the masquerade ball to notice their absence. He just wanted a few minutes alone with her, a few minutes to find out what her life had been like in the years he'd been away. If he could just hear she was happy, then maybe that would be enough for him. Maybe.

* * *

'Lady Somersham,' a deep voice said quietly in her ear, 'I'm sorry to interrupt.'

It was another gentleman she did not know, with a simple black mask and a serious expression. She turned to him, smiling apologetically at the two older ladies she had been conversing with.

'Your father is a little indisposed. He has been asking for you.' The message was delivered quietly, discreetly, but Francesca knew her two companions had heard every word. Feeling her heart sink, she summoned a breezy smile.

'Please excuse me, ladies,' she said.

'He is in the library. Shall I escort you?'

Francesca shook her head. As much as she would like someone to share the burden of her father with, a stranger at a ball was not the right person. Not for the first time she wished her mother could be persuaded to go out in public, but she hadn't attended a ball or event since Francesca's debut ten years earlier.

'Thank you, it is a kind offer, but I should see to my father on my own,' she said, feeling a ball of dread in the pit of her stomach. Over the past few months, during the time she'd been only in half-mourning and allowed again at social events, her father had been *indisposed* four times. On one particularly cringeworthy occasion she'd had to enlist the help of a very kind footman to carry him out to their waiting carriage.

The messenger let go of her arm as they exited the ballroom and motioned to one of the doors on the left. 'He's in there,' he said, before bowing, then disappearing back into the ballroom.

Francesca took a moment to compose herself before she reached for the handle. Sometimes her father was a violent drunk, but most of the time he was emotional and downcast when he'd imbibed too much. In some respects this was worse than when he lashed out. Seeing the man who had been the backbone of her family throughout her childhood break down and cry was hard to bear.

'Father,' she said, adopting a sunny smile as she entered the room. Everything was quiet and dark, not even a solitary candle flickered. Francesca paused, listening for some sign that her father was in the room, conscious or not. There wasn't even the hint of heavy breathing.

'You came.' A deep voice startled her from the direction of the glass doors on the other side of the room. As she peered through the darkness she could see they were open and a man was silhouetted in them.

'What are you doing here?'

'This is where we agreed to meet,' he said.

Remembering the offer of a quiet liaison on the private terrace, Francesca frowned.

'I'm looking for my father.'

'There's no one else here.'

She swallowed, feeling her mouth go dry as she realised what a precarious position she was in. If she was sensible, she should feel scared, being alone with an unknown man. If she was sensible, she would turn around and head out of the door and back to the ball.

Against every ounce of common sense she possessed, she stepped further into the room.

'You tricked me,' she said, trying to catch a glimpse of the man's face. She should know everyone who was invited to this ball. Her social circle was surprisingly small, with the same hundred or so people being invited to each ball or social event. It was irritating her that she couldn't place him, not even when she felt as though she knew him.

'I gave you the freedom from your own conscience to come and meet me.'

'You tricked me.'

She saw him grin in the darkness, a flash of white teeth, and heard a low chuckle.

'Maybe a little,' he conceded. 'But you wanted to come. It was just the consequences of being found here with me you wanted to avoid.' The confidence emanated from every bit of him—he was certainly a man who knew what he wanted.

'Goodnight,' she said firmly. Part of her *had* wanted to come, to be wooed by a mysterious stranger and feel that giddy freedom of being irresponsible for one evening, but she wouldn't ever tell him that.

He crossed the room quickly, moving from the glass doors to her side in six steps, placing his hand over hers as she reached for the door handle.

'Five minutes,' he said. 'Give me five minutes and I promise you won't regret it.'

'I know I would regret it,' Francesca murmured, feeling the heat of his hand through her glove. He was standing close and she could sense the power of his body, but she didn't feel scared at all. If she'd been cornered by anyone else she would be panicking, wondering if they would allow her to leave with her virtue unscathed, but she felt peculiarly at ease with the man standing next to her, as if she'd known him her whole life.

'Who are you?' she asked.

'Spend five minutes with me and I'll tell you,' he said, his voice no more than a whisper in her ear.

Indecisively she glanced down at where her hand still rested on the door handle. What she should do was walk out of the room and never think of this man ever again. She should seek out her future husband and ensure he agreed the details of their marriage with her father and saved her family from financial ruin.

Slowly she turned around so she was standing chest to chest with the mysterious man.

'Five minutes?' she asked.

'Five minutes.'

'Then you'll remove the mask.'

'You have my word.'

Francesca stepped to the side and around her companion, leading the way to the glass doors and the terrace beyond.

The terrace was lit by the flickering light of a few lanterns, placed at strategic intervals along the stone balustrade. It was cold, icily so, but the air was crisp and dry and the sky clear. All in all, quite a romantic spot her mysterious companion had chosen.

'Why am I here?' she asked as he came to join her, resting his arms on the stone balustrade and looking out over the garden.

'Only you can answer that question,' he said.

Thoughts of her impending marriage to a man she could not stand, of wanting to escape, to have one night, even one moment of freedom, of adventure, flashed through her mind.

'Why did you ask me here?' she corrected herself.

'I wanted to be with you. Alone. Away from the other guests.'

'Why?' she asked, her mouth feeling peculiarly dry and the question coming out as a little breathless rush.

He looked at her with a half-smile on his lips and she felt all the air being sucked from her body.

'Can a man not want to get to know a woman away from the prying eyes of society?'

Francesca laughed. 'No.'

He shrugged. It seems a foolish rule that two people can never be alone together. How do you ever truly get to know someone?'

'You don't.'

'How do you know if you want to further an acquaintance then?' he asked.

'You don't,' she said, knowing that she was

standing too close when she could feel the warmth of his body next to hers, but was unable to step away. Never was she this reckless, but there was something both charismatic and comforting about the man standing next to her. He made her feel like she wanted to fall into his arms, feel his lips on hers *and* spill her deepest secrets.

Francesca felt a wave of sadness wash over her. This would never be her life. She was moving straight from one unhappy marriage to another which promised to be even worse. There was no room for a reckless liaison, no room for this sort of scandalous behaviour. Normally that didn't bother her, but tonight she wanted more than she could ever have.

'How then am I supposed to find out what's caused the sadness in your eyes?' he asked.

Glancing up at him in surprise, she wondered if she were that transparent that he could read her every emotion. 'I am in mourning,' she said, wondering if he would accept that as an explanation.

'Did you love your late husband very much?'

She thought of his indifference to her, his belittling. His downright contempt as the years went on and she didn't produce the heir he was so eager for.

'No,' she said.

'Then why the sadness?'

Looking up again, she wondered why she felt so easy in his company. He was a stranger, a man too confident and self-assured for his own good, a man she should feel wary around, but she didn't. Instead she felt as though she wanted to spill her deepest, darkest secrets.

'Surely a woman like you has everything?' he pressed. 'Wealth, family, servants to do your every bidding.'

'Appearances can be deceptive,' Francesca said. It had been a long time since either her late husband or her family had been wealthy. All the money had been squandered in failed investments and business ventures years ago. Living back at her parents' house had been depressing after being mistress of her own household, but it was made even worse when she'd explored the empty rooms which had once been filled with luxurious items of furniture, when she'd seen all the servants except the cook and two maids had been dismissed.

'So you're sad because your family is not as wealthy as it once was?' he asked.

Francesca laughed. If only it were that simple. She wouldn't mind the lack of money, not if she had some say in her life to come. Seven years she'd endured her first marriage. It had been loveless and, although Lord Somersham had never been violent towards her over the years, his resentment had grown as she failed month after month to get pregnant. He'd belittled her, bullied her, made her hate him more with each passing day. She doubted her next marriage would be any better.

'I don't want money,' she said quietly, 'I don't care about fine dresses or jewels. I don't even need a lady's maid to dress my hair and press my clothes.'

'What do you want?' he asked the question quietly, turning his masked face towards hers.

'I want to be happy. To not be forced into another awful marriage, to have the freedom to choose who I spend my time with and how.'

'You're a widow, surely you have some degree of choice in the matter.'

'No.' She didn't, not if she wanted to save her family from complete ruin. She didn't want to spill all the sordid family secrets, no one needed to know that her father owed various lenders debts the size of a small country.

The man next to her looked pensive, as if some great debate was raging inside him.

'I should be getting back,' she said.

'No.' He caught her hand, holding it softly. 'I'm sorry, I should not have pried.'

'Will you remove your mask?' she asked, peering up at him.

'I don't think you really want me to.'

'Of course I do, I feel as though I know you...'

'Wouldn't it be better to have this one mystery, this one little bit of magic?' He looked down at her with dark eyes and she had the overwhelming urge to ask him to hold her. She thought there might be something rather comforting about having those strong arms wrapped around her.

He was still holding her hand, she realised, and his thumb was tracing lazy circles across the satin of her glove. She wondered if he could feel the places the material had thinned and almost frayed—it had been a very long time since she'd had money to spend on new clothes.

'Can you hear the music?' he asked.

With her head tilted a little to one side she listened. Coming from the open doors of the ballroom on the other side of the house were the first soft notes of a waltz.

'Lady Somersham, will you grant me this dance?'

Placing her hand in his, she felt her body

tremble as he pulled her in closer and began to dance. He was a natural, guiding her expertly around the small space with just the pressure of his hand in the small of her back. As the music swelled Francesca felt her worries begin to melt away until it was just her, her mysterious companion and the waltz.

After a minute she glanced up at him and found him gazing down at her. Again she felt that bubble of recognition, this time deeper inside. She felt at ease with this man, she realised, as if they had been lifelong friends.

'I feel as though I know you, Ben,' she said, seeing the easy way he smiled and wondering if she was being foolish. Surely there was no way he could be the Ben of her childhood, the boy she had loved and lost all those years ago. He'd been transported to Australia, all because of her father's actions, and he probably hadn't even survived, let alone made his way back here eighteen years later.

He spun her, pulling her in closer at the same time, and for a moment they were chest to chest. She could feel his heart beating through his jacket. And then the music moved on, he relaxed his grip and they were a more decorous few inches apart again.

'Perhaps you do,' he said. 'Or perhaps I just remind you of someone.'

'Ben…' she said quietly, all the time looking up into his eyes for some sort of confirmation.

He smiled at her, but his expression gave nothing else away and she sighed. She was probably just being fanciful. For so many years she'd longed to see her friend again, longed to hear that he'd survived, that he'd thrived despite what her father had done to him.

As the music slowed Francesca wished this moment could last for ever. While she was dancing there was no Lord Huntley pushing for marriage, no debts, no family falling apart under the strain. It was just her, the strong arms around her waist and the music. Soon it would be back to reality, back to everything she wished to escape.

'Thank you, Lady Somersham,' her companion said, bowing and placing a kiss on her gloved hand. 'It has been a pleasure to make your acquaintance tonight.'

It was over. The fantasy was shattering and soon it would be as if this moment had been nothing but a dream.

'Your mask?' she asked, already knowing he would refuse.

He hesitated and she saw the internal debate

raging as a flicker of uncertainty in his eyes. 'Best not. Best to have one little mystery in life,' he said.

She didn't protest. Maybe he was right. Maybe it was better not knowing who he was, that way she could make up her own story.

He raised his hand as if he was going to stroke her cheek, but his fingers paused less than an inch from her face. Instead he smiled sadly.

'Goodbye, Frannie,' he said and then he was gone.

Francesca felt the air being sucked from her lungs as her whole world tilted. *Frannie*—only one person had ever called her that.

'Ben,' she called out, but already he had gone. Disappeared into the darkness like a phantom.

Chapter Three

'Why the long face?' Sam Robertson asked as he came and sat down in one of the comfortable armchairs in Lady Winston's drawing room alongside Ben and George Fitzgerald. Lady Winston was Fitzgerald's aunt and their hostess for their time in London. She'd been kind to them, accepting Ben and Sam as if they were her relatives alongside Fitzgerald.

Up until recently Ben had been staying at her town house alongside his two friends, but he'd craved a little privacy to conduct his affairs and had rented a set of rooms nearby. He did, however, drop in most days for at least one meal, or to partake in the particularly delicious mid-afternoon snack Lady Winston insisted on serving. The platter of cakes, scones and biscuits was enough to keep ten men going for an entire day, but between the three of them they often devoured it completely.

'Do you remember when we were on the transport ship together,' Ben said after loading his plate up with biscuits and cakes, 'I told you about the girl I used to be friends with? The one whose father falsely accused me of stealing the family jewellery.'

'Of course. Francesca, wasn't it?'

He nodded. 'I saw her last night. I talked to her.'

'Did she remember who you were?' Robertson asked.

'It was at the masquerade. I was wearing a mask.'

'The lady in violet,' Fitzgerald said, understanding dawning in his eyes, 'The one you asked me to escort to the library.'

'Did you want her to remember you?' Robertson asked.

Ben shrugged, trying to act nonchalant. Of course he'd wanted her to remember him. For so long she'd haunted his dreams and, if he was completely honest, she was one of the main reasons prompting his return to England. He had needed to see she was happy, that her father hadn't completely ruined her life as well.

Now he had set eyes on her again, his feelings were even more complicated. As they'd danced on the terrace the night before he had seen the recognition slowly dawning in Francesca's eyes and he'd been all ready to reveal his identity to her, but then an unfamiliar stab of uncertainty had stopped him. She was a lady, the daughter of a viscount. He might be a wealthy landowner now, but his origins still meant he was an imposter in society. What if she shunned him? He'd taken the easy way out, the coward's way, and had slipped away before she confronted him about his identity.

'Did you tell her who you were?' Fitzgerald asked.

He shook his head. 'I planned to…'

'So what happened?'

Ben shrugged. 'She probably doesn't even remember me anyway.'

'Unlikely,' Robertson said. 'Surely she'd remember the man her father had falsely arrested?'

At the end of that last summer before Ben had been arrested there was a robbery at Elmington Manor, Francesca's childhood home. A large amount of jewellery was stolen, along with some cash and other small valuables. The hue and cry was raised and the magistrate along with other upstanding men in the community began their search.

After a week a small locket had been found in Ben's possession. It had Francesca's initials on it and immediately Ben had been arrested. He'd begged his accusers to just go and ask Francesca, to confirm that she'd given him the locket as a gift, as a token of their friendship.

The magistrate refused, no doubt eager to stay in favour with Lord Pottersdown, but one day a week into his incarceration Francesca had turned up anyway. She told anyone who would listen that Ben was speaking the truth—she had given him the locket. Over and over she told the magistrate that her father had set the whole thing up, that he had framed Ben in a desperate attempt to cover his own debts. Of course, no one had listened. She was just a girl, a ten-year-old who was obviously infatuated with a common thief.

Eventually her father had arrived and dragged her away. Ben would never forget the moment the door of the county gaol closed behind her; in that moment, his heart had broken. Three months later he was sent to the hulk ships that lined the Thames and a year after that he was aboard a transportation ship to Australia.

In the eight years of his sentence and the ten

years since he'd acquired his freedom he hadn't ever been able to forget his childhood friend. He'd dreamed of coming back for her, to rescue her from her cruel father. As he'd grown older he'd let go of any thoughts of rescue, knowing that by now Francesca would be living her own life, but he'd never given up the hope that one day he might see her again.

What he hadn't expected was the attraction he'd felt for her. When he'd last seen her they'd both been children. He had loved her, there was no denying that, but in a way one friend loves another. Now he felt something much more primal, much more pressing. He desired her. Francesca was beautiful now, sleek and elegant and graceful. When they'd danced, he'd felt raw desire for the woman in his arms and it had taken all his self-control not to kiss her there and then on the terrace. Even though once they had been very close he knew it was unlikely a woman of Francesca's status would allow herself to be seduced by him.

'So you're just going to leave it?' Robertson asked, his voice a touch incredulous.

Ben shook his head. He couldn't leave it like that. He had just needed to regroup, that was all, decide what he actually wanted from Francesca before he saw her again.

'She was very pretty,' Fitzgerald said quietly. Probably the most perceptive of the three friends, George Fitzgerald had a way of seeing past the façade and getting to the heart of a problem.

'She's changed a lot,' Ben said carefully.

'And she's a widow...'

'Not that kind,' Ben said quickly. She was a respectable woman, he knew that much, and he also knew how reputation mattered to the ladies and gentlemen of society.

'Fair enough. Isn't she engaged, though?' Fitzgerald asked.

'Not yet,' he said, thinking of the boorish man he'd met fleetingly the night before. He couldn't imagine the girl he'd once known married to such an oaf and likely that was the source of sadness in her eyes. She'd said as much, with her desire for a little freedom in her choice, in her life.

'Then you have a window of opportunity, surely?' Robertson said.

'I do,' he said quietly. First he needed to work out what he wanted from Francesca—only then would he seek her out again.

Taking a deep breath, Francesca looked up at the building in front of her. It was in a de-

sirable part of London, the street lined with
trees and well-dressed men and women strolling
along the pavements arm in arm. Really,
she shouldn't be nervous.

Telling herself not to be so silly, she crossed
the road and climbed the five steps that led to
the front door. There she hesitated, not knowing
what the correct etiquette was when visiting
a gentleman's rooms.

Francesca had been an unmarried debutante
for two years, unhappily married for seven, and
then a widow for almost a year now. That made
ten years of adulthood in which she had never
visited a gentleman's rooms. Many of her contemporaries
would whisper and giggle about
their affairs, taking pleasure in sneaking off
behind their husbands' backs to meet their lovers,
but she had never done anything like that.
So she lifted the knocker and let it drop a couple
of times, all the while feeling completely
out of her depth.

'Good morning, miss,' a pretty young girl
said as she answered the door. She was dressed
in a French maid's uniform that had been popular
for a certain set of the *ton* to instruct their
maids to wear a couple of years earlier.

'I'm here to see Mr Crawford,' Francesca
said quietly, hoping no one would overhear.

'I'll see if he's in, miss, if you'd like to wait here.'

The maid indicated a spot in the hallway where a couple of chairs had been set out for waiting visitors. Francesca perched, ready to flee at the slightest sign of anyone recognising her.

Two minutes later the maid returned, almost skipping down the stairs.

'Mr Crawford will see you,' she said. 'Follow me.'

Feeling increasingly nervous with every step, she followed the young maid up two flights of stairs to the top floor of the building. There, lounging against the door frame of an open door, was Ben. Without the mask it was unmistakably him, the boy she'd called her closest friend throughout their childhood. He gave her a half-smile, full of charm, and despite her nerves Francesca felt her heart flip inside her chest.

'Lady Somersham,' he said, his voice low, 'What a pleasant surprise.' He didn't look surprised to see her, he didn't look as if anything in the world could ruffle him, especially not the mere reappearance of an old childhood friend.

'Mr Crawford,' she greeted him formally, her upbringing taking over as her mind went completely blank. She wanted to reach out, to touch his face, trace the lines with her fingers and convince herself he was really there and not just a figment of her imagination.

'I think you can call me Ben, Frannie,' he said with that roguishly charming smile. 'It's not as though we're strangers.'

He was right. They were far from strangers, but the boy she'd known had grown up into a man she didn't much recognise. A man her body was reacting to in a most inappropriate way.

'What brings you to this part of town?' he asked, still leaning against the doorframe.

With her eyes narrowing, Francesca took in his appearance. He was wearing a shirt and trousers only, no jacket and no necktie or cravat. His shirt was half-untucked and opened at the neck, revealing a hint of the bronzed skin of his chest underneath.

A moment of realisation dawned and her hand rose involuntarily to her mouth. It was the middle of the day, but that didn't mean to say he didn't have company.

'It's a bad time…' she began to say, starting to back away. How could she be so foolish? He was a grown man, a man who wasn't tied by the expectations of society like she was. She felt unexpected jealousy and quickly tried to tamper it down before it could show on her face.

'Not for me.' Ben caught her by the hand, then stepped back, motioning for her to enter his rooms first.

They were sparsely furnished with just the essentials. A small sitting room with a couple of chairs alongside a writing table and then a bedroom leading off the sitting room with a bed and wardrobe. It didn't look as though Ben had brought much of his own to personalise the space, but if the rumours were to be believed he had only recently arrived from Australia and as such probably wouldn't have much more than his clothes and a few of his dearest possessions with him.

'Would you like me to call for something to drink?' he asked, motioning for her to take one of the chairs. He perched on the windowsill, leaning casually back against the glass.

Now she was here, Francesca didn't know what to say. At the ball three nights ago when she'd realised who the mysterious man in the mask really was she'd barely been able to believe it. *Ben*, the boy she'd loved ever since she could remember. The one she'd carried in her heart all these years, never daring to hope she might see him again. And now he was here, in the flesh. All six foot of him, and he was grinning at her like they were twelve again.

'You're looking well, Frannie,' he said softly.

His words and his tone unnerved her. His voice was low and gravelly and it cut through her body and penetrated her soul. There was something about the way he looked at her that made her want to throw herself into his arms and find out just how strong the taut muscles were. Ben had aged well and barely looked his thirty years; only the faint few lines around his eyes gave away the life he'd lived already.

Self-consciously she touched her hair. Ten years ago she'd been considered a diamond of the Season. That was after hours of her maid taming and curling her hair and strapping her into beautiful dresses, but Francesca had still felt like a fraud. Then she'd been more at home in breeches and a shirt with her hair loose and streaming out behind her.

Now she was twenty-eight. Many of her friends had children the same age as she'd been when Ben was sent away. She was no longer young, no longer so smooth and polished. Years of living with a man who gradually resented her more and more had caused her to age a little. Ben, with his handsome tanned face and muscular physique, was probably used to pretty young things throwing themselves at him.

'So are you,' she said.

It was true. The boy she remembered had been all arms and legs. Tall for his age but skinny, with a cheeky grin that had been too big for his face. He'd been tanned then, too, a consequence of spending every waking hour running through the countryside.

The man in front of her bore a passing resemblance to that boy, but the changes were innumerable. He was taller now, with long legs and a broad body, no longer skinny, but a frame filled with hard muscle. His hair was still the same dark brown and his eyes a dark, deep green, but his face had changed over the years. The smile was still there, but layered behind the cheekiness was years of experience and Francesca knew instinctively it had charmed hundreds of women.

'You left the masquerade without saying anything,' she said, not knowing how to start. She could hardly come out and tell him she'd thought about him every day for the last eighteen years.

'I didn't want to embarrass you,' he said quietly.

Francesca nodded slowly, feeling the pain at

the instant reminder in their difference in circumstances. It had always haunted them, always kept them apart even as children. Again and again her father had threatened to have Ben whipped if he caught her running wild around the estate with him again. He wasn't deemed suitable company for the daughter of a viscount. Now was no different, not really. Francesca was expected to marry well again and keep herself scandal-free until then. Socialising with an ex-convict would hardly be keeping a low profile.

Lord Huntley. She'd almost forgotten about him in the heat of the moment. The man she was destined to marry as soon as her mourning period was over. He would be livid if he knew she was here. He might even call off the marriage. Even though she despised the man she *had* to marry him. Yet still she could not bring herself to leave.

'Sit down, Frannie,' he said, motioning to one of the chairs. She obeyed, glad to sink into the soft fabric. This whole encounter had drained her already and a seat was welcome while she worked out what she had wanted when she came to see Ben.

'How are you here?' she asked. There were so many things she wanted to know, so many questions she barely knew where to start.

'I took a ship from Australia,' Ben said, grinning as she rolled her eyes at him. Already she was beginning to feel more at ease.

'You know that's not what I mean.'

'I think my life story might be a little too long for you to listen to.'

'I don't need your life story,' Francesca said, leaning forward in her chair, 'Not all of it at least. Just what you've been doing for the past eighteen years.'

'This and that,' he said. 'I'm more interested in you.'

'This and that isn't a proper answer.'

'I served my sentence,' he said and Francesca noted the subtle flash of pain in his eyes as he remembered the years he must have spent toiling under the hot Australian sun. 'Then I was lucky enough to be taken in by a kind man who mentored me and showed me how to thrive in a hostile land. I had good friends and I built a life for myself out there. A good life.'

What he wasn't saying was the pain he must have felt at everything he'd left behind. His father and siblings, people who cared for him, people who loved him.

'How about you?' he asked.

'I was married,' Francesca said, wondering how to condense the last unhappy decade and a half into a few sentences. 'And now I'm a widow.' It was depressing when she said it like that. Eighteen years Ben had been gone and all she had to show for it was a dead husband she hadn't much liked and now the prospect of another marriage she was being forced into.

'My Frannie,' Ben said, slipping from his chair and kneeling in front of her. With callused fingers he reached up and stroked her cheek, and Francesca instinctively closed her eyes and sank into the caress. She didn't know this man, not how he was now, but everything about him seemed right. Her body and her heart were telling her to fall into his arms even though she'd barely exchanged a hundred words with him. 'Such sadness,' he said, 'What can I do to make you smile again?' The words were almost a whisper and conjured up thoughts of all sorts of inappropriate actions. She could almost feel his lips on her skin, his hands on her body, his legs entwined with hers. Unconsciously she leaned forward ever so slightly, catching herself at the last moment and recoiling sharply.

'I need to go,' she said, the words catching in her throat. Thoughts of Lord Huntley flooded into her mind and she had to blink away the tears. He was her future, not the man in front of her.

Lord Huntley with his wobbling jowls and mottled skin. What a contrast to Ben who was the embodiment of vigour and health. At the masquerade his eyes had seemed to penetrate to her very soul and today she felt as though his lips were teasing her, inviting her in.

'I'm sorry,' she said and stepped towards the door.

Her hand was on the doorknob when she felt a soft touch on her arm. He must have moved as quickly and silently as one of the big cats that she'd seen the previous year at an exhibition. The black panther had stalked around the tiny cage as if constantly on the lookout for prey.

'Wait,' he said. His fingers burned through the material of her dress and she felt the heat of his skin on hers. Taking a deep breath to compose herself, she turned and found Ben standing directly behind her. They were close, far too close for propriety, but she'd thrown all notions of good behaviour away when she'd knocked on a bachelor's door. Slowly she raised her chin so she was looking into his eyes.

It was a mistake. The moment her eyes met his she knew it was futile to resist. It might not be today or this week, but one day she would succumb to those eyes, to the man behind them.

'I missed you, Frannie,' he said, raising a

hand and tucking a stray strand of hair behind her ear. His fingers lingered, caressing her neck like the most intimate of lovers, and it took all her self-control not to sigh with contentment.

'I missed you, too,' she found herself admitting. She needed to get out of his rooms, needed to escape before she did something she would regret. Something that would put her whole future, the future of her entire family, in jeopardy. 'But I can't see you again.'

'Lord Huntley?' Ben asked, an amused look in his eyes.

'He wouldn't approve.'

Ben leaned in, his breath tickling her ear. 'Sometimes it feels good to be just a little bit bad, doesn't it?'

Francesca swallowed, knowing if she tried to speak her voice would come out as a series of squeaks instead of words.

'I should go,' was all she managed to repeat eventually. Ben smiled and leaned forward, kissing her cheek with a gentle brush of his lips. Francesca was mortified by the small sigh that managed to escape from her throat and knew she was turning pink.

'If you wish,' he said, his eyes never leaving hers.

Nervously she groped for the doorknob again,

her fingers slipping in her anxiety to get away. After two more attempts she had it gripped in her hand and twisted, almost falling out into the corridor. She'd hoped the spell he seemed to hold over her might break if she put a little distance between them, but it didn't seem to make any difference. With a hurried little curtsy that made her feel completely ridiculous, she scurried off down the hall, feeling his eyes on her back the entire way.

Chapter Four

Ben pummelled the punchbag, feeling the wonderful burn in his arms as the seconds ticked by. He was at the Smith-Hickory Boxing Club, a rundown boxing gymnasium close to Charing Cross. It was owned by a rugged middle-aged man called Kit Hickory, who looked as though he'd taken one too many punches in the face as a young man with a crooked nose and a marked asymmetry. It wasn't a gentleman's boxing club—Ben had been in one of those when he first arrived in London and had left after a few minutes. That sort of boxing was more prancing and pontificating than actual punching and defending.

Here he felt at home, among the working-class men, the men eager to take their frustrations out on the punchbags and their fellow patrons. Ben didn't feel uncomfortable when he attended the events of the *ton*, but it wasn't his world. This was more where he belonged.

'Lighter on your feet,' Kit Hickory called as he walked around the gym. 'Punch, punch, duck. Guard up. *Guard up!*'

The older man was shouting at the two youths fighting in a roped-off boxing ring. They were good, made better by Hickory's coaching, both destined to be local fight champions one day soon.

Turning back to his own punchbag, Ben began to punch again, feeling the tension seep from his shoulders and neck as he hit the bag over and over. He was annoyed at himself. Francesca's visit had unbalanced him and he hated to be unbalanced. These past ten years since finishing his sentence he'd strived to always be in control, to always be the one calling the shots. Frannie had challenged that.

Although he had expected to be affected by seeing his childhood friend again, he had never thought she would cause such a reaction inside him. Every waking moment he thought of her, of the graceful way she glided into the room, the way her cheeks pinkened when she was thinking something inappropriate. He had always prided himself on being in control of his emotions, on never letting anyone too close. It was a lesson he'd learned on the convict ships, to look after yourself before anyone else, and the only people he normally made exceptions for were the men who were more like brothers than friends: George Fitzgerald and Sam Robertson. Now all he could think about was making her his. Every time he looked at her he felt his body react to her. These past few nights he'd woken in a hot sweat after very erotic dreams where she'd done unspeakable things. Dreams that meant he'd had to douse himself in cold water as soon as he woke.

It wouldn't be easy, Francesca had been raised to be a dutiful wife and daughter, free from even the faintest hint of scandal. She might desire him—he'd seen that raging in her eyes during both their meetings—but she wouldn't allow that to jeopardise her duty.

Throwing a particularly hard punch, he let out a deep growl. Duty be damned. After everything they'd been through surely they deserved at least a few weeks of happiness.

'Women troubles?' Hickory asked quietly behind him.

Ben grunted. He didn't particularly want to share his deepest thoughts with the reprobate that ran the boxing club. They would likely be halfway round London within a day.

'Loosen up your shoulders,' Hickory said. 'It'll give you more power behind your punch.'

The older man moved on and Ben took a few deep breaths, trying to let the tension ease from his shoulders. He tried a few softer, experimental punches and immediately his thoughts wandered back to Francesca. The way her entire face lit up when she smiled, the light smattering of freckles over her nose that she'd had as a child and still had now, no doubt to her dismay. The soft curves of her body and the hair that he wanted to pull from its immaculate style and run his hands through as he kissed her into submission.

Then there was the sadness in her eyes, the sense that the intervening years had not been easy for her either. He found himself drawn to her, wanting to know her body and soul.

Closing his eyes, he stepped back. 'Enough,' he murmured, unwinding the strapping from his hands. This needed to stop. Somehow he needed to exorcise these thoughts, whether by fulfilling his fantasies or finding a way to move on from the woman who had haunted him for so long.

Francesca peered out from behind the curtain that covered the window of her carriage. It was hired, their family carriage having been sold many years ago, but her father had insisted on hiring one and a set of horses for the duration of the Season. *For appearances*, he'd said. Just like almost everything else they did. Their house was furnished *for appearances*. She had fine clothes *for appearances*. And they threw lavish dinner parties *for appearances*. All of it just served to make their money problems worse and Francesca was under no illusion that people didn't know quite how in debt they were.

Slouching back, she felt the despair she always had when she thought about money. Their family had once been one of the richest in England, but years of gambling, poor investments and poor judgement on her father's part had landed them in the position they were in now. Her marriage to Lord Somersham had been arranged with the idea that his wealth would trickle through to her family, but he'd ended up being just as poor a custodian for the family money as her father. The last few years of her marriage had been a familiar cycle of borrowing and the calling in of debt. When her husband had died the title had passed to some distant relative, but there had been no bequests, no tidy little allowance for his widow, meaning that once again she'd had to return home to her parents, once again a pawn in her father's quest for more money.

Sometimes she thought about refusing, thought about withdrawing from society, perhaps taking up a position as a governess or companion. She didn't want fine things, didn't particularly enjoy the continuous cycles of balls and dinner parties and nights at the opera. Then she thought of her sister, twenty-year-old Felicity, the lively, kind girl who saw everything with those huge brown eyes. She deserved a chance. And the only way she would get that chance was if Francesca married Lord Huntley.

She wasn't sure what arrangement Lord Huntley had made with her father, but she had extracted the promise from him that he would provide a decent dowry for her sister, allowing Felicity a modicum of choice about her future husband.

Trying to push the thought of another unhappy marriage from her mind, she glanced out of the window again, straightening as she saw Ben emerge from the darkened doorway. Already everything about him seemed familiar to her, his gait, his stature, even the way he turned the collar of his coat up to combat the icy temperatures.

She wasn't quite sure why she was here. It

mortified her when she thought of how she'd fled from his rooms in Gower Street, her imagination filled with images of him embracing her, kissing her, doing all the things a widowed lady shouldn't. She should have left it at that, but she found herself drawn to him, unable to leave him behind entirely, but not able to trust herself to see him face to face again.

As he passed the carriage, head bent against the cold wind, she sunk back against the seat. She'd just needed to see him again, to convince herself that it hadn't been a dream. For eighteen long years she'd agonised over his fate, imagining him a broken man, worn down by years of hard labour and then the difficult life of an ex-convict. Never had she imagined the confident and seemingly successful man that he'd turned out to be.

A few steps down the road he paused, turned quickly and in a couple of paces was back by the side of the carriage. Before Francesca had a chance to react he'd swung open the door and hopped inside.

'Lady Somersham,' he said, settling back on to the seat opposite her. 'What brings you to this part of town?'

She'd preferred it when he'd called her Frannie.

'I…' she started to say, but couldn't think of any lie convincing enough.

'It would appear that you are following me,' he said, fixing his eyes on hers and making her squirm under the intensity.

'No,' she said quickly, although that was an outright lie. She had been following him and right now she couldn't think of any other excuse as to why she might be in this part of town, peering out of her carriage just as he left whatever establishment he'd just been in.

'Boxing club,' he supplied helpfully.

'What?'

'You were wondering where I've just been.'

Feeling completely flummoxed, Francesca took a deep breath and composed herself. She was a lady, the widow of a viscount, the daughter of a viscount. Probably the future wife of an earl. All her life she'd been coached to stay calm and serene whatever the world threw at her. Surely she could do that when faced with Ben Crawford.

'I was following you,' she said slowly, giving him a half-smile as if they were conversing about something as dull as the weather.

'Couldn't keep away?' he asked.

Francesca felt her stomach drop away from her as she realised it was the truth. She hadn't been able to keep away from him. Whatever she told herself, whatever lies she concocted to cover this embarrassing little episode, she'd just wanted to see Ben one more time.

'I wanted to apologise,' she said.

'You have nothing to apologise for, Frannie.'

'For my father. What he did to you…'

'That's his sin to bear the burden of, not yours.'

'I tried everything I could,' she said quietly.

When she'd heard Ben had been arrested for theft she'd confronted her father, who had promptly slapped her so hard she'd been knocked senseless for a few seconds, then he'd bundled her into her room. For days she hadn't been allowed out, but eventually one of the maids had taken pity on her and unlocked the door. Francesca had headed straight for the county gaol and there had told anyone who would listen that Ben was innocent.

He had been accused of stealing jewellery from her family. None of it had been found in his possession, except one small locket. *Her* locket, the locket she'd given to him as a token of their friendship earlier that summer. The magistrate hadn't listened when she had tried to explain and within half an hour her father arrived to drag her off home. The last time she'd seen Ben had been through the bars of a cell.

For eighteen years she'd agonised about her part in his conviction, wondering if she'd just shouted a little louder, begged a little harder, if things would have turned out differently.

'I know, Frannie. I've never blamed you. You were just a child.'

'So were you,' she said, her eyes coming up to meet his.

As their eyes connected she felt her body react to his gaze and was reminded neither of them were children now. Francesca had images of Ben slowly undressing her, of their bodies coming together and his lips on her skin.

'Perhaps…' Ben said, but trailed off.

'Yes?'

'I know our time together is limited,' he said slowly. 'I know you have to marry Lord Huntley.'

She nodded, not wanting to be reminded of it, but knowing there was no getting away from her fate.

'Perhaps we could find a way to make the most of the weeks we have left,' he said.

'What do you propose?' she asked, hearing the slight wobble to her voice and trying to stop herself from imagining a whole host of wonderful, but not entirely respectable, pastimes.

He smiled, holding out for a long few seconds before answering. 'Eight days for eight years,' he said.

Frowning with confusion, she waited for him to explain.

'You give me eight days of your life, one for every year of my sentence.'

'And what do we do with these eight days?'

There was a mischievous glimmer in his eyes as he shrugged. 'Whatever we want.'

It sounded wonderful. Eight days to be free, to do whatever she wanted. After that she would have to accept her fate, but for just a little while she could pretend her life was on a different track. He held out his hand to seal the bargain and tentatively Francesca placed her fingers in his.

'When do we start?' she asked, trying to ignore the warmth of his hand on hers. Neither of them was wearing gloves despite the icy temperatures and it was the first time she'd felt his skin against hers. His fingers were a little rough, probably from the years of physical work, and his hand engulfed hers completely.

'Tomorrow.'

Tomorrow was as good a day as any. She had

to remember she only had a few more weeks of freedom anyway. In six weeks her year of mourning finished and then she didn't doubt her father would waste any time in arranging her marriage. She would likely be Lady Huntley within three months with no opportunity to go running after her childhood friend.

'Tomorrow,' she agreed.

Only then did he release her hand, placing it softly back in her lap. He was a man of contradictions. Physically powerful but gentle in his touch. Gone through so much suffering, but outwardly charming and jovial. And an ex-convict who could blend in at society events. He was a confusing man to be around.

'Until tomorrow,' he said, leaning over. For a moment she thought he was going to kiss her. She felt her lips part in anticipation and her heart begin hammering in her chest, but then he reached for the catch on the door, threw it open and hopped down.

'How did you know it was me in here?' she asked as he went to shut the door. 'When you came out of the boxing club?'

She didn't think he'd caught sight of her in the darkness of the interior.

'Who else would be following me?' he asked. 'I barely know anyone else in London.'

With a smile and a wink he spun on his heel, striding off down the street. As she watched him go Francesca thought she even heard him whistling a jaunty tune. Trying not to think too much about what she'd just agreed to, she leaned out and instructed the coachman to take her home. Really she should be feeling dread and regret at her agreement to his proposal— no respectable lady would agree to it—but as she searched her emotions she could only find excited anticipation.

Chapter Five

Sitting at the small writing desk in his room, Ben tried to concentrate on the letter he was supposed to be writing to the man he'd left in charge of his farms while he was away in England. He'd left detailed instructions, so detailed the stack of paper was the size of a medium-length book, with Andrew Phillips, his very capable second in command. The man was trustworthy, sensible and good-natured, but still Ben didn't feel easy about leaving him for so long. Every week he wrote the man a letter with further instructions and since being in London had received a few updates sent months before from Australia. He'd always found it difficult to trust anyone but himself, but so far it would appear Mr Phillips was doing a good job.

It was almost eleven and, unless she had changed her mind, Francesca would likely be making an appearance soon. He'd spent half the morning trying to pretend to himself he was indifferent to her and the other half wondering what had possessed him to make the silly suggestion the day before. Eight days. Eight days spent in her company. Already he could barely keep his thoughts from the gutter when his mind wandered to her—spending more time with her wasn't likely to help matters. He knew he would find it difficult to keep his hands to himself for eight days and Francesca wasn't the sort of woman who would give up her virtue to a man she would soon have to say goodbye to.

'Remember, you're in control,' he muttered to himself. That was a lie. He found her so attractive he had struggled to stop himself from kissing her the last time they'd been together. What he was worrying about was getting to know her more and then not wanting to leave. She'd made it clear soon she would be marrying Lord Huntley so he was under no illusion that they would ride off into the sunset together. Perhaps during these eight days she would irritate him and then his attraction towards her would fade. He'd never had a problem moving on from women before. His relationships were always short and fun, ending before either party had the chance to develop a lasting affection for the other. Although none of them were Francesca...

Quickly he finished the letter he was writing and tidied the desk. His rooms were always meticulously clean and tidy—probably from the years spent living on top of scores of other men. He'd got used to hiding away anything precious to him and keeping his limited living space clean despite the less-than-sanitary conditions.

Crossing over to the window, he peered out, catching a glimpse of the muted grey skirt of one of Francesca's mourning dresses. It seemed a strange tradition to him, wearing dull colours to signify your distress at the death of a loved one. Or in Francesca's case the death of a husband it would appear she didn't like very much at all.

He waited, listening as the maid answered the door downstairs. Already he'd instructed her to allow Francesca up and after a few seconds he heard quiet footfalls on the stairs.

There was a pause, as if she were hesitating, wondering if this was really such a good idea after all, then a knock on his door.

'Good morning,' he said, summoning his sunniest smile. She looked nervous.

'Good morning,' she said, her voice much more composed than her expression.

'Come in, sit down. Would you like a drink?'

'Yes, please,' she said, exhaling, some of the tension seeping from her at the normality of the offer. Perhaps she'd imagined him ravishing her as soon as she walked through the door. The thought had crossed his mind, but he wasn't that immoral. He might want to lead her to the bedroom and strip off her ugly grey dress to see the woman underneath, but he knew that couldn't happen and he would be foolish to spend too much time torturing himself.

'I'll go fetch some tea.'

He left her standing nervously looking around for somewhere to sit. As he descended the stairs he took his time, trying to figure out what he wanted from the woman upstairs in his rooms. They had been so close as children, the best of friends, and Ben had known every last thing about Francesca. Now he knew hardly anything about her. He wanted to get an insight into her life, to see the woman she'd become. Of course, he wanted more than that. He'd wanted more from the moment he'd set eyes on her again, but he would have to tread carefully. Francesca was a lady, and a woman with a strong sense of right and wrong to boot.

He might want to strip her off and join her on the bed, but he had to be wary of where their relationship might lead them. In a few weeks she would be engaged to be married again and he was under no illusion that at that time he would have to fade into the background.

Quickly he tasked the maid with making some tea, asking for it to be brought up when it was ready. His rooms were part of a small establishment, there were only three other residents. They all shared the services of Hetty, the quiet but efficient maid who cleaned twice a week, showed in visitors and kept the place running smoothly. It was ideal for him, peaceful and discreet with no rules about who could visit. Some of the places he'd looked at had a strictly men-only policy which seemed absurd to him—the freedom to have whichever visitors he chose was one of the reasons he'd moved out from Lady Winston's house.

Taking the stairs two at a time, he made his way back to his rooms, wondering what exactly he was going to do with Lady Somersham for the eight days he'd asked of her.

Running her fingers nervously across the back of one of the chairs, Francesca watched the door close behind Ben. Tea would be wonderfully fortifying, and perhaps if she just sat down her legs might stop shaking.

She was under no illusion as to why she was so nervous. Ben hadn't come out and said the words as such, but she had made discreet enquiries and knew a little about his reputation, and she suspected he had certain ideas about them becoming reacquainted. The idea that their friendship might not be just an emotional one had both thrilled and petrified her. The only man she'd ever been intimate with was her husband. There had been no affairs, no lovers, and towards the end of her marriage—thankfully—hardly any intimacy even with Lord Somersham. Not that she was complaining, her husband had been all about duty. He'd taken his pleasure without a single thought for the woman underneath him.

For her part, she couldn't believe she was considering having an affair with this man she barely knew—but she was. The past few days, Ben had invaded her every thought and she knew that for once she was going to be reckless. Soon her life would be about duty and responsibility again, but for a few short weeks she was going to enjoy getting to know Ben again. Even if the thought gave her butterflies in her stomach.

Nervously she moved around the room. She felt unsure of herself and a little inadequate. Ben was probably used to women who knew what they were doing in the bedroom, women who knew how to please a man of the world. She knew nothing of the sort; each and every one of her encounters with her late husband had been disappointing, and she knew she was in no position to compete with the women Ben would normally spend his time.

Perhaps she should just show him she understood what they wanted from one another. Of course, she wanted to get to know the man Ben had become, but perhaps she should show him she was ready to become an active participant in a more physical relationship as well?

The idea thrilled her and Francesca felt herself blushing. She wasn't supposed to be so scandalous, so reckless, but she was beginning to understand the excitement in the eyes of her friends who had conducted affairs over the years. With her mind made up she stepped through to the bedroom.

Quickly she unfastened her dress, pleased she'd chosen a simple grey sack-like thing to wear for ease of undressing. Underneath she wore a chemise and petticoats and a fine pair of stockings to try to combat the icy temperatures. The petticoats she took off, folding every-thing neatly and placing them on a chair, then she slipped in between the sheets and waited.

Apprehension mixed with excitement. Never before had she done anything so scandalous, anything so ill advised. She'd always been a good girl, doing everything her family had asked of her, everything her husband had com-manded her to. Now she was nervous, but mak-ing this decision herself felt freeing.

The door opened and from her position she could just see Ben re-enter. At first he didn't see her, glancing around the sitting room with a frown on his face.

'Tea will just be…' He trailed off as he caught sight of her. His eyes widened and im-mediately Francesca knew she had made a mis-take. 'What are you doing in my bed, Frannie?' he asked, his voice low. She noticed he hadn't taken a single step towards her and was hold-ing on to the back of one of the chairs so firmly his knuckles were turning white.

The blush seemed to start at her toes and work its way up her entire body until the skin of her cheeks were burning.

'I thought…' she said, trailing off as she re-alised she couldn't actually voice what she'd thought.

Slowly, trying not to draw attention to the movement, she pulled the bedsheets a little further up so they touched her chin.

The seconds seemed to stretch into hours as neither of them moved. Then she felt a thrill of excitement and nerves as he moved towards her. Gently he sat down on the bed, making no move to touch her, and for the first time she wondered if she had read the situation wrong. Perhaps he didn't desire her, perhaps he still thought of her as the ten-year-old girl he'd known all those years ago. Perhaps the gossips had it wrong and he was happily married and faithful to his wife.

'Frannie,' he said, his voice strained, 'you have no idea how much I want to get into that bed with you.'

She waited, wanting to hear exactly what it was that was stopping him.

'But if I do, then it might jeopardise our chance to get to know one another again.'

'When you said…' she started speaking, but couldn't finish the sentence.

His eyes raked over her and she watched as he swallowed and gripped the sheets as if having to hold himself back. A thrill of excitement travelled through her body as she realised she did this to him.

'I want you,' he said, his voice like crushed rock. 'But I don't just want your body.'

'I'm practically engaged…' Francesca said, wondering if she had led him to believe there could be anything long-term between them.

'I know that,' he said, 'And I will respect your engagement. *When* it happens. But I don't just want to tumble into bed with you and then go our separate ways.'

'What *do* you want?' she asked, her fingers edging closer to his. It was hard to resist this man whom she felt she knew so well, but knew was largely a stranger.

'I want to know you, Frannie. Find out what you've been doing these years. See what makes you smile, what makes you cry.'

'Why?' she asked, almost afraid to hear the answer.

'I've missed you. Eighteen years I tried to forget about you and I couldn't. When I return to Australia in a few months I would like to have some new memories to take with me.'

The mention of his return to Australia pulled Francesca back from indulging in some romantic but ridiculous fantasy of them riding off into the horizon together. They had eight days— eight days to become reacquainted and make the most of each other before he returned to his life and she moved on to the next stage of hers.

'I need to get dressed,' she said, unable to meet his eye.

'Go ahead.' He gestured to her clothes on the chair, but did not turn around or make any move to give her some privacy for at least thirty seconds. Then he growled something under his breath and moved out of the bedroom.

Closing her eyes to compose herself, she sat up in bed, letting the bedclothes drop from her chin and feeling her skin prickle under her chemise as the cool air of the room chilled her. She felt a little disappointed that her first foray into the scandalous world of affairs had ended so sedately, but she had to concede Ben was right. It would be good to get to know him, to find out all the things she'd had spent the past eighteen years wondering about. And if she read the look in his eyes correctly, it wouldn't be long before they had another opportunity to enjoy one another in a more intimate fashion in any case...

Resting his head against the cool plaster of the wall outside his rooms, Ben took a deep breath to steady himself. Never before had he walked away from a beautiful woman in his bed. Then again, never before had his heart pounded every time he looked at a woman.

Be careful, he cautioned himself. He hardly knew the woman, but he knew himself. This wasn't how he reacted to a woman, however attractive. He'd never had trouble resisting someone before, never found it hard to move on. It had only been a couple of days since Francesca had waltzed back into his life, but already he was finding it hard to imagine her married to another man while he returned to Australia.

'You should have kissed her,' he growled to himself. When he had first seen her in his bed he had wanted nothing more than to tumble her back between the sheets and spend days getting to know her intimately. It had taken all his willpower to resist and even now he was regretting it a little.

Despite the desire that still raged through his body, he knew he'd made the right decision. Ben was under no illusion that in a couple of weeks they would have to go their separate ways and he didn't want to jeopardise any of that time by causing Francesca to feel rushed into a physical relationship. In a week or two things would be different and they would be ready to enjoy each other's company in every way possible. But today he'd seen the apprehension in her eyes, the nerves. *When* they tumbled into bed together there would be no uncertainty, no doubt in her mind that it was the right thing.

Closing his eyes, he saw the image of her sitting up in bed, clothed only in a simple cotton chemise. That would certainly haunt his dreams in the weeks to come. Of course he shouldn't have looked. He should have been a gentleman and turned away. But it had been hard enough walking out through the door—he wasn't going to torture himself over one look.

'I should go,' Francesca said, slipping out of his rooms and passing him quickly.

Instinctively he reached out and caught her by the arm, feeling her stiffen under his touch.

'Where are you going, Frannie?' he asked.

For a moment he thought she might flee without answering him.

'I just thought…'

'Come back inside and drink your tea,' he said, gripping her hand in his and caressing the skin on her palm with his thumb. 'We have a lot to talk about.'

'Surely you can't want me to stay after…' She gestured in the direction of his rooms, her cheeks turning that delightful shade of pink again. She blushed at the slightest embarrassment and it was something he was finding rather attractive.

'Come back inside,' he said.

She hesitated.

'You can even take your clothes off if it makes you more comfortable.'

He saw the flash of panic in her eyes before she realised he was joking. The old Frannie, the one he'd known all those years ago, would have come back with a witty quip of her own, but it seemed that years of socialising with the richest and most powerful people in the country had stolen her sense of humour.

'Tea?' Hetty asked, coming up the stairs with a tray and breaking the tension between them at just the right moment. Francesca exhaled, glanced at him and nodded once before turning and making her way back into his rooms. Trying not to notice the enticing sway of her hips, he followed her inside. It was going to be a long few weeks and he only had himself to blame.

Chapter Six

Francesca sipped her tea in silence, feeling her own awkwardness overshadow the entire situation. Ben had been gentle as he'd turned her down and ejected her from her bed, but it had still been a rejection and it was still embarrassing to think she'd offered herself to this man and he'd said no.

'Shall I pour?' she asked, grasping for something normal to focus on.

'Go ahead.'

Out of the corner of her eye she saw him sit back, stretching his legs out in front of him and placing his arms behind his head. He looked like a cat stretching out by a warm fire and she felt a pang of nostalgia. This was how he'd always sat, even as a child. She could remember him flopping down into a fireside chair and relaxing completely.

'How do you take your tea?' she asked.

'Just a little milk,' he said, reaching out for one of the biscuits the maid had placed on the tray beside the teapot.

Once the tea was made she handed over the cup, trying to ignore the rush of heat she felt as his fingers brushed against hers. She doubted Ben even noticed, he seemed calm and unperturbed, watching her from under his long eyelashes.

'What exactly did you have in mind?' she asked when it became apparent that Ben wasn't about to start a conversation. 'When you proposed we spend time together?'

He shrugged, reaching for another biscuit. They did look good. Francesca resisted—she might have been able to get away with a biscuit with her tea when she was a young debutante, but now she was a little older she had to watch what she ate to maintain her figure. She eyed Ben and tried not to snort. He didn't seem to be plagued by the realities of ageing. In fact, she'd wager he looked better today than he had a decade ago. Some men had all the luck.

'What do you normally do with gentlemen of your acquaintance?' he asked. 'Apart from testing out their beds, of course.'

She looked up sharply, but Ben was studiously admiring his cup of tea, just the hint of a smile on his lips. He'd always teased her when they were children. It was one of the things she'd liked best about him. Most of the other local children were too cautious to make friends with the daughter of the nobility and, if they did happen to run into her, they were polite but not really friendly. Ben had been different, he'd always treated her like just another village child, teasing her or challenging her as he would anyone else.

'I don't socialise with gentlemen,' she said. 'I'm a widow, certain standards are expected.'

'From whom?'

'From my family, society, everyone really.'

'From your husband-to-be?'

'Lord Huntley?' she asked. 'Nothing has been confirmed yet.' There was the slimmest chance that she might escape that horrible fate, although she wasn't overly hopeful. 'But, yes, he does expect me to behave in a particular way.'

'And if you didn't, the wedding would be off?'

She nodded.

'Are you tempted to be a little scandalous?' he asked.

Once or twice the thought had crossed her mind. It would be easy to engineer a situation to look like she'd been caught in a compromising position. Lord Huntley wouldn't tolerate too much in the way of public disgrace and she would be free from the proposed marriage. Oh, it would be wonderful not to have to worry about what her married life would be like with the ageing, pompous, overbearing man, but she knew that the alternative was worse. Without Lord Huntley's money her family would be completely ruined. They would lose their house and her sister, her beautiful, sweet little sister, would lose the dowry Lord Huntley had promised to provide. So she had to accept her fate and try to make the best of it.

'If only…' she said. 'But no. Once I'm out of mourning I expect everything will be arranged.'

They fell silent for a moment, but despite everything that had happened between them it wasn't an awkward silence.

'What *did* you mean when you proposed I give you eight days for the eight years of your sentence?' she asked, looking at him directly for the first time since he'd convinced her to return to his rooms.

For a long moment he looked at her, his eyes so intense she felt a shiver despite the roaring fire only a few feet away.

'Honestly?' he said. 'I've no idea.'

She wondered if he felt it, too, the irresistible pull between them—and, looking into his eyes, she was almost certain he did.

'You don't have to go through with it if you don't want to,' he said. 'You have enough in your life making you unhappy—the last thing I want to do is add to that.'

'No. I want to do it.' And she realised she did. She wanted to get to know the man she hadn't been able to forget all the eighteen years he'd been away. 'But perhaps we can postpone our first rendezvous until tonight,' she suggested.

'Am I going to come back from dinner to find you in my bed again?' he asked.

'No.' She held his gaze this time.

'Shame,' he murmured, but she knew he only said it to provoke her.

Quickly she stood, bade him farewell and moved towards the door. Before she could open it Ben had darted across the room, placing his hand on the doorknob and opening the door for her. Momentarily she wondered how he'd gone from convict to gentleman, where he'd learned to blend in with the cream of society so well, but now wasn't the time to ask.

'Until tonight,' he said and Francesca felt his eyes follow her down the stairs until she was out of sight.

* * *

'Do you know what you're doing?' George Fitzgerald asked as he lounged back in one of Ben's chairs, warming his feet by the fire. It was still icy out and the month of February was looking to be no warmer than the January. Ben had vague memories of the cold of an English winter, but after so many years spent in the milder conditions in Australia it had come as a bit of a shock. It was true that the climate in New South Wales wasn't constant sunshine, but the winter temperatures didn't dip to anywhere near this low.

'Probably not,' Ben admitted, trying for the third time to tie his cravat. It was a delicate item of clothing and something he had not had cause to wear until their arrival in London a month ago. However, Francesca had sent a note instructing him to dress in evening wear so here he was.

'You're playing a dangerous game.' Fitzgerald said. 'She's basically betrothed. In a few weeks, you'll have to give her up.'

'This was never going to be a long-term situation.'

Fitzgerald snorted. 'I saw the way you looked at her, Crawford, you're besotted. And I've never seen you besotted before.'

Shrugging, he concentrated on the cravat, avoiding Fitzgerald's eye in the mirror. Besotted was putting it too strongly. He admired Francesca, desired her, thought about her from the moment he woke up until the moment he went to bed, but he wasn't besotted. It would be wonderful to spend a month or two with Francesca, but he would leave her behind at the end of it. She would marry Lord Huntley and he would return to Australia.

'Be careful,' Fitzgerald said.

'I will.'

'When are you going to see your father?' Fitzgerald asked, changing the subject as if sensing Ben didn't want to talk about his complicated acquaintance with Francesca.

'He's in Yorkshire for another two weeks, I'll go back and see him when he gets home.'

His father had been estate manager to Francesca's father, Viscount Pottersdown, at the time Ben had been accused of theft. He'd lost his job and his status as well as his son, but the man was resilient and talented. It wasn't long before he'd found another position with the Earl of Harwich, initially as an assistant to the Earl's steward, but then slowly taking on more and more responsibility. He now oversaw all the

Earl's estates, hence why he was up in York-shire at the moment.

Ben was both excited and dreading seeing his family again in equal measure. It had been so long, with only the irregular correspon-dence that reached Australia to link them, and he wondered if the years and their different ex-periences would have put too much emotional distance between them.

'Will your brothers be home?'

Ben nodded. He had two younger brothers, both of whom had been little more than infants the last time he'd seen them. They now were men in their early twenties, full grown with lives of their own. They worked for his father, overseeing the Earl's vast estate in Essex, and according to the information in his father's let-ters both still lived in the same village they'd grown up in.

The only two members that would be miss-ing were his mother, who had passed away when Ben was nine from a weak chest, and his elder sister. She'd been the oldest, the one he'd looked up to and wanted to emulate when they'd been children, but his father had in-formed him she'd passed away in childbirth a few years earlier.

'It'll be worth it,' Fitzgerald said quietly. 'Of course it will be hard, but it will be worth it.'

'We're all different people now,' Ben said. 'Who knows what it will be like?'

'Different people, but still family.' Fitzgerald rose, looking at the clock on the wall. 'I'd better let you set off,' he said. 'Try not to break too many hearts tonight.'

'It's never my aim...' Ben said with a grin, happy they'd moved on from more painful subjects.

'Come for breakfast tomorrow,' Fitzgerald said. 'Aunt Tabitha is asking after you and Robertson is falling for the daughter of the man he hates most in the world. Not that he'll admit it yet. He needs something to distract him.'

'I'll call at eight.'

'Enjoy your evening.'

As Fitzgerald left, Ben spent a moment looking in the mirror. He looked almost unrecognisable, with the cravat and jacket on top of a pressed white shirt. It was very different to the clothes he wore while out on his farms. Although he employed hundreds of workers now he still got his hands dirty each and every day. To his mind that was the only way to run a successful business.

Trying not to think about the evening ahead,

or the sense of anticipation he felt deep inside, he left his rooms. He would not give in to the more primal urges he felt every time he looked at her.

Chapter Seven

Peering out through the door of the carriage for the twentieth time, Francesca forced herself to remain calm. It was only Ben, and if he could get past her mortifying behaviour earlier that day then so could she.

As she saw his tall figure come sauntering down the steps she felt her pulse quicken and all the nerves she had been trying to suppress bubble to the surface.

'Good evening, Lady Somersham,' he said, giving a formal bow before hopping up into the carriage beside her. He looked smart and suave, every inch the gentleman even though Francesca knew he wasn't.

'We're not going far—would you prefer to walk?' she asked. The evening was cold but bright, and suddenly she realised she would prefer not to be cooped up in an enclosed space with Ben. She might do something foolish.

'That sounds wonderful,' he said, getting down from the carriage and holding out a gloved hand for her to take. She quickly instructed the driver where to wait for them before hesitantly placing her hand in the crook of Ben's arm.

'Where are we going?' Ben asked as they began to walk along the pavement. Their pace was brisk to try to stave off some of the inevitable chill and, not for the first time, Francesca felt envious of men's more practical clothing. Ben's boots and thick coat over his evening wear would keep him considerably warmer than her pretty-but-thin coat and satin shoes.

'To a dance. At the Assembly Rooms.'

She'd been unsure where to take Ben and had agonised over the decision for hours. Then she'd decided just to take him somewhere she enjoyed spending the evening.

'Ah, the famous Almack's,' Ben said.

'No, not quite,' Francesca said quickly. She felt his eyes on her as he turned his head towards her in question. 'I wasn't granted a voucher this year,' she mumbled, hoping he wouldn't ask any more.

Glancing up, she saw him frown, 'You're

going to have to explain,' he said. 'I've got no idea what you're talking about.'

Sighing, she swallowed the memory of her dented pride. 'To gain entry to Almack's each week you need a ticket. To get a ticket you need a voucher which proves you are on the approved list of people allowed in to Almack's that Season.'

'The approved list?' Ben asked, his lips turning up into that smile that did strange things to her knees. 'And who decides who gets approved?'

Francesca grimaced. 'There is a group of Patronesses and they vet applicants, deciding who to grant vouchers to each year. I think the idea is that one might socialise at Almack's knowing that everyone is your social equal.'

'How dreadful,' Ben murmured. 'So why didn't you get a ticket?'

It was a deeply personal question, but from Ben she'd begun to expect no less. He wasn't constrained by the rules of good etiquette and just came out and asked what he wanted to know.

'Any number of reasons,' she said, trying to keep the disappointment she'd felt from her voice. 'Father's debts or drinking habits, our declining position as a family in society. It could

be anything, really. Although I've always suspected it's because Lady Golding's husband
pursued me quite relentlessly when we were
debutantes and she's never quite forgiven me
for making her feel second-best.'

'Something as petty as that?' Ben asked. 'It
sounds like you're better off out of it.'

'Mmm…' she murmured non-committally.
With her head she knew he was right. She
shouldn't want to socialise with such a shallow and cruel group of people, but the snub had
hurt. Knowing that she'd been judged and found
wanting by her peers, whatever the reason, had
injured her probably more than it should.

Every Wednesday the cream of society was
off dancing and socialising at Almack's and
she was excluded.

'I suppose it's hard to be pushed out,' Ben
said perceptively, 'when it is something you've
always been part of.'

She nodded. It was exactly that.

'Plus I love to dance and that was one of
the only places I could go without a chaperon
and dance without having to worry about any
scandal.'

'So where are we going tonight?' Ben asked.

'When I found out I wasn't going to be
granted a voucher for Almack's I looked around

for other Assembly Rooms that held regular dances and I found DeFevrett's. It's not far from St James's and they hold a dance every Wednesday just like Almack's.'

It was an entirely different atmosphere as well as an entirely different clientele. Whereas Almack's was filled with the titled and wealthy all dressed in their finest, DeFevrett's catered to the upper-middle classes. At first Francesca had felt uncomfortable and out of place, but slowly she'd realised that with all her peers spending their night socialising at Almack's there was no one to spot her attending the less well-to-do dance and had begun to enjoy herself. The first few weeks she'd persuaded Lucy Winthrow, an old friend who had once been a companion to Francesca's grandmother, to come with her, to act as an unofficial chaperon and make the whole thing a little less scandalous if she did get found out. As the weeks went on Francesca's confidence had grown and now she felt happy to attend just with Ben as her guest.

'Are you sure you're just not too embarrassed to take me as your guest to Almack's?' Ben asked, grinning at her.

'I think you'd actually go down well there,' Francesca replied. 'The patronesses seem to favour a good-looking man, even if his pedigree isn't quite as noble as some. It's me they have an issue with.'

They crossed the street and hurried towards the Assembly Rooms, Francesca's pace quickening further as she realised she couldn't feel her toes.

At the door she produced her ticket and felt the familiar soaring of her mood as they stepped inside and heard the first jaunty notes of the quartet who would provide the music for the evening's dancing.

'First drinks are served and there is the chance to socialise a little, and then the dancing will start in half an hour.'

They walked arm in arm through the entrance hall and into the ballroom proper. Around the perimeter were a few groups of people, but from past experience Francesca knew in this early part of the evening most of the guests would be gathered around the card tables in the third room.

She nodded a greeting to a few of the regular attendees, men she'd danced with and women she'd talked with. All in all most were friendly and it was certainly a more welcoming atmosphere than at Almack's.

'Who do you normally dance with?' Ben

asked, eyeing the gentlemen who were dotted around the room.

Anyone who asks, Francesca thought, but didn't say. When you loved to dance as much as she did you weren't overly picky about partners.

'Just like a society ball, really you should wait to be introduced before a man asks you to dance,' Francesca said, but in fact the rules were a little looser here. She'd danced with plenty of men who she'd never met before. If her mother knew she'd be scandalised, as would the rest of society, but for Francesca the risk was worth it.

'Correct me if I'm wrong, but you take a big risk to come here. If anyone found out, wouldn't you be the subject of scandal and speculation?'

'Yes.'

'But you do it anyway.'

'I love to dance.'

If she was honest there was more to it than that. An unconscious desire to have a little freedom in her choices, to be the one to decide where she went and when. To be able to choose whether to accept or refuse a dance partner herself without always having to think whether her actions might damage the family in some way. For so long she'd shouldered responsibility for her father's mistakes, but here she didn't have to worry about any of that.

And the risk that she might get caught and exposed as a shameless widow who socialised below her class, that just made it all the more appealing.

Ben chuckled. 'You always did like taking risks, Frannie,' he said.

When they'd run around as children she'd never had a problem with taking risks, with her and Ben as bad as each other, spurring the other on to climb higher, jump further, be that little bit more mischievous. Things had been different as she'd grown up. Her mother had withdrawn more and more, leaving the responsibility of running the household and raising her younger sister to Francesca. And then her father had revealed he'd lost all the family money and it had been down to Francesca to marry well to try to save them. It hadn't worked out, with Lord Somersham almost as skilled at losing money as her father, but she'd done her bit all the same.

'Shall we get a drink?' Francesca asked.

He let her lead him to the room where refreshments were served and they both took a glass of the brightly coloured punch that was offered. Ben took one sip and handed it back to the young woman who'd served it and after tasting the artificial sweetness Francesca did the same. With replacement glasses of lemonade in their hands they wandered around the room, waiting for the dancing.

'Would you like a game of cards while we wait?' Ben asked.

'No,' she said a little too vehemently, causing Ben to look at her with a raised eyebrow. 'No, thank you,' she said more calmly, 'But please feel free to play if you wish.'

Her heart sank a little when she thought he might. Both her father and late husband were unlucky and unskilled when it came to cards, but more importantly they both seemed to think they were much better than they were. It was just another example of their poor judgement, and Francesca had spent many a painful evening watching an increasingly desperate Lord Somersham bet money they did not have in an attempt to claw back some of what he'd lost already.

'When I have you for company?' he asked. 'A man would be a fool to leave you for a game of cards.'

'Does that charm come naturally or do you work to say what a lady wants to hear?' she asked.

'Completely natural,' he said with the smile that made her heart flip inside her chest. 'Never trust a man who has to work to give a lady a compliment.'

'I'd wager you've left a string of broken hearts behind you,' Francesca murmured.

'A gentleman never breaks a lady's heart,' he said, but from the slight shift of his eyes she knew it was true. He probably told himself he only got involved with women who understood the short-lived nature of any affair they would share together, but she would wager her only remaining set of pearls that no matter how hard they tried the women always fell in love with him.

'Only cherishes it?' Francesca asked. From his expression she could see he had never let anyone get close, let alone take responsibility for their happiness. She felt a pang of sadness. As a boy, Ben had been warm and loving, with genuine affection for his friends and family. He deserved more than passing flings, he deserved true love after all he had suffered.

'When a lady entrusts me with her heart I will let you know,' he said quietly and Francesca felt her pulse quicken and her skin flush.

'I hear the music,' Francesca said, glad for the distraction. 'Shall we dance?'

Obligingly he gave her his arm, leading her

back to the main room where couples were beginning to assemble.

'How do you know how to dance?' Francesca asked.

'When I was a young boy I had an irritating young girl who would follow me around,' he said, keeping a completely straight face. 'She loved to dance and to oblige her I learned the steps to one or two of the most common dances. I merely had to refresh my memory before returning to London.'

'You used to follow me,' she murmured, 'not the other way around.'

'I remember it rather differently.'

For a moment everything was easy between them and Francesca found herself smiling a true smile for the first time in a very long while. Then the dance began and she was swept away in a flurry of steps and laughter.

Chapter Eight

As he watched her laughing and smiling Ben felt an unfamiliar tightening in his chest. It had pained him to see Francesca looking so sad at the masquerade ball and he wanted to banish for ever that despair from her eyes.

He'd only been momentarily surprised at her choice of where to take him this evening. She'd always loved to dance, but more than that Francesca had always been a bit of a rebel. Over the years she might have suppressed that part of her, but he wasn't surprised to find she still did a few of the things she shouldn't, even if it was carefully hidden from the people who might judge her.

'The mauves and greys have gone,' he murmured in her ear as they joined hands at the end of a particularly energetic dance.

'Just for tonight.' She grimaced. 'Just while

no one of significance can see me and start to gossip.'

'Blue suits you,' he said, admiring the contrast of her almost-black hair with the deep blue of the evening gown she was wearing.

'Is that a compliment, Mr Crawford?' Francesca asked.

He leaned in closer, 'Although I much prefer you in white.' He waited until she remembered the incident earlier where she'd stripped down to her white cotton chemise to get into his bed and watched her cheeks colour.

'A gentleman would never mention *that* ever again,' she said primly.

'I'm no gentleman, Frannie, and you'd do well to remember that.'

Her eyes widened a little before narrowing almost completely.

'You're toying with me,' she said. 'No one toys with me.'

'They should. It's great fun.'

'Fun isn't expected for a widow.'

'Even a widow who disliked her husband?'

'Be quiet,' Francesca hissed and Ben could see it took all her self-restraint not to punch him on the arm as she had when he'd teased her when they were children.

He was actually enjoying himself. Here in

a stuffy Assembly Rooms, mixing with the snobby upper-middle classes with the woman whose father had ruined his childhood on his arm, he was enjoying himself.

'Care for some air?' he asked.

'Only if you promise to behave yourself.'

'You wouldn't like me if I did.'

She mumbled something under her breath, but allowed him to escort her through the now-crowded room to the terrace at the back of the Assembly Rooms. It was cold outside and Ben could see his breath on the air, but it was a welcome change from the heat of the room. He watched as Francesca leaned elegantly against the stone balustrade that separated the terrace from a small courtyard a few steps below. Without thinking he pushed himself up on to the balustrade, sitting on the cool stone, his feet still touching the ground.

'Get down,' Francesca hissed.

'Why?'

'You're not supposed to sit up there.'

'Who says?'

She spluttered, then regained control of herself. 'I do.'

He grinned. 'Don't pretend you don't wish you could be up here with me, sitting comfortably and resting your weary feet.'

Opening her mouth to deny it, just to be perverse, Francesca thought better of uttering the lie and pressed her lips together again.

'If you get me thrown out, I won't be very happy,' she said.

'Surely once you're married again, once you're Lady Huntley, they won't be able to deny you a voucher for Almack's,' Ben said.

She shrugged and he could tell it was a subject she didn't want to discuss, but he pushed on nevertheless.

'Lord Huntley is an earl, isn't he? So you will be a countess?'

'Can we talk of other things?' she asked, turning so her back was against the balustrade and she was looking back inside the Assembly Rooms. 'Or, better still, dance some more.'

'In a minute. I want to know why you're even considering marrying a man like Huntley.'

'You say it like I have a choice.'

Ben knew there were many reasons people got married—for money, connections, even love—but he was intrigued to know why Francesca was allowing herself to be trapped into another unhappy marriage.

'Don't you? You're a widow, a woman, not a scared young girl who has to do her father's bidding.'

'I might be a widow, but I have no independence. Lord Somersham left me no provision in his will. He was completely broke. The title and lands have gone to his second cousin, but there was no money to go with it.'

'So you still rely on your father to support you?'

She nodded.

'And that's why you have to marry whomever he chooses?'

'No.' This was said vehemently and Ben wondered whether to push her further.

'Why then?' he said. 'Make me understand.'

'My father owes a lot of money,' Francesca said quietly.

From the rumours Ben had heard that was an understatement. Lord Pottersdown had more debt than all the inhabitants of a debtors' prison and then some.

'Lord Huntley has offered to clear the worst of the debts,' she said, 'and provide a dowry for my sister.'

Ben screwed up his face as he searched for a name. The little girl had been no more than an infant when he'd been sentenced to be transported and he'd only ever seen her from a distance with the nursemaids or nanny.

'Felicity,' he said eventually.

'Yes. She's twenty and the sweetest, most wonderful young woman.'

'With no dowry.'

It seemed ridiculous to him, this business of a dowry, but he knew in society it was one of the most important factors when agreeing on a match between two people.

'No one has offered for her,' Francesca said sadly. 'Or at least no one in the least bit acceptable. They don't want to tie themselves to our family.'

'And you feel like this is all your responsibility? To keep a roof over your parents' heads, to provide a dowry for your sister?'

'Of course it is. They're my family.'

'You deserve to be unhappy so they can live better lives?'

'Someone has to make that sacrifice,' Francesca said and it was clear from her tone that it wasn't going to be either of her parents. She was the responsible one, the one caring about the happiness and survival of everyone else but herself.

Ben pushed himself down from the wall and waited for Francesca to turn to him. She looked radiant even with the frown on her face. In the moonlight her skin was pale and perfect, contrasting beautifully with her full, rosy lips. He wanted to see her smile again, even though he felt an almost uncontrollable desire when she did. As she turned towards him her arm brushed against his and he knew from her expression that she felt the same frisson of excitement as he did every time their bodies touched. He wondered for a moment what it would be like to have her in his bed and with absolute certainty he knew it would be incredible. Part of him regretted refusing Francesca earlier that afternoon, but he knew it was only a matter of time before they would fall into each other's arms.

'Couldn't your sister marry Lord Huntley?' he asked, trying to distract himself from the spot just above her collarbone where he could see her pulse ever so faintly. It was tempting to place his lips there, to taste the sweetness of her skin, but he had to remember they were in a public place.

'No,' she said vehemently. 'That is not an option.'

He waited for her to elaborate.

Sighing, Francesca continued, 'He has a reputation—there are rumours.'

'What sort of rumours?'

'He was married before and his wife seemed to have rather a lot of accidents.'

'He beat her?'

Francesca shrugged, 'As I say, there are rumours, but who really knows what goes on behind closed doors?'

'Frannie, are you telling me you wouldn't let your sister marry this man, but you're willing to risk a lifetime of beating and abuse?'

She shrugged, but wouldn't meet his eye.

Ben let out a disgusted sigh. It wasn't his place to care, he knew that, but some part of him wanted to wrap her up in his arms and protect the girl he'd once loved.

'Let's forget this,' Francesca said, forcing a smile on her face. 'Let's dance.'

Ben could tell by the set expression on her face there was no reasoning with Francesca now so he offered her his arm. He shouldn't interfere; she was perfectly capable of making her own mistakes, but the thought of her spending the rest of her life with a man like Lord Huntley made him feel nauseous.

They stepped back into the Assembly Rooms, the temperature inside at least twenty degrees warmer than the freezing air outside. Francesca just wanted to dance, she didn't want to think about the way her life was going to be in just a few short months, she didn't want to think about the rumours that circulated detailing Lord Huntley's first wife's *little accidents* or the possessive way her future husband already looked at her. When she danced, especially when she danced in Ben's arms, she could forget all these worries and get lost in the music.

Turning to suggest they ready themselves for the next dance, Francesca stiffened, her whole body seizing up with panic. Without any explanation to Ben she let go of his arm and rushed behind a pillar, flattening her back against the cool plaster.

'I thought you wanted to dance?' Ben said casually, regarding her with a frown.

'Lord Huntley,' she hissed. 'He's here.'

There was no reason for the man who was determined to become her future husband to attend DeFevrett's—on the contrary, it should be a place a man of his class and status vigorously avoided. The only possible reason he could have for coming here was her. Someone must have seen her, someone must have told him of her less-than-acceptable behaviour, and here he was, seeking her out. Whether to reprimand her or end his association with her she wasn't sure, but she didn't want to wait around to find out.

'Looking for you?' Ben asked as he casually took a step back and cast his eyes around the room. 'So he is. He's standing by the entrance looking like someone has stolen his favourite toy.'

'Someone has,' Francesca muttered. 'I need to get out of here.'

'There's no way to sneak past. We'll have to go out through the back.'

For a moment the burden of getting out of this impossible situation didn't seem quite so heavy as she realised Ben was right there beside her.

'Move slowly, but keep your head down,' he instructed her, 'You don't want to draw attention to yourself.'

Doing as he commanded, they strolled back the way they had come, Francesca trying to keep the panic she was feeling from overcoming her and making her run, which she knew would be counter-productive. Once back out on the small terrace they paused and Ben took a moment to glance over her shoulder into the ballroom they'd just left.

'He's coming this way,' he murmured, no hint of panic or stress in his voice. Either he was very good at controlling his emotions or he felt the stakes weren't that high.

'There's no other way out,' Francesca said,

looking round the enclosed area. Beyond the terrace there was a drop of a few feet to a small, square courtyard. On the opposite side of the courtyard was a wall, separating the Assembly Rooms from the street on the other side.

'That depends on how desperate you are not to be found,' Ben said, grinning at her.

She narrowed her eyes, wondering if he thought they could scoot around the back of Lord Huntley and make it to the front door while he was distracted.

'I can't be found here,' she said.

'Come on.' He grasped her hand and before she could protest had pulled her up on to the stone balustrade. Without a backward glance he dropped the few feet to the courtyard below, turning and motioning for her to follow him. Hesitating, Francesca took a deep breath, if they were trapped in the courtyard there would be a scandal of momentous proportions, it would be much worse than Lord Huntley merely finding her socialising with people not of her class at DeFevrett's. However, there was a chance, even just a small chance, that Ben could get her out of here.

It all came down to whether she trusted the man in front of her. He was not obliged to help her, but instinctively she knew he would do everything in his power to help her escape. His feelings for her might be complicated, but he was a good man, that much she could tell already from their short reacquaintance. Ben wouldn't let Lord Huntley catch her without a fight.

Hoping he would catch her, Francesca pushed off the balustrade, falling the few feet into his waiting arms. He swung her down with ease, grabbed her hand and pulled her across the courtyard.

'Ready to climb?' he asked. She nodded. It had been years since they'd last climbed together, boosting each other up haystacks or into the lofts of old barns, but as she placed her foot into Ben's hand she felt ten years old again and as if she were invincible. Deftly he lifted her up, waiting until she had hooked a leg over the top of the wall, managing to disentangle her skirts at the same time.

A shout from the other side of the courtyard made her glance back, but quickly she dropped her head so no one would be able to identify her. A small crowd was forming on the terrace, watching their escape attempt. She had to hope Lord Huntley wouldn't appear until they were out of sight.

Ben used the branches of a nearby tree to

help him clamber up the wall as easily as a monkey, dropping down the other side as soon as he'd reached the top. He held out his arms for Francesca and this time she didn't hesitate to drop into them.

As her feet hit the floor he grabbed her hand and together they darted through the darkened alleyways. Francesca felt a surge of relief and an uncontrollable giggle burst from her lips.

'Do you think he saw us?' she asked, trying to get her laughter under control.

'No,' Ben said, pausing. The main street was just a few feet away, but here in the darkness of the alley it felt like they were the only two people in the world.

'My coat,' Francesca said, as the cold air penetrated through her dress, reminding her of what she'd left behind.

'I will go back for it tomorrow,' Ben promised, turning to her. Francesca's back was against the wall, the freezing bricks making her shiver, but as his eyes met hers she couldn't help but giggle again. She hadn't behaved so badly in her entire adult life.

'You're a bad influence,' she murmured.

'Perhaps,' he said and something in his eyes darkened as he looked at her. Francesca felt the whole world slow and fade into the background so the only thing left was the man in front of her. 'Frannie,' he murmured, reaching up and touching her cheek with his cupped hand.

Francesca closed her eyes as he moved towards her, knowing that his lips would find hers instinctively. They brushed against hers and inside Francesca felt a rush of elation like never before.

'Who goes there?' an annoyed shout came from the direction of the Assembly Rooms and quickly they sprang apart. Ben gripped her hand again and pulled her out on to the street. The moment between them had passed, but Francesca knew she would never be able to forget it. It had been a stolen moment in a mad evening, but a moment of perfection all the same.

'Definitely a bad influence,' she murmured.

'I wasn't the one who suggested we go to the Assembly Rooms,' he said, 'Or who insisted on getting out of there without a peer of the realm catching me.' Eyeing her with a barely repressed grin, he offered her his arm again. 'Come, let's get you home.'

They walked briskly to combat the cold and with their heads bent to try to prevent anyone from recognising them. Fifteen minutes and they were in streets Francesca recognised and within twenty they were in the small public gardens opposite her father's house.

'Will you be safe from here?' Ben asked, looking out from their hidden spot behind a tree to the darkened house beyond.

'I will…' She paused, wondering how to say everything that was clamouring for attention in her mind. And wondering if he might kiss her again before he left. 'Ben…'

'Frannie.'

'I'm sorry,' she said, feeling her heart thumping in her chest.

'Don't apologise, it was fun.'

'Not for that, not for tonight. For what my father did eighteen years ago. For ruining your life.'

He looked at her and for a moment she wondered if he might turn his back on her and walk away.

'Do you know,' he said, tucking a stray wisp of hair behind her ear, 'I had quite forgotten all about that.'

'I don't want you to hate me,' she whispered.

'I don't hate you, Frannie. I've never hated you. You didn't do anything wrong.'

'But my father…'

'Hush,' he said, his fingers coming up and brushing against her cheek. Francesca felt her heart leap in her chest and her skin tingle under his touch. 'You are not your father, or responsible for his actions.'

'I should have done more.'

'I don't hate you, I could never hate you,' he said again and as she looked into his eyes she believed him. She felt safe in his arms, content, as if she was meant to be there, and as his head lowered towards hers there was no way she could have stopped her lips coming up to meet his.

He kissed her softly, his lips brushing against hers, feeling velvety and smooth and causing a fiery heat to rise up inside her. She'd been kissed before, but never like this. Never had her entire body responded to a kiss with such passion. Ben murmured her name, kissing her again and again, until she was sure she had lost all reason.

When he pulled away Francesca felt like crying out, but just about managed to maintain some sort of composure.

'Why did you do that?' she asked, hearing the breathless quality to her voice and coughing to try to cover it up. It wouldn't do to let Ben see how much that one kiss had affected her.

'I wanted to,' he said.

Opening her mouth to reply, Francesca found

she was lost for words so instead gave a short, sharp nod. She didn't quite believe he'd kissed her not once but twice now merely because he'd wanted to, but she couldn't find the words to demand a further explanation.

'I shouldn't have done that,' she said after a couple of seconds, 'I'm almost engaged.'

'Almost…'

'And I'm in mourning.'

'It was just a kiss, Frannie, nothing more.'

Feeling herself deflate a little, she tried to rally. To him it might have been just a kiss, something he went around doing all the time, but for her it had been wonderful, exquisite, and felt as though it had awoken every nerve in her body.

'You shouldn't kiss me,' she said.

'I've never been good at following the rules.' He shrugged, 'And I happen to find you very attractive.'

'But earlier…' She trailed off at the memory of him rejecting her as she lay half-undressed in his bed.

'I didn't want to rush things. If you decide to come to my bed, I'd like to think we could come out on the other side as friends. I don't want you to have any doubts, any second thoughts.'

She spluttered, her eyes widening. 'If I decide to come to your bed?' she repeated.

Ben shrugged. 'We're both adults, there's a spark between us, it is up to you if you want to pursue it.'

'I am a daughter of the nobility and the widow of a viscount,' Francesca said, focusing in on the spark of humour in his eyes. She wasn't sure if he was teasing her or if the offer was a genuine one, but she wasn't going to let herself be embarrassed any further. 'This morning was a momentary lapse of judgement. It will never happen again.'

'As you wish,' he said so calmly she wanted to thump him.

'I think I should bid you goodnight,' Francesca said, knowing she should get away from him before she said something she regretted. Or kissed him again. 'It was nice to see you have done well in life, but perhaps we should go our separate ways.'

She turned, only to have his hand dart out and catch her gently on the arm.

'What about the other seven days?' he asked and this time she knew he was struggling to keep an entirely straight face.

She looked up at him, feeling her pulse quicken. As much as she might pretend and postulate, she wasn't going to do anything to shorten the time they could spend together.

'I shall pen you a note,' she said as haughtily as she could muster, then marched off before he could say anything more.

Chapter Nine

'Lord Huntley to see you, my lady,' the butler announced and Francesca had to suppress a groan. She'd barely slept, her mind rebelling against her sensible side, and images of Ben kissing her, touching her, laying her back on the bed and making love to her, had occupied her thoughts for most of the night. The problem of Lord Huntley, and his tracking her to De-Fevrett's, hadn't even crossed her mind. Now she would have to try to work out what he knew and what she would be able to get away with.

'Oh, joy,' Felicity said drily from her position on the window seat.

'Lady Somersham,' Huntley said as he burst into the room, glancing at Felicity, but barely sparing a nod in her direction. 'You have some explaining to do.'

'My lord?' Francesca tried to sound as meek

and guileless as possible while the man she was probably going to have to marry paraded round the room as if he owned the place. Remembering the large debt her father owed Lord Huntley, she realised he probably did own some of Number Twelve Park Square and a large proportion of their country estate, too.

'Oh, dear, is something amiss, Lord Huntley?' Francesca asked.

'Where were you last night?' he demanded.

'Last night,' she mused as if it were half a year ago.

'Here,' Felicity said without looking up from the book she was reading, 'With me.'

'What?' This had evidently thrown Lord Huntley and he was looking round the room as if searching for inspiration.

'We spent the evening doing a little embroidery and Francesca sang after dinner. It was a very pleasant evening,' Felicity said.

'Is this true?' Lord Huntley asked, turning back to Francesca.

'Of course. You know I'm still in mourning for my late husband. I still spend most of my evenings in and Felicity was kind enough to keep me company last night.'

'We'll talk about this preposterously long mourning period later,' Lord Huntley murmured, 'Right now I want to know why I heard reports of you frequenting an inappropriate dance.'

'Oh?' Francesca said mildly. 'And what dance is that?'

'Assembly Rooms called DeFevrett's. It caters to those of the middle class who have an inflated view of their own importance and status.'

'DeFevrett's?' she mused, beginning to enjoy herself now. 'No, I can't say I've ever heard of it. Who on earth gave you the idea I might go there?'

'A rumour,' Huntley said, frowning as if he didn't quite believe her.

'They must have been mistaken. And you think I went there last night?'

He grunted, only now deigning to sit down on the armchair that had seen better days with upholstery that had been carefully repaired more than once.

'Was there anything else, Lord Huntley?' Felicity asked. It was bordering on rude, but Francesca's sister had never had any time for the man who had initially asked for her hand in marriage before settling on Francesca instead.

'It's high time we announced our engagement,' Lord Huntley said. 'I'm fed up of all this dilly dallying.'

'The correct mourning period must be observed,' Francesca said, repeating the line she'd been using for the two months Lord Huntley had been pushing for a date. It wasn't as though she had even accepted his proposal yet, it would be bad form to do so before the mourning period for Lord Somersham was up, but everyone around her—her father, her mother and Lord Huntley himself—seemed to think the marriage between them was a certainty.

If she was honest, it probably was a certainty, but she was still hoping for a miracle before she had to formally agree to the engagement.

'How long is left?' he asked brusquely.

'Six weeks.' Only six weeks of freedom before she would have to wake up to this man every morning and promise to obey him, serve him, love him and honour him. It made her feel sick to her stomach.

He grunted again and promptly stood. 'I need to finalise things with your father. I shall call again next week—please ensure he is sober.'

'Of course, Lord Huntley,' Francesca said, knowing nothing she could say or do would have be able to influence that.

They waited until he had left before both Francesca and Felicity let out long exhalations.

'I can't believe you're actually considering marrying *that*,' Felicity said.

Francesca couldn't tell her sister she was doing it for her. If it wasn't for Felicity she might be able to finally leave her parents to sort out their own mess, but she couldn't condemn her lovely younger sister to a life of misery. Without the dowry Lord Huntley had promised to provide Felicity she might never get a proposal from a decent gentleman.

To ensure her voice didn't betray her emotions Francesca just shrugged.

'Where were you last night?' Felicity asked, sitting up on the window seat and putting her book down so she could focus all her attention on her sister.

'Just out,' Francesca said, fiddling with a frayed piece of cotton on her dress.

'At the Assembly Rooms? The inappropriate one?'

'It was just a dance,' she said, 'Nothing scandalous.'

'I didn't know you had it in you,' Felicity said, a new admiration dawning in her eyes.

'He was there,' Francesca said quietly, 'Lord Huntley. He was there looking for me.'

His behaviour terrified her a little. If he was this obsessive about her movements even before they were engaged, what would he be like when they married? Lord Somersham hadn't been a particularly pleasant man, especially as the years went by without Francesca producing the heir he so desperately wanted, but he had expressed his displeasure with his words and his obvious contempt for her. Never had he thought to control who she saw or where she went and never had he raised a hand to her.

There were rumours about Lord Huntley and how he'd treated his first wife. According to the gossips she'd often been incapacitated after some awful accident, much more often than one could expect in the course of a few years. Francesca knew she wouldn't be alone if Lord Huntley did turn out to be a cruel husband, there were many men who raised a hand to their wives behind closed doors, but that didn't soften the dread she felt whenever she thought of her inevitable nuptials.

'I take it from his appearance here today he didn't actually see you.'

'I was able to sneak out.' She remembered Ben's cool handling of the situation, the way he'd not hesitated to assist her in escaping Lord Huntley. She could still feel the pressure of his hands around her waist as he helped her down from the wall, the easy way he'd caught her and lifted her. And then, of course, there were the kisses.

The kisses that she'd been obsessing about ever since she'd returned home the previous evening. Francesca had been unable to think of anything else, no manner of distraction had worked. Over and over again she'd relived every moment, picturing how Ben had held her, how his lips had felt on her own, how her heart had hammered in her chest. Never had she been kissed like that and she knew she would do almost anything to feel the same just one more time.

'Who did you go with?' Felicity asked, pulling Francesca back to the present.

'Lucy,' she fibbed. Their grandmother's companion, when their grandmother was still alive, had chaperoned Francesca to many balls and events when her mother had been indisposed. She was now a happy spinster in her early forties who over the years had been more of a mother to Francesca and her sister than Lady Pottersdown, who spent all her time secluded in her room.

'I would have come with you,' Felicity said with a grin.

'You, young lady, need to avoid any hint of scandal,' Francesca said in her sternest voice.

Felicity was so carefree and innocent. Sometimes a little too carefree and innocent. She went through life thinking nothing bad could ever happen to her and that meant sometimes she took unnecessary risks.

Once Francesca had been like that, too, but over the years she'd been forced to step up, to be the responsible one. Their mother spent almost all her time ensconced in her bedchamber and their father was either getting them into further financial trouble with one of his doomed schemes or drowning his sorrows in the bottom of a whisky glass. Sometimes Francesca wished she could go back to the days where all she had to consider was which dress to wear or how to spend her morning, but that seemed a lifetime ago.

'Mr Crawford to see you, Lady Somersham,' the butler announced.

Francesca shot up from her chair and started to tell the butler to show Ben into another room, but he'd already stepped out to let Ben in.

'Aren't you popular this morning?' Felicity murmured, her eyes fixed on the door and a little smile on her lips.

'Good morning Fran—' Ben started, but cut himself off as he caught sight of Felicity on the window seat. 'Lady Somersham,' he corrected himself. 'And this must be Miss Felicity—a pleasure to make your acquaintance.'

As soon as her eyes met his she was taken back to the moment of their kiss before she'd left him the night before. She remembered every vivid detail and by the smile on Ben's lips he knew exactly what she was thinking.

'I trust you are both well?' he asked. For a boy who'd spent eight years as a convict worker in Australia he did a good impression of being a gentleman.

'Very well, thank you,' Felicity said, her eyes sparkling with glee. Inwardly Francesca groaned. Her sister was always telling her to go out into the world and enjoy herself, to mix with people who made her happy and Francesca knew she would do everything to find out more about Ben and his interest in her. 'Mr Crawford,' Felicity said slowly. 'Are you the same Mr Crawford who is friends with Mr Robertson?'

'I am. Do you know Mr Robertson?'

Felicity shrugged, a non-ladylike gesture that made Francesca smile every time she saw it.

'I'm friends with Caroline Yaxley and Georgina Fairfax. I believe Mr Robertson is acquainted with Lady Georgina.'

If the rumours were to be believed, the two had been caught in a mildly compromising position and it was only the intervention of Lady Winston, Fitzgerald's aunt, who had saved the pair from much more salacious gossip.

'He is,' Ben said, barely able to keep the smile from his face. 'In fact, I am due to be attending a house party at Lady Georgina's family estate this weekend with Mr Robertson. Will you be there?'

'No,' Felicity said with no hint of malice in her voice. 'Her mother did not think me suitable.'

'Ah. That is a shame.'

'Was there a reason for your visit, Mr Crawford?' Francesca asked, pulling him back to the present.

'I wanted to return your coat.'

Francesca's eyes widened and quickly she glanced at her sister. There was no good reason for Mr Crawford to have her coat.

'There really was no rush,' she managed to ground out.

'I thought you might be in need of it. Unless you have a whole wardrobe of coats.'

He knew very well that she didn't. Over the years she'd conserved the best-made pieces of clothing, lovingly mending them when sleeves frayed or seams became loose, but still she only had a skeleton wardrobe left now. And he was right, it was her only coat.

'Where on earth did you leave it, Francesca?' Felicity asked, her eyes dancing with amusement.

'At the Assembly Rooms,' she said, hoping her quick answer would be enough for her sister, but knowing it would not.

'How kind of you to return it, Mr Crawford. Did you enjoy the dancing last night?' Felicity asked.

'Very much so. Your sister is an excellent dancer.'

Knowing she'd been caught out in a lie, Francesca sat back in her chair and gave up. Felicity would have the details from Mr Crawford in no time, there was no point in trying to stop her. Her sister would have done well as an interrogator in the war, Francesca had never known anyone able to keep information from her for long.

In a move that surprised her, Felicity stood, executed a brief and sloppy curtsy and moved towards the door.

'Please excuse me, Mr Crawford, I've got to be…somewhere else.' She didn't even bother coming up with a convincing lie.

Left alone, Francesca tried to avoid Ben's

gaze but after nearly half a minute of silence she had to look up.

'You look lovely this morning, Frannie,' he said, his eyes flitting over her face.

'Stop it,' she muttered.

'Stop what?'

'This.' She gestured to him, not really sure herself what she was asking him to stop.

'You want me to stop being me?'

'Yes. No. I don't know. Sit down.'

He did and she tried to ignore the grin on his face.

'So that was the sister you're giving up your life for,' he said as he flopped down on to the sofa next to her. He was far too close and his proximity meant she couldn't think straight. Subtly she tried to shift so their legs were not touching.

'Shush,' she said, glancing at the door. She wouldn't put it past her sister to be listening outside.

'She seems nice. Resourceful. Independent. Able to make her own decisions.'

'She's twenty years old.'

'The same age as you when you married Lord Somersham.'

'And look how happy that made me,' Francesca murmured.

'Have you asked her if she wants you to sacrifice the rest of your life for her?'

'Of course not. And it's none of your business.'

He shrugged as if agreeing with her, then leant in and started to trace a lazy pattern across the back of her hand with his fingers.

'Ben,' she said, not knowing herself if she was asking him to stop or begging him to continue.

'Frannie.'

'We can't do this,' she said, wishing she didn't believe her own words. Her body wanted to lean in to him and succumb to every pleasure he was offering.

'We can,' he said. 'We're both consenting adults, free and unfettered.'

That was technically true. She was a widow and still had not formally accepted Lord Huntley's proposal, even though in her heart she knew it was only a matter of time.

'It would be a fun way to get yourself out of marrying Huntley,' he murmured.

'Stop it.'

'Your choice,' he said, sitting back. 'Where are you taking me today?'

'I thought we could have a little break from each other today,' Francesca said sweetly. She knew she needed some distance to think rationally about the kiss they'd shared the night before. Time and distance to lock it up in a box where it couldn't ever escape and plague her thoughts like it did now.

'The sun is shining, it might be cold, but you've got your coat back. I can't think of a better time to get out in the fresh air together.'

'I find myself a little tired from last night.'

He grinned and she felt herself blushing, knowing exactly what he was thinking.

'Rest today, then,' he said. 'I'll pick you up tonight at nine for an evening of mystery.'

'Nothing scandalous?' she asked.

'I promise.'

Reluctantly she nodded. At least she would have the day to get hold of her emotions and talk some sense into herself. There would be no kissing, no discreet but passionate affairs, no wishing for something that could never be.

'Until tonight,' Ben said, taking her hand and planting a kiss just below the knuckles. 'And I promise to be on my best behaviour.'

Ben took his place at the table across from his friends and grinned. Cards were his speciality, he rarely lost a game and over the years had made a fair amount of money from his opponents. He liked to play games where you read the other players, used the skills of understanding body language and subtle changes in demeanour rather than relying on luck. He had two rules: always know when to bow out and only to play while it was still fun. He never broke these rules and as a consequence had never lost any large sums of money in a card game or felt the need to stay when he really should leave.

Sam Robertson and George Fitzgerald had seen him play numerous times and as such the three friends only ever played for fun, with no money involved. It was an opportunity to sit together, share a drink and reconnect when their lives were all so hectic.

He'd known both men for well over a decade. Sam Robertson he'd met on the transport ship on the way to Australia. They'd been two of the youngest convicts, both still children. Immediately they'd formed a friendship that had stayed solid throughout the harsh conditions of the transport ship, the cruel realities of life under the guards as convict workers in Australia, and slowly life had got better as they'd served their sentence and became free men.

Their friendship with George Fitzgerald had come a little later, when the boys had been assigned to work on his father's farm. Mr Fitzgerald, the younger son of an impoverished baron in England, had been fair and kind, treating the boys as people rather than animals under the yoke. One day while working in the fields to bring in the harvest Ben and Sam had spotted a venomous snake ready to spring towards George. They tackled it, saving George from a deadly bite. From then on Mr Fitzgerald had treated them more like sons than convicts, insisting they share lessons with George and slowly giving them the love and kindness to make them believe there was good in the world again. Although Mr Fitzgerald had passed away a couple of years ago the three men were still as close as brothers. Ben found he didn't trust many people in the world, but Robertson and Fitzgerald he could always rely on.

'All set for the house party?' Ben asked.

'As much as I'll ever be,' Robertson replied, grimacing as he looked at his cards.

One of the main reasons they'd returned to England after so long away was Robertson's desire to confront the man who had falsely accused him eighteen years ago and had him convicted of theft. This weekend Ben had agreed to travel to Hampshire with his friend to Lady

Georgina's house party, the daughter of the man Robertson wanted revenge on.

Ben's main motivation for agreeing to go was to keep an eye on Robertson and ensure his friend coped when he confronted the old Earl, but he wouldn't deny it would be good to have a little time away from London, some space to think and consider what he wanted from the rest of his time in England.

Francesca. That was what he wanted. He wanted her in his arms and in his bed. He could deny it all he liked, but the attraction he felt for her was overwhelming in its intensity.

'How is Lady Somersham?' Fitzgerald asked mildly as Robertson stood to fetch some drinks.

'Well, I believe,' Ben said.

'You believe?'

'I'm not privy to her innermost thoughts.'

'Yet,' Fitzgerald murmured, 'I'm curious as to why you're spending so much time with her.'

Ben leaned back in his chair and ran a hand through his hair. He was curious, too. If he could understand his own motivations, it might make the whole Francesca situation much easier to contain and cope with.

'We merely want to renew our friendship, to find out what each of us has been doing all these years. And Lady Somersham has asked

me to accompany her to some events,' Ben
fibbed, knowing it was he who'd pushed for
the eight days together. 'What gentleman could
deny her that?'

'You've never wanted to be a gentleman in
your life, Crawford,' Fitzgerald said.

'True.'

'Outings, eh?' Fitzgerald asked, a suggestive
glint in his eye.

'Not like that,' Ben said quickly, trying to
suppress the image of Francesca in his bed, the
way her chemise had clung to her curves as
she'd sat up, the beautiful flush to her cheeks
as she'd awaited his arrival.

'Are you sure you're not in love with her?'

Ben nearly choked on thin air he was so surprised by the question.

'I've only known the woman five minutes,'
he said, hearing the defensive note to his voice.

'Twenty-odd years,' Fitzgerald corrected
him. 'You've only been *reacquainted* for five
minutes. And in the eighteen years you've been
away you haven't been able to forget about her,
have you?'

'I'm not in love with her,' he ground out. Perhaps once, perhaps when they'd been children
he *had* loved her in the way one could in child-

hood. But now he felt a myriad of other emotions, but certainly not love.

Fitzgerald shrugged. 'Fair enough.'

'What's fair enough?' Robertson asked, re-entering the room with three glasses of whisky.

'The mysteries of Crawford's heart.'

'You're going to have to let someone in one day,' Robertson said, placing the glass of whisky down in front of Ben.

'I thought we were here to play cards,' Ben said, not looking at his two friends.

'This is more important,' Robertson said, sitting down and swinging his chair back on to two legs. It was a habit he'd had since they were youths together and it still riled Ben. He grabbed the chair, set it back on four legs and ignored Robertson's grin. 'You don't trust anyone, you have affair after affair after affair and never do you let a woman get close to your heart.'

'You two aren't exactly good role models for a settled life,' Ben murmured.

'We're not talking about us. And Fitzgerald is peculiarly well adjusted,' Robertson said, 'Must have been something to do with spending his childhood with his family and not among a bunch of convicts.'

'Strange how much of a difference that might make,' Fitzgerald said.

'The next woman you have in your bed, pause for a moment and ask yourself what is stopping you from feeling something deeper for her,' Robertson said.

Ben grumbled something incomprehensible and thankfully his two friends settled back down to play cards again. He didn't need their insights into his emotions. He knew he was a little stunted when it came to initiating a deeper relationship. No doubt it stemmed from being torn from his family at such a young age. That, and his feeling that he didn't quite belong anywhere. He was a wealthy man, influential in his own way, yet most certainly not a gentleman. And class seemed to be the thing that mattered when it came to marriage. Even though he was wealthier than half the men that considered themselves the cream of society in England, he would never be deemed worthy enough or refined enough for their daughters.

He only had to look at Francesca—for her, Lord Huntley was considered a decent match, despite his age and rumoured issues with anger. Huntley had an old family name and pure pedigree and that elevated him above anything Ben could ever be. It made Ben feel sick that it was such an inconsequential thing that mattered. Anyone could inherit a family name—it was much harder to build a successful business from nothing.

He shook his head. Even thinking of a future with Francesca was ridiculous. Instead he would enjoy the eight days they had together and hope the memories would last a lifetime.

Chapter Ten

'Goodnight, Father,' Francesca called as she slipped out through the front door. To keep up the pretence she was going to a dinner party hosted by one of her widowed friends she was wearing an evening gown and thin satin shoes again, but had her thick coat thrown over the top despite it being frayed along the hem in numerous places. She wasn't sure where Ben was going to take her tonight, but she had a feeling it would be outdoors. It was easier to hide from curious eyes somewhere outside, although even just a few steps from her front door she was already shivering. The winter had been colder than usual, with snow every few weeks and the rivers and ponds in the city freezing over on numerous occasions.

Quickly she checked left and right, paranoid someone might be watching her go off to meet an entirely unsuitable man, and then hurried off down the street. Ben was waiting for her in a carriage at the corner and as he saw her approaching he opened the door and hopped down. Not for the first time she felt her insides flip when she saw him and she had to pause and compose herself before she took another step.

'Good evening, Frannie,' he said, leaning forward and giving her an entirely inappropriate kiss on the cheek. She felt the skin tingle where his lips had been and quickly tried to hide her blush.

'Behave yourself,' she admonished.

'There's no one here but us,' Ben said. He was right. On a night like tonight no one was lingering outside and all the carriages had their windows closed and curtains drawn against the freezing temperatures. 'Come inside.'

He helped her up, waited until she was settled on the seat before he stepped inside and sat down next to her. It was intimate, their legs touching through the multiple layers of clothing, but on the seat opposite was a large package taking up most of the room.

'Where are we going?' Francesca asked, trying to ignore the warmth emanating from his body. It would be so easy to sink into his arms, but she knew she would struggle to ever come up again.

'It's a surprise,' Ben said as the carriage set off.

'What's that?' She motioned to the parcel on the opposite seat of the carriage.

'A present. You will need it tonight.'

'A present?'

'Nothing extravagant,' he said, 'But I couldn't expect you to venture out on a night like tonight and not keep you adequately warm.'

Images of him tumbling her into his bed, a roaring fire across the room and their bodies perspiring from the heat they generated filled her mind and hastily she looked away.

'Can I see?' she said. It had been a long time since anyone had bought her a present. In the early days of their marriage her husband had bought her one or two trinkets, but nothing extravagant, and even that had stopped when their relationship had begun to sour. As he'd got more and more into debt he'd withdrawn further into himself until even a civil greeting had been too much to expect. Lord Huntley wasn't a man for presents either. To him their proposed union was a business deal, to be conducted with her father with no sentimentality involved whatsoever.

Reaching across to the other seat he pulled the package towards them, resting it on his lap.

'Open it,' he said quietly, taking her hand and placing it on the string that held the parcel together.

Pulling at the knot, Francesca opened the package, frowning as the paper fell away and a swathe of beautiful deep red material cascaded out.

'It's a cloak. A thick one. Something to keep you warm this winter.'

Francesca felt the tears building and struggled to contain them. It was the most thoughtful present. He must have seen the almost threadbare condition of her coat and of course he would know the rumours about her family's dire financial situation.

'Ben,' she said, hearing her voice catch in her throat, 'it's too much.'

He turned to her, none of the usual humour or light-heartedness in his eyes, and shook his head.

'A person needs to be warm, Frannie, it's a basic human need.'

Wondering what else he considered a basic human need, she looked down, running her fingers over the soft material.

'Thank you,' she whispered. 'It's the nicest present I've ever received.'

'Now I know you're lying,' Ben said, the grin returning to his face. 'I remember a young girl who once told me the best present she'd ever received was a baby piglet.'

Immediately Francesca smiled. It *had* been her best present. Ben had given it to her when she was eight years old. It had been the runt, unable to fight its way through the rest of the piglets to get to its mother's milk. She'd loved that piglet, nurtured and cared for it for two years as it grew until her father had declared the now almost adult-sized pig too big for the house and demanded she take it back to the farm on the edge of the estate.

'You're right,' she said, 'Porker was better than a cloak. But I doubt I'd get away with having a pig for a pet now.'

'Society wouldn't approve?' Ben asked.

'I think it would be frowned upon.'

'Perhaps you should do it anyway,' he said, his hand resting on the soft material of the cloak just an inch away from hers. 'Perhaps you should decide you don't care one iota what society thinks and do what makes you happy instead.'

'Wouldn't that be nice,' Francesca said.

'I'm serious, Frannie. People here seem to make so many important decisions on what *looks* right. Take your marriage to Huntley.'

'Proposed marriage,' she murmured the correction.

'It wouldn't make you happy. You're only doing it to save your family from the shame of financial ruin.'

'That is a pretty good motive,' she protested.

'Not good enough. Let them sell the houses. Let them sell all the land. Sell everything. Live in a little cottage somewhere. Stop spending money they don't have keeping up a pretence of wealth. Then you might be able to choose a life where you're not tied to a man with a reputation for being unkind to his wives.'

She looked down, not wanting to admit how accurate Ben was with his statement. Her father did focus too much on wanting to keep up a pretence of wealth. Their house in London and estate in the country had only a couple of rooms furnished, those which might receive visitors. The rest of the rooms were empty shells. Everything they did was to try to show the world they were *normal*, even when the act of doing it put them further into debt. On a few occasions Francesca had wondered about just running away from it all, finding employment as a companion or governess for a few years and saving up for a little cottage at the coast somewhere. If it wasn't for her sister she might have done so already. Although she knew that she would find it difficult adjusting her expectations of life. She wanted to be free, but for so long she'd lived life as a lady—as the daughter of a viscount and then Lady Somersham. To become someone who worked for a living, that would be hard to accept, even though she suspected in the long term she would be happier.

'I don't want to argue about this,' she said. 'You know why I'm doing it. Can't we just enjoy this evening?'

'As you wish,' he said, capitulating easily. For a moment she wondered why he was so concerned about her future and she felt a flurry of hope inside her. It had been a very long time since anyone had put her needs first.

They continued the journey in silence for a few more minutes, Francesca aware of Ben's body every time he shifted, every time his leg innocently touched hers.

'Are we going to one of the pleasure gardens?' she asked.

'Have some patience and you'll find out,' he said, infuriatingly not giving anything away.

'Ranelagh Pleasure Gardens?' she asked. 'Or Vauxhall, perhaps?'

Vauxhall was a little less upmarket, with a cheaper admission price, but would probably afford them more anonymity. There were rumours about what couples got up to there, with plenty of dark avenues and secret gardens, but most of it was probably grossly exaggerated. Silently she chastised herself for the bubble of anticipation at the thought of escaping somewhere private with Ben. She was a widow, a respectable lady, and in a few short weeks she would likely be engaged to be married once more. As much as she might want to be reckless, to indulge her baser desires, she knew that once again she would have to deny her own wants and needs and do what was right.

'Patience,' Ben said again and she saw the grin on his face as she glanced sideways. Patience never had been one of her virtues. She'd always wanted to know things immediately, to be told exactly what was happening.

'It's too late for a stroll in the park,' she mused, thinking perhaps it wasn't a pleasure garden after all.

'Mmm...' Ben murmured non-committally.

'And I wouldn't need a cloak if we were going somewhere indoors.'

'Unless it was very cold indeed,' Ben said, looking as though he were enjoying himself immensely, teasing her by withholding the knowledge of what they were going to do with their evening.

'It wouldn't hurt to tell me.'

'It would ruin the surprise.'

'What if I don't like surprises?'

'Everyone likes surprises. Just some people are too impatient to wait for them.'

She huffed, sat back and twitched the curtain, peering out of the window to see if she could find any clues as to where they were going.

Only ten minutes later the carriage slowed to a stop and Ben hopped out, turning to help her down before reaching up to fetch the package with her new cloak. As she looked around, puzzled as to why they'd stopped in a pleasant but quiet residential street, he draped the cloak over her shoulders, his fingers tickling her neck as he adjusted it. Francesca looked down, feeling the warmth from the luxurious garment already making a difference to her cold body.

'Ben...' she said quietly, trying to convey the myriad of emotions that were fighting for supremacy inside her.

'It's only a cloak, Frannie,' he said, offering her his arm.

It wasn't only a cloak, though. It was the most thoughtful gift anyone had ever given her.

'What are we doing here?' she asked, looking around.

'It's not quite Ranelagh or Vauxhall,' he said, smiling at her confusion, 'But I thought they might be a little too public for us to be seen together.' He paused, slid his hand into hers and then pulled her along the pavement to the quietest end of the street. 'Here. Shall I give you a boost up first?'

Frowning with confusion, Francesca looked at the wrought-iron railings that surrounded the private gardens for the residents of the street. It was like a small park, but the gates were locked and only those with keys could get inside.

'You don't mean in there?' she asked.

'Unless you're not up to it,' Ben said, a hint of challenge in his voice.

It was what they'd always done as children, challenged the other to more dangerous and more difficult pursuits, and Francesca felt the years falling away as she looked at Ben. For just one night she didn't want to be Lady Somersham, she wanted to be someone reckless and fun.

'It's you I'm worried about,' she said, moving up to test the sturdiness of the railings and feel the cold metal beneath her hands. 'You're not as young as you used to be.'

'None of us are.'

'Some of us carry it better,' she said, tapping a gloved hand on the metal.

'Cheeky minx. I wouldn't worry about me, my body has been honed by years of hard labour, while you've been sitting around idle in your drawing rooms and ballrooms.'

'How do you know I don't break into private gardens every week?'

'Sometimes I feel I know you better than I know myself,' he murmured in her ear.

She shivered, knowing everything about this evening was dangerous. There was the physical danger of climbing over the iron railings into a place they were not allowed. The danger of being caught together somewhere they had no excuse to be, but most of all the danger of being alone with a man she was finding it supremely hard to resist.

Everything in Francesca's life had schooled her to guard her virtue, to never allow herself to let her desires and emotions overcome her common sense, but here she was with a man she found incredibly attractive, allowing him to escort her into a dark and secluded garden. She knew if he tried to kiss her again she would be powerless to protest and deep inside she knew there was nothing she wanted more than to feel his lips on hers again.

'On to that tree?' Francesca asked, eyeing the railings critically. They were shoulder height, but at one corner a tree branched out over them, providing an easy route into the gardens.

'Have you got the strength?'

'Of course.' She wasn't entirely sure if she did, but was determined to give it her best try. Although she kept active, dancing while in London and walking and riding in the country, none of her pursuits required the upper body strength needed to climb a tree.

'I'll be right behind you,' he said, offering his hands to boost her up.

Placing one foot in his hand, she felt him lift her and carefully she caught hold of the tree branch, pulling herself up on to it until she was sitting comfortably with her legs dangling over the gardens beyond the railings. She watched as Ben jumped, caught hold of the tree branch and pulled himself up, the muscles straining the seams of his coat, but otherwise no other outward signs of the effort it must have taken.

Lithe and nimble as a cat he skirted along the

branch, swung himself around her and dropped to the ground on the other side of the railings.

'I'll catch you,' he said, holding out his arms.

Just as she pushed herself off the branch Francesca realised she had no fear. She *knew* he would catch her, knew he wouldn't let her fall. She wouldn't jump into the arms of Lord Huntley or have contemplated trusting her late husband in this way.

'Nice work, Lady Somersham,' he said, setting her on the ground, but not hurrying to remove his arm from around her waist.

'I break into private gardens all the time,' she said, finding her footing and adjusting her new cloak. 'Climbing trees and vaulting over railings isn't much of a challenge.'

'I'll have to find something to stretch you next time,' he murmured.

He took her hand and, although they were both wearing thick gloves to protect themselves from the freezing temperatures, Francesca felt a rush of blood to her fingers at the intimacy of the gesture. Most men offered their arm or would content themselves merely with walking side by side with a lady, but Ben took her hand as boldly as if there were nothing strange in the action.

Slowly they meandered along the path, having to take care in the near-total darkness to avoid any obstacles.

'The stars look different from here,' Ben said as they paused to look up at the sky. 'You wouldn't think it, it's the same sky after all, but they look different here to how they do in the Australian sky.'

'Is it very different there?' Francesca asked softly. Ever since they'd become reacquainted she'd wanted to ask about his life, to find out what he'd been doing all these years, but she'd been too afraid. Too afraid that it might have been nearly two decades of hell because of her father and that he might resent her even just a little for it.

'I can't think of two more different places,' he said. 'England is so ordered, so structured. Australia is just wilderness. Even the settlements are nothing more than a collection of buildings.' He paused and Francesca saw his eyes softening. 'The countryside though, Frannie, that's where you fall in love with the country.'

She hardly knew anything about Australia. After learning of Ben's sentence eighteen years ago she'd tried to find out as much as she could about the country on the other side of the world, but information was thin on the ground. Hardly anyone who had been had ever come back and the reports that were published were mainly from the voyage where it was first discovered. Her imagination had supplied images of vast swathes of scrubland, dry and dusty with no redeeming features.

'It's beautiful. There's fields and farmland just like here, but so much more. There are beaches of golden sand and the ocean is brilliant blue. The mountains near Sydney are misty and cool and although I've never been the interior of the country is meant to be filled with miles upon miles of orange sand and great rocky out-crops. One day I will venture to the very centre of the country and see for myself.'

'You plan to go back?' she asked. Swept up in the passion of the past few days she'd forgot-ten his return to England was temporary.

'Of course. It's my home.'

'You have work there? A family?' Francesca found she was holding her breath. A lot could happen in eighteen years. Ben might be mar-ried with a brood of children for all she knew.

He laughed. 'Work, yes, a family, no.'

'And these friends you came over to England with, they're planning on returning, too?'

'Robertson and Fitzgerald. Yes. We all have farms to run.'

Francesca found her eyes widening. 'You run a farm?' She wasn't sure what she expected Ben to have been doing the last ten years after his sentence was completed, but even though he was an intelligent man she never imagined he might be making a success of his life. It took a special type of man to turn his life around after serving eight years for theft and being transported to Australia.

'I own a farm,' he corrected her. 'Actually, lots of farms.'

'How?' she asked, feeling such a mixture of emotions that she barely knew where to start dealing with them. Of course she was happy his life hadn't been completely ruined by her father's actions, but she felt a sense of loss and panic at the thought of him leaving. It wasn't her place to want him to stay, wasn't her right to miss him, but still she knew she would. In a couple of months she would be married again and he would return to his home in Australia. That was how things had to be, but it didn't mean she had to be happy about it.

'Luck,' he said, 'and a little work.'

She doubted much of it had been luck. He was a determined man and underneath the humour and easy-going attitude she would wager there was a man who worked harder than he let on.

* * *

Ben watched as Frannie screwed up her face, steeling herself to ask the next question on her mind.

'So it hasn't all been terrible?' she asked quietly. 'Not every single moment?'

He stopped and turned to her, waiting for her to lift her eyes to meet his in the darkness.

'No,' he said softly, 'It hasn't all been terrible.' It was difficult to resist kissing her. With her face turned up to his and that look of forlorn concern in her eyes he just wanted to cup her chin and kiss her until she forgot all her worries.

He had suffered greatly over the years, with the terrible conditions of the hulk ship and even worse on the transport ship, then the years of hard labour under a hot sun supervised by cruel and petty guards, but he realised in his own way Francesca had been suffering, too. It was clear she felt guilty for not being able to save him all those years ago despite doing everything a ten-year-old girl could do. Added to that were the years of unhappiness foisted on her by her father and her husband.

Ben knew he'd weathered the hard years and come out stronger on the other side and now he knew the worst of his life was behind him.

Francesca still might have her hardest years ahead of her.

'I survived, Frannie,' he said softly, raising up one hand and letting his fingers trail down her cheek, 'The first few years were terrible, but I survived.'

She nodded, not able to tear her gaze away from his.

'And then life began to get better. I've got six huge farms, great friends and my freedom. No one judges you in Australia for being an ex-convict—over half the population have such beginnings.'

'But you lost so much,' she said. 'Your family. Your childhood.'

There was no way he would ever get his childhood back, but one of the main reasons he'd returned to England was to see his family. In a few short weeks his father would return home and Ben would make the journey to Essex to see the man who'd done everything in his power to show Ben he hadn't been forgotten even though he was half a world away.

'I haven't lost my family,' Ben said quietly. 'And I try not to dwell on the loss of my childhood.'

She nodded, her movements shaky.

'I always imagined the worst…' she said quietly. 'It was terrible never knowing what had happened to you.'

'Hush,' he said as she buried her head in his shoulder. He suspected she was crying, trying to hide the tears from him, and feeling a rush of sentimentality he wrapped an arm around her and pulled her in even closer.

Waiting while she composed herself, he found his fingers trailing instinctively across the nape of her neck. It was warm under the fur lining of her new cloak and her skin was as soft as the finest velvet.

'Ben,' she murmured, emerging from his shoulder. It was phrased half as a question, half as a plea, and he knew if she looked up at him with those beautiful blue eyes he wouldn't be able to stop himself from kissing her.

Slowly she looked up and even in the darkness he could see the desire and confusion mixed in her gaze.

Ben knew a lot about desire. Since he'd gained his freedom he'd promised not to ever deny himself pleasure whenever the opportunity arose, as long as it didn't damage anyone, of course. He'd conducted numerous short and pleasurable affairs, always making sure they ended before either party became too invested in the relationship. He'd felt desire before, of course he had, but never had he wanted a woman quite like he wanted Francesca.

'Come,' he said, grabbing her hand and pulling her through the gardens to a spot of grass under the trees. Quickly he helped her unclasp her cloak and lay it on the ground, lowering Francesca down on to it before lying down beside her.

Above them the bare branches of the trees swayed in the breeze and as Ben reached out and pulled Francesca towards him he caught a glimpse of the moon emerging from behind a cloud.

Slowly, as if they had all the time in the world, he kissed her. Beneath his lips he felt hers open, inviting him in, her arms wrapping around his back and pulling him closer.

'What are we doing?' she whispered in between kisses.

'Life is for enjoying, Frannie,' he murmured in her ear, 'Let me help you enjoy it.'

Slowly he trailed a hand inside the coat she was wearing, the threadbare one she'd kept on under her cloak, feeling the warmth of her skin just underneath her collarbone. As he kissed her she fiddled with the fastenings, opening up the coat and allowing him access to her body. At this simple gesture he felt himself grow even harder, with every nerve in his body stimulated and on edge.

Loving how Francesca moaned as he bent his head to trail kisses along the neckline of her dress, he pushed the material as low as it would go, revealing the smooth swell of her breasts. Taking his time, with Francesca's hands tangled in his hair, he kissed lower and lower. Tugging less gently, he tried to pull her dress even further down, but the material was too stiff and the fastenings too tight.

'Don't stop,' she begged, her fingers still tangled in his hair.

Underneath him he felt her hips rise in an instinctive movement, pushing against his, and in that moment he would have done anything for a soft bed and warm covers. He wanted her so badly, but even he was too much of a gentleman to expect a lady to make love on the freezing ground of a public garden.

'Soon,' he whispered, pulling away, pausing only to kiss her one last time.

As his body stopped touching hers he watched her face, waiting for the inevitable transformation. For a few minutes Francesca had been caught up in her desire, not caring that her actions were scandalous and they'd been reckless in a public place. Now, with her sensibilities returning, she would pull away from him and regret their intimacy.

Quickly she shuffled backwards, as if trying to put as much distance between her and Ben as possible. Her hand struck a tree root and she let out a cry of surprise, stopping where she was.

'What are we doing?' she whispered as she hugged her hand to her chest.

'The inevitable,' Ben murmured. Deep down he'd known all along this was where they'd end up. Not exactly here, in this private garden, but certainly in each other's arms. He'd felt Francesca's pull the moment he'd set eyes on her again and somewhere inside he'd always known that they would not be able to go their separate ways before they'd quenched the desire they had for each other.

'Nothing is inevitable,' she snapped. 'It was foolish and reckless, but certainly not inevitable.'

'Whatever you say, Frannie,' Ben said, knowing that she didn't believe her own words.

He stood, offering her his hand. For a moment she looked like she was thinking of refusing.

'It's not inevitable,' she said as she allowed him to pull her up.

'I've seen how you look at me, Frannie,' Ben

said, suddenly wanting to shock her, to show her she didn't have to always abide by society's rules. 'Don't try to pretend you're anything but an eager participant. We both know I only have to kiss you here and you'll fall into my arms again.' He kissed her on the neck, just below the earlobe, and felt her shudder with anticipation.

Quickly she pulled away, her eyes filled with anger and defiance.

'You're so arrogant,' she hissed, evidently trying to keep her voice down due to where they were despite her anger. 'You think any woman, no matter what class difference there is, will just fall into your arms as soon as you smile in her direction.'

He shrugged. 'In my experience they do.' Pausing, he caught her hand, lowering his voice to a more soothing level. 'And what's this obsession with class, Frannie? Your whole life is governed by rules and society and wanting to be perceived in a certain way. People are people, whether they are rich or poor, well educated or illiterate.'

'You wouldn't understand.'

'Try me,' he said, pulling her to face him.

She looked so lost, so forlorn that he regretted his outburst. He'd just wanted her to admit that she was just as human as he, that she had the same desires, the same needs, no matter how hard she tried to bury them.

'All my life I've been expected to behave in a certain way. To dress appropriately, to speak in the right way, to be interesting to gentlemen, but not *too* interesting. Every single day of my life I've been told again and again to conform.'

He watched her, saw the pain on her face and realised that she must have struggled with society's expectations over the years.

'A wife should run a comfortable home for her husband. A wife should conduct herself with dignity and decorum at all times. A wife should never question or nag her husband as to where he's been. A wife should provide and raise well-mannered children.'

'That's the expectation?' Ben asked.

'Yes. And I know I don't *have* to conform, but in reality I do. This is my world, Ben. If I break the rules, I'd be shunned by everyone I know, cast out. What would I do then?'

'And that's why your family are so insistent on maintaining the pretence that everything is well, even when they are in so much debt.'

'What would they do with a small country cottage? My father is a viscount, brought up to be a leader of men. He has been told throughout his life that he is important, he matters. To take that away from him would destroy him.'

'And you?' Ben asked quietly.

'Who knows? I'm not brave enough to leave everything behind and I don't want to desert my family.' She sounded resigned to her fate. 'But I don't think I care like my parents do, not about keeping up appearances. Everyone knows we are in debt anyway. I find it ridiculous the pretence we go through, incurring more debts just to make it seem like everything is normal.'

'What would society say if they saw you in here with me?' Ben asked, leaning in and placing a gentle kiss on Francesca's cheek. She didn't pull away this time, instead her whole body sank into his.

'I don't think I'd get many invitations, my social calendar would look rather bare.'

They both fell silent for a few minutes, contemplating her answer.

'Come,' he said eventually, guiding her gently along the path again, 'Let's enjoy the gardens.'

The argument that had sizzled between them was now almost entirely forgotten, but Ben knew their kiss was not. As he led her down one of the well-manicured paths he could feel her heart beating hard inside her chest. One day he would get her to see that her happiness was more important than leading a conventional life. And one day very soon he would kiss her again somewhere he wouldn't feel guilty for stripping her naked and spending the whole night making love to her.

Chapter Eleven

'Don't make eye contact,' Caroline Yaxley whispered, 'or we'll never be rid of him.'

Francesca was sitting with her sister and Miss Yaxley at the perimeter of the ballroom, thoroughly enjoying herself. When she'd been a debutante Francesca had revelled in the friendship of a close and lovely group of female friends, but over the years they'd lost contact, mainly due to her late husband's dislike of her going out and enjoying herself. Felicity and Miss Yaxley were huddled together, talking so fast about so many topics it was hard to keep up, but their faces were alight with excitement making them both look beautiful.

'He's such a bore,' Felicity said, casting her eyes down to the ground. 'I can make small talk until I'm blue in the face, but it's so difficult with Mr Witherington.'

Glancing surreptitiously over her shoulder, Francesca identified the gentleman in question—a pallid and uncertain-looking man in his mid-thirties.

'Don't look,' Felicity and Miss Yaxley whispered together, pulling Francesca round to face forward again.

'Anyway, the Duke proposed and Georgina accepted him, even though she's completely in love with someone else,' Caroline said, sighing dramatically.

They were discussing the house party Felicity hadn't been invited to the previous weekend, the one Ben had disappeared off to. *Ben.* Francesca felt the heat rise in her cheeks as she remembered their illicit embraces shared in the private gardens. She should never have been so reckless, so bold, but she couldn't bring herself to regret her actions. Every day and every night since she'd found herself thinking of him, remembering how he tasted, how his lips felt on hers, imagining what else might have happened between them had they been somewhere more private and a little warmer.

'Good evening, ladies,' a deep voice said from just behind them. Francesca felt herself stiffen and hoped her sister, with her all-seeing eyes, wouldn't notice her reaction.

'Mr Crawford,' Caroline gushed, 'How wonderful to see you.'

Feeling a momentary pang of jealousy, she wondered how well Ben knew Miss Yaxley. They'd been at the house party together and everyone knew there were different rules outside London.

'Any news on Lady Georgina?' Ben asked cryptically.

Miss Yaxley shrugged, then sighed. 'She's stubborn, always has been.'

'I have a feeling things will work out all the same,' Ben said. 'Now, ladies, you must excuse me, but I am going to deprive you of Lady Somersham's company. She promised to teach me how to dance a Scotch Reel.'

'You're dancing again,' Felicity said with a smile.

Francesca nodded, not able to do anything else. Really she shouldn't be dancing at balls until her mourning period had completely finished. It was one thing to attend as a chaperon, quite another to be seen gaily prancing around with another man on her arm while she was still meant to be remembering her late husband. Still she felt the frisson of excitement she always did when given the opportunity to dance and allowed Ben to assist her to her feet.

'How was the house party?' Francesca asked, not wanting to pry, but unable to help herself.

'A disaster. Robertson made a complete mess of everything,' Ben said with a sigh, 'He has fallen head over heels in love with Lady Georgina, but was too much of a fool to admit it and now has ruined everything.'

Although she hadn't met Sam Robertson she knew a little about him from how Ben spoke of him and the rumours that circulated in society. He and Lady Georgina were of completely different social classes and it was unlikely a romance between them could ever work out, but she felt sorry for Ben's friend all the same.

'Still, he's a lucky devil with a smooth tongue, I have a feeling he'll persuade Lady Georgina to pass over her Duke before the week is out.'

'Surely not?' Francesca asked, shocked at the idea of the daughter of an earl breaking off her engagement to a duke for a man of a much lower social class. It was the stuff of fairy tales, and romantic in theory, but everyone knew fairy tales couldn't be translated into real-life moments.

'Let's hope so. He's a good man, one of the best. I doubt I'd still be alive today if it wasn't for him. I want him to find some happiness.'

'You met him in Australia?' Francesca asked as they circled the ballroom, waiting for the announcement of the next dance.

Ben shook his head. 'On the transport ship. I'd already served almost two years on one of the hulk ships on the Thames and I was a shadow of my former self by the time we were actually transported, but meeting Robertson saved me.'

'He was a young boy, too?' She desperately wanted to know more about his life after his conviction, but didn't want him to relive the worst parts unnecessarily.

'Even younger,' Ben said with a grimace. 'I was twelve when I was convicted, he was just ten.'

'And you stayed together throughout your time in Australia?'

'We did. Our first job was north of Sydney Cove, digging a road. Then after that we were taken as convict workers to Mr Fitzgerald's farm.'

'The Mr Fitzgerald I've met?' Francesca asked with a frown. They seemed such good friends, not like convict worker and landowner.

'His father. Mr Fitzgerald was a good man. Perhaps the best man I've ever had the good fortune to know.' The words were said solemnly and Francesca could tell they were heartfelt and genuine. 'He saved me. He saved *us*, Sam and I. He plucked us from the awful abyss that all convicts stare into at some point of their sentence and taught us there is good in the world.'

'He sounds like a wonderful man.' Francesca felt the tears welling up, threatening to spill down her cheeks, and heard the thick quality to her voice. Ben had only needed someone like Mr Fitzgerald to rescue him because she'd not been strong enough to save him from her father's cruel machinations.

'He was...' Sam paused, his solemn expression turning to a grin as George Fitzgerald approached them.

'Lady Somersham,' Fitzgerald greeted her, 'a pleasure as always.'

'We were just talking about your father,' Ben said.

'Ben...' Francesca paused, then quickly corrected herself. 'Mr Crawford was telling me how he saved him and Mr Robertson.'

'Always was a sentimental fool,' Fitzgerald said with a sombre shake of his head. 'Has Crawford told you the story of why he took him and Robertson under his wing?'

Shaking her head, Francesca waited for either man to continue.

'He got it into his head those two reprobates were heroes,' Fitzgerald said, keeping a straight face, but only just.

'What Fitzgerald isn't telling you,' Ben said, cutting in, 'is he was foolish enough to nearly be killed by a poisonous snake and Robertson and myself put our own lives on the line wrestling the monstrous beast to the ground and saving his life.'

'A mild exaggeration,' Fitzgerald murmured, 'But there *was* a snake and it did spring and if it had bitten me it would have been deadly.'

'Do we regret it?' Ben asked, dodging a punch on the arm from Fitzgerald, and Francesca found herself laughing as the two friends grinned at one another.

'You two wouldn't know what to do with yourselves without me,' Fitzgerald said.

'It's true,' Ben said once Fitzgerald had taken his leave. 'He's a good man just like his father and, when Robertson and I were at our lowest, they showed us how to be human again.'

She wanted to ask more, wanted to learn every little detail about the time he'd spent in Australia, but at that moment the music started up from the next dance and Ben pulled her forward. For now she would have to content herself with that little insight into his life.

Breathless and laughing, Francesca looked radiant as they finished the dance with a curtsy and a bow. She was a wonderful dancer, her body moved instinctively and her feet never missed a step, but what really made her a pleasure to dance with was the light in her eyes, the pure enjoyment and the happiness when she was dancing to the music.

'Lady Somersham,' Lord Huntley said disapprovingly as Ben escorted her from the dance floor, looking for a glass of something cool to refresh them both.

'Lord Huntley, what a surprise. I did not expect to see you tonight,' Francesca said and Ben could hear the note of panic in her voice.

'I decided to attend at the last minute,' Lord Huntley said with a dismissive wave of his hand. 'I see you are dancing.' It was a simple comment, but his voice was loaded with meaning.

'I am,' she said after a moment's hesitation. After all, she could hardly deny it.

'My fault, I'm afraid,' Ben said cheerfully. 'I rather bullied her into it.'

Lord Huntley turned to him for the first time with an air of interest.

'I don't think we've had the pleasure of an introduction,' he said, his eyes narrowing ever so slightly. Their meeting a few weeks earlier evidently hadn't made much of an impression on the Viscount.

'Lord Huntley, this is Mr Crawford,' Francesca said. He saw her hesitate before adding, 'He is an old friend of the family, we've known each other since childhood.'

Lord Huntley inclined his head, out of habit more than politeness, but Ben saw the shrewd and calculating look in his eye.

'Mr Crawford,' he said slowly, 'I was under the impression you've only recently arrived in the country.'

'That's right,' Ben said, appraising the older man. He might appear bombastic and pompous, but there was an observant man underneath the bluster.

'I'd be interested in how you and Lady Somersham have managed to maintain a friendship with you not residing in the country,' he said.

Francesca gave a nervous laugh and Ben felt his heart shrivel a little. This was the man she was going to marry. This cruel old bully who would slowly squeeze the life out of her until there was no more vibrancy, no more free spirit. She'd be crushed under the weight of his constant disapproval. She deserved so much more than a lifetime of misery with Lord Huntley.

'Letters,' Ben said shortly. 'Lady Somersham is a fantastic correspondent.'

'I wouldn't know,' Lord Huntley murmured, looking at the woman he was determined to make his wife. 'Letters make it all the way to Australia, then?'

'I hope so,' Ben said, 'otherwise the weekly instructions I send my land steward are a little pointless.'

It would be foolish to underestimate the man standing in front of them. He already knew more about Ben than anyone else in London and that made Ben uneasy. He obviously distrusted Ben and would probably do anything to ensure he and Lady Somersham didn't spend any more time together.

'Seeing as you are dancing now, I will take the next dance,' Lord Huntley said, addressing himself to Francesca. It was said as a statement rather than request to dance and Ben saw the moment of rebellion flare in Francesca's eyes before she submitted and nodded demurely.

'Of course, Lord Huntley.'

'I'm sure you'll be going back to Australia soon,' Huntley said over his shoulder. 'It is a pity you'll miss the wedding.'

'A shame,' Ben murmured, watching Francesca's stiff posture as they walked away.

They lined up for the next dance and Ben gave a snort of disgust when the musicians struck up for a waltz. It was the most intimate of dances allowed at a society ball, a wonderful dance where it was perfectly acceptable to hold your partner in your arms while you swept them around the dance floor, and now Francesca was being subjected to dancing it with Lord Huntley.

'They don't look very well matched,' Fitzgerald said as he came to stand next to Ben.

'He's not the sort of man I'd wish upon anyone,' Ben said quietly, unable to tear his eyes from the Lord Huntley's oversized hands resting on Francesca's waist.

'Especially not someone you care for,' Fitzgerald murmured.

Ben began to protest, but found his friend had already slipped away. And if he was honest he *did* care for Francesca. Every day he spent with her, he found it harder to deny the depth of the feelings he had for her. It wasn't just desire that clouded his mind every time he looked at her, it was something much more than that.

'Don't be a fool,' he murmured to himself. Francesca had made it perfectly clear where her priorities lay. She would put saving her family from the shame of financial ruin and securing her sister a dowry above her own happiness. And that meant there was no future for them.

It wasn't even just the money that separated them. Ben was a wealthy man now, but what he didn't have was the pure bloodline a woman like Francesca was meant to marry into. He could never be truly accepted into her world, even though it was ridiculous to be separated for such an inconsequential detail.

Friendship, he told himself. That was what they'd had when they were young and that was what they were building now.

And if he hated the idea of Francesca spending even one second in another man's arms, well, he could put that down to the concern of a friend rather than jealousy.

Forcing himself to turn away, he'd only taken one step when he came face to face with Felicity, standing there beaming at him with Miss Yaxley on her arm.

'Walk with us,' Felicity requested, smiling sweetly in an expression that was reflected on Miss Yaxley's face as Ben looked from one to the other.

'For some strange reason I feel nervous all of a sudden,' Ben said, offering an arm to each of the young ladies.

'We're just curious,' Miss Yaxley said.

'How do you know my sister so well, Mr Crawford?' Felicity asked.

'After such a long time out of the country.'

'I wouldn't have thought you would remember many people from your childhood.'

Ben waited in case there was any more, his head already spinning from the double act of Felicity and Miss Yaxley.

'Has your sister not told you?' he asked.

'She's being very coy. Apart from saying she knew you from years ago she's been very tight-lipped.'

'Irritatingly,' added Miss Yaxley with a smile on her face. 'But rumour would have it that you've been out of the country for eighteen years, which would have made Lady Somersham only ten when you left.'

'And that seems rather young for such a friendship to endure,' Felicity added.

Ben shrugged. 'I don't know what to tell you ladies.'

'The truth,' Felicity said quickly. 'How do you know Francesca?'

'We were friends in childhood,' he said simply.

'And…?' Miss Yaxley asked.

'And nothing.'

Felicity sighed, 'I told you, Caroline, it was too much to hope for.'

Caroline scowled and shook her head in disappointment. 'So you haven't been corresponding all this time?'

'I'm sorry to be a disappointment, but, no...' He paused, but realised he needed to know what they were talking about. 'What was too much to hope for?'

Felicity waved a dismissive hand, 'Oh, that you'd been in love with Francesca for eighteen years and had come back to rescue her from the clutches of the evil Lord Huntley.'

Ben felt his eyes widen before he could gain control of himself.

'Shame,' Miss Yaxley said, shaking her head. 'It would have been romantic.'

'And an answer to the Huntley problem.'

'The Huntley problem?' Ben asked, feeling exhausted by the two minutes of conversation. He wondered if the young women were always like this and realised he didn't want to find out.

'You know,' Felicity said, nodding her head towards the dance floor where Lord Huntley still had Francesca in his arms, *'the Huntley problem.'*

'No one wants Lady Somersham to marry Lord Huntley,' Miss Yaxley said dramatically.

'Well, Father does and Lord Huntley,' Felicity corrected her friend, 'But no one whose opinion should actually matter does.'

'Have you spoken to your sister about this?' Ben asked, wondering if Felicity knew her sister was mainly doing it to provide her with a dowry.

'Francesca still thinks I'm about eight years old. She won't discuss it with me—I think she thinks she's protecting me.'

'Soon it will be too late,' Miss Yaxley said ominously.

'Perhaps you could talk to her,' Felicity suggested, turning to Ben.

'I think you overestimate our friendship,' he murmured. He didn't want to tell the young woman in front of him that he had already expressed unease at Francesca's choice of future husband and been unable to sway her opinion away from the decision. 'Perhaps you should talk to her about her motivations behind the marriage.'

Felicity regarded him for at least twenty seconds without saying anything before she groaned. 'She's doing it for me, isn't she? To protect me or some such nonsense.'

'I really think you should ask your sister,' he said.

'If she's marrying that old goat purely to protect me, I will not be very happy,' Felicity said to Miss Yaxley.

'It's the sort of thing she'd do,' Miss Yaxley agreed. 'Sacrifice herself so you could have a better future.'

'I bet he's promised to provide a dowry for me,' Felicity said, pursing her lips together. 'Francesca is always talking about me marrying some nice young man and getting out of the way of Father's *ill-advised schemes.*'

'Even if it means she'll spend the rest of her life miserable,' Miss Yaxley said with a sad shake of her head.

'Thank you, Mr Crawford,' Felicity said, relinquishing his arm. 'Please excuse me, I have a sister to go and batter some sense into.'

Both young women curtsied and hurried off, their heads bent together as if they were plotting and scheming. Feeling a little dazed at the speed of the conversation, Ben moved to the edge of the ballroom, found a convenient marble pillar to lean against and took a moment to straighten his thoughts.

His eyes searched for Francesca in the crowd and he saw her finishing the waltz and curtsying prettily to Lord Huntley. Ben knew she would be angry at him for letting her sister come to the conclusion that Francesca was marrying Lord Huntley to provide a better life for her, but he couldn't have done much more. Maybe Felicity could talk some sense into her sister.

Chapter Twelve

Stretching out in one of the comfortable armchairs, Ben read through the latest letter he'd written to his farm manager, checking he'd left nothing out. There were crops to be harvested at this time of year, but knowing how long it would take for the letter to reach Australia Ben's instructions were focused more on the planting and care of the land in the Australian winter, many months from now.

He was just tucking the letter into the envelope when he heard voices downstairs and sat up to listen. Not many of the residents ever got any visitors and he was already up out of his chair and heading for the door when there was an abrupt rap.

'Good morning,' he said with a smile as he opened the door.

Normally the maid who looked after the residences in this building would come and announce any visitors, but this time it looked as though Francesca had pushed through despite the maid's protests to knock on his door herself.

'How dare you?' she asked without any form of greeting.

Ben stepped back, allowing her space to enter. Hesitating, she seemed to weigh up the options, eventually deciding this wasn't an argument she wanted to have in the corridor, so entered his rooms.

There was a mixture of anger and indignation on her face and immediately Ben knew this would be about him letting slip to Felicity the night before that Francesca was only marrying Lord Huntley out of some notion to provide her sister with a better future.

'It wasn't your right,' she said as she turned on him as soon as the door closed behind her.

'Would you care for tea?' he asked calmly, motioning for her to take a seat.

She ignored his question and didn't move towards the armchairs. With a shrug he walked past her and sat down, causing her lips to purse.

'It is my decision who I marry and why I have decided to marry them,' she said with fire in her eyes.

Ben loved her like this. She was so animated,

so beautiful, not the downtrodden woman she was forced to be by other men. Francesca would never speak to Lord Huntley like this and it saddened him to think she was soon to be condemned to a life where she was the inferior one in the relationship, not allowed to speak her thoughts or air her grievances.

'Your sister guessed,' he said. 'She's a very intelligent young woman and she knows you well.'

'You could have denied it,' Francesca said.

'I wasn't going to lie. And perhaps Felicity deserves to know what you are planning on sacrificing for her future.'

'She doesn't need to know, she's just a child.'

'You were married by her age,' Ben reminded her gently. 'And I'd served eight years for theft and started building towards a better future.'

'Felicity is young and innocent,' Francesca ground out.

'I think she's more worldly wise than you give her credit for. She's been living with your parents for all these years, too.'

As he watched some of the anger left Francesca and she slowly sank down into one of the armchairs.

'What did she say to you?' Ben asked quietly.

Running a hand over her brow and down

the angle of her jaw, Francesca took a moment to answer.

'This morning she came into my room with a tray of tea and toast,' Francesca said, 'And then proceeded to question me with military levels of inquisition about my motives for considering Lord Huntley as my future husband.'

'What did you tell her?' Ben asked.

Francesca sighed. 'I tried to satisfy her curiosity while still remaining vague, but she wasn't having any of it, thanks to you, I presume. She accused me of being a martyr.'

Ben laughed, picturing Francesca's overly dramatic sister calling her a martyr.

'She's not entirely wrong,' he murmured.

'I am not martyring myself for her. I'm just giving her a chance of a better future.'

'At the expense of your own.'

'I don't want to have this argument with you again. I'm angry because of what you told Felicity.'

Ben shrugged. 'I apologise for making you angry, but I'm not sorry your sister knows what you are planning.'

'You are infuriating,' Francesca said through clenched teeth.

'What if your sister doesn't want to ever get married? What if she wants to travel the world, or work as a governess or set herself up as a merry spinster? You haven't asked her, have you?'

'Don't be ridiculous.'

'It's not ridiculous. You're sacrificing your happiness for something you don't even know your sister wants.'

'Of course she wants to get married. That's what all young ladies do.'

'Just because it is the norm doesn't mean it's what she wants. Think about it—if you could have anything, any future you desired, would you really choose matrimony to a society bore?'

Francesca hesitated 'We don't have a choice,' she said eventually. 'It's not like we can just buy up land and start a farm or go to university and learn a profession. We're women. Our options are severely limited.' Shaking her head, she took a few fortifying deep breaths. 'We're held back at every turn, told to be quiet, to follow orders, to obey others. Just look at what happened when I tried to defy my father and speak out to defend you. No one listened. Because I was a girl.'

'I know,' Ben said, a hint of conciliation in his voice. 'And I also understand the demands of society for you to conform, but some of those limits are put in place by you.'

She opened her mouth as if to protest, but slowly closed it again without saying a word. He saw the sadness in her eyes, saw the hurt and pain and uncertainty and instantly he was on his feet, wrapping his arms around her. Resting her head on his chest, she burrowed in to him and Ben felt a pang of sympathy for her. All she was doing was trying to make the best decisions for her family, despite not having many attractive options. He just wished she wasn't going to throw away her entire future in the process.

'How did you leave it with your sister?' he asked softly, giving in to the temptation to bring one of his hands up to run through her silky hair.

He felt Francesca grimace into his chest before she spoke. 'Felicity is refusing to accept any dowry Lord Huntley provides.' She sighed and shook her head. 'It's just her little protest. I'm sure when some young gentleman catches her eye she will take the dowry to smooth the path.'

Ben wasn't so sure and he could tell by her tone Francesca wasn't entirely convinced either.

'So you marched all the way over here to tell me off?' he asked, smiling into her hair.

He loved that she could be so natural with him. It was healthy to be able to voice your feelings of dismay or irritation. Although he'd never been in a relationship that lasted long enough to have first-hand experience of this, he'd had the best role models. Fitzgerald's parents, the kindly couple who had taken him and Robertson in after the boys had saved their son from the bite of a deadly snake, had been wonderful role models. The couple had both grown up in England with all the rules and expectations of society. The older Mr Fitzgerald was the second son of an impoverished baron and as such his wife was from the upper echelons of the gentry. However, years of living in Australia, surviving where many others couldn't, had meant their marriage was a partnership. It was equal, with both parties having a say in the decisions and no one overruling the other. Of course they argued and disagreed, but in a healthy way, and always they came together at the end of it to find some mutual agreement and way forward.

If Ben ever settled down, that was the sort of relationship he wanted. With a wife not afraid to speak her mind with him.

Glancing down at Francesca, he found himself imagining what it would be like to wake up to her every morning. It was a tempting fantasy, but he knew it could never be anything more than that.

'Perhaps I should show you how sorry I am for upsetting you,' he murmured and felt her stiffen in his arms.

'How would you do that?' she asked, her voice coming out as no more than a whisper.

'I can think of one or two ways.'

As she hesitated, looking up at him before nodding, Ben felt the desire almost overwhelm him. He'd found women attractive before, but never had he felt this level of desire. It was as though he *needed* to be with her, to show her pleasure and to know every inch of her.

Gently he led her into his bedroom, seeing the flush of anticipation on her cheeks and pausing to look into her eyes.

'Are you sure?' he asked. He needed to check now, when he was still lucid, still able to stop himself. Soon he would be lost in her, oblivious to everything except how their bodies and souls were meeting.

'I'm sure,' she said with an unwavering voice. He had to remember she wasn't a shy virgin, she'd been married for years and as such wouldn't be a stranger to the bedroom.

'Come.' He held out a hand, waited for her to take it, then pulled her towards the bed. Softly he kissed her, reining in some of the passion he felt so as not to overwhelm her entirely. Her lips were warm and inviting, welcoming him in, and before long he was lost. All he could think about was the woman in his arms.

Frantically he pushed at her dress, trying to expose a little more skin, but it was laced up tightly and refused to budge.

'Poor choice of clothing,' he murmured into her ear as he spun her round to fight with the fastenings. A giggle turned into a groan as he caught her earlobe in his mouth, nipping it as he fiddled with her dress.

'I didn't dress for ease this morning,' Francesca said as she caught her breath. 'I wasn't expecting this.'

Neither had he been, although he'd fantasized about this moment long enough. Every night he'd woken up hard with desire after dreaming of this.

With a swell of triumph the dress came loose and he managed to push it down to her hips. Francesca did a little wiggle to help the garment on its way and soon it was pooled around her feet. Carefully he lifted her over it, his hands encircling her waist and feeling the warmth of her skin through the cotton chemise she wore.

Ben took a moment to look at her, still far from naked with a collection of petticoats, a cotton chemise and legs clad in white stockings, and he could begin to catch glimpses of her body underneath. Forcing himself not to rush, he ran his hands over her body, loving how she inhaled sharply as his fingers brushed over her more sensitive areas.

As he kissed her again he felt her hands tugging at his jacket, pulling it off over his shoulders before untucking his shirt from his waistband.

'I'm not finished with you yet,' he said, lifting her gently on to the bed, taking his time to rid her of the petticoats before he got to work on her stockings. Slowly he rolled them down her leg, marvelling at the creamy skin underneath. She'd always been tall and her legs were long and slender, just begging to be kissed.

Underneath him Francesca sighed as his mouth met the skin of her legs and she clutched at his shoulders as he worked his way from calf to thigh. Unable to resist, he pushed her chemise higher, revealing the skin all the way to her abdomen, and carried on planting kisses as her hips writhed beneath him.

As his lips skimmed the very top of her thighs he felt her gasp in surprise as he brushed against her most sensitive place. Instinctively he knew that she had never been worshipped as she should, that her husband had never focused on her pleasure, and he felt inordinately pleased that he would be the one to give that to her.

Slowly at first he kissed her, his fingers circling and dipping as her body writhed beneath him. He could feel her hips coming up to meet him, the movement instinctive and natural, and as her breathing quickened he felt her tense, clutch hold of his shoulders before letting out a deep moan of pleasure.

Only once her hips had fallen still did he move, manoeuvring himself so he was above her, looking down into her flushed and beautiful face.

'What...?' she started to say, but couldn't seem to put her question into words.

'You deserve to be worshipped,' he whispered in her ear, kissing along the angle of her jaw and down her neck, tasting the sweetness of her skin. Quickly he pulled off his shirt and in one swift movement rid Francesca of her chemise, too, taking a moment to memorise every wonderful inch of her body.

He felt her hands on his chest, fingers dancing across his skin and delving lower to the waistband of his trousers. Deftly she unclasped them, pushing them down and looking up into Ben's eyes at the same time.

She was beautiful, with her hair escaping in

rebellious tendrils around her face, her cheeks flushed from desire and her lips rosy from being kissed.

'I want you, Ben,' she said quietly but firmly, pulling him down towards her. He loved her determination, her certainty.

Unable to hold himself back any longer, he pushed inside her, groaning at how wonderful it felt. Francesca's hands encircled his back, pulling him in further, and together their bodies began to move in rhythm. It was as though they were made for each other, they fitted together perfectly.

Again and again their bodies came together until he felt Francesca clutch at his back and tighten, a quiet moan escaping from her lips. That was enough to send Ben over the edge and for a long minute he knew nothing but pleasure.

Slowly, as his breathing started to return to normal, he lay down beside Francesca. Normally he made it a rule never to fall asleep with a woman after making love. It complicated things, gave people unrealistic expectations, but today he couldn't have done anything differently even if he wanted to. There was no way he could get up and leave Francesca alone in his bed, he had an overwhelming urge to gather her to him, to spend the rest of the day baring his very soul to her, letting her see every vulnerable part of him.

'Ben,' she said, resting her head on his chest and tracing a lazy pattern on his abdomen. 'Is it often like that?'

He kissed her head before answering.

'No,' he said. 'Not quite like that.'

As he lay there with Francesca on his chest he felt as though his whole world had shifted. It would be difficult when he had to walk away from this woman.

Francesca must have dozed for she felt heavy and unwilling to move when she woke up.

'Good afternoon,' Ben said from his position at the end of the bed. He was dressed and had a sheaf of papers in his hand as if he'd been reading them while he waited for her to wake.

'What time is it?' she asked, feeling the panic rising up inside her.

'Only two.'

She'd slept for nearly three hours. Self-consciously she pulled the sheets up a bit higher, aware that she was completely naked under the bedclothes while Ben was sitting there with his dignity intact.

'I should be getting back home soon. I said I was going shopping with an old friend.'

Ben nodded and she felt a stab of disappointment. Part of her imagined him gathering her up in his arms, promising they'd never be parted again and whispering his undying affection in her ear. Quietly she snorted. *That* was never going to happen. Ben had made it quite clear over their short acquaintance that his relationships with women were short-lived only. He would give them affection and share pleasure, but he didn't get emotionally attached, not in a lasting way. Eight days, that was what he suggested they spend together, and after that they would disappear from one another's lives again.

As she shuffled off the bed, pulling the sheets closely around her, she wondered at the direction of her thoughts. She shouldn't be thinking of a future with Ben, her path was already decided. When she'd kissed him she'd known exactly how things were going to end up, and it wasn't with a walk down the aisle—at least not with him.

'I have seen you naked,' Ben remarked mildly, 'so if you'd prefer not to break your neck hopping around in that sheet, that would be acceptable.'

Looking at him with her best haughty expression, she said nothing. He was enjoying this—she could tell by the barely repressed grin on his face. Deciding to shock him, she stood straight, dropped the sheet and looked him in the eye, challenging him to hold her gaze.

He couldn't. Within three seconds his eyes had dropped to her body. She refused to blush, despite the heat already creeping into her cheeks, and waited for his eyes to come back up to meet hers.

'Perhaps you shouldn't have done that, Frannie,' he murmured, dropping the papers he was holding on to the floor and moving towards her.

'In your own words, you have seen me naked,' she said, finding it difficult not to sink into him as soon as he came close. 'There should be nothing surprising for you here.'

'Not surprising,' he said. 'Awe-inspiring, desire-inducing, but not surprising.'

Gently he ran his fingers over her shoulders, making her skin feel on fire and before she knew what was happening he'd tumbled her back on the bed, his mouth seeking hers.

An hour later Francesca got up again, this time dodging the hand that tried to pull her back to bed.

'I have to go,' she said with a giggle.

'Don't. Spend the whole night here with me.'

'They'll send out a search party,' she said,

trying to sound stern as she struggled into her layers of clothing.

'You could send a note,' Ben suggested.

'What would it say? Don't worry, I'm spending the night with a man of questionable morals and giving him my virtue?'

'That would just about cover it,' Ben said, rolling over on to his back and grinning. 'Will anyone have missed you?'

Francesca considered and shook her head. As a widow she had a little more freedom than she had when she was a debutante. It was perfectly acceptable for her to lead her own life without informing her father of her every last move. Of course it wasn't perfectly acceptable to spend the day naked in a man's rooms, but no one would ever need to know that.

Finally dressed, she perched down on the edge of the bed, letting her head drop back as Ben came up behind her and kissed her neck.

'Do you regret this, Frannie?' he asked softly.

'No.' The word came out quickly, but she realised it was the truth.

Never before had she considered an affair, not throughout her marriage and not since her husband had passed away. It just hadn't been something she did. Although she hadn't loved her husband, she did believe in the marriage vows she'd uttered and they'd included being faithful until death.

What she didn't feel was any regret about their intimacies today. One day soon she would be married again, but until then, or more precisely until she had given her promise to another man, there was nothing wrong in enjoying herself a little.

'Do you?' she asked.

'Never.' He kissed her again on the neck and she felt the heat beginning to rise in her body. It was almost too difficult to pull away.

'I should go,' she said, standing reluctantly.

'When shall I see you again?' Ben asked.

Feeling elated that he didn't want to get rid of her as fast as possible and then never see her again, she considered.

'Felicity has persuaded Father to let her host a dinner party tomorrow night. Lord Huntley has sent his apologies so will not be there. Would you like to attend?' Too late she realised the foolishness of the invite. It was her father who had lied and condemned Ben to eight years' hard labour and transportation for theft, there was no way he would ever want to be in the same room as the man.

'It would be my pleasure,' Ben said.

As she turned to look at him she noticed a

steely expression on his face and wondered what she had just done.

'Father might not even be there...' she said, trying to work out why he had accepted. It wasn't as though she could withdraw the invite now.

'All the better,' he said serenely. 'Until tomorrow, my dear Frannie.'

She rose and moved to the door, pausing as she heard his footsteps behind her. With her hand on the doorknob she turned to find him right behind her, completely naked and completely unabashed.

'Goodbye,' he said, kissing her until she forgot what she was meant to be doing.

'Goodbye,' she said once he'd released her and quickly slipped out through the door, pausing on the landing to compose herself before she made her way down to the street.

Chapter Thirteen

With great interest, Ben stood for a moment and regarded the façade of Francesca's father's house. It was a little shabby looking, with the door needing a coat of paint and the railings peeling and starting to rust. Certainly not up to the standards of the other houses in the street.

He had not hesitated in accepting the invitation to dinner, even though it would mean spending an evening in the company of the man responsible for sending him to Australia as a convict. Eighteen years ago Francesca's father had accused him of stealing a large stash of valuables from the country estate. Of course Ben had been innocent and the only item found when he'd been searched was the small locket Francesca had given him the summer before as a token of her affection, but it had been enough for the magistrate who had uprooted the twelve-year-old Ben from the family home and thrown him in jail.

Ben had begged the magistrate to ask Francesca, to hear that the locket had been given as a gift and not stolen. The magistrate had refused, but a few days later Francesca had broken free from her father's imprisonment and made her way to the jail. She'd told anyone who would listen that Ben was innocent, that the locket had been a gift, but it hadn't been enough. Francesca had been dismissed—after all, she was just a girl and it was her word against the word of a viscount.

Ben would never forget the moment Francesca was dragged away. It had been the last time he'd seen her and the moment that had sealed his fate. A week later he'd been found guilty of theft and sent first to the hulk ships on the Thames and finally to Australia.

His father had tirelessly continued to dig into the case after Ben had been sent away and in one of his letters years later he told Ben he thought it was all a scam on the part of Lord Pottersdown who, it would appear, had taken out some sort of insurance against the valuable items in his home and claimed when they had gone missing, no doubt also selling the items quietly at the same time to get double their worth.

Over the years he'd thought about Francesca's father rather a lot. At first he'd been bitter, swearing he would get his revenge on the older man, but after a while the bitterness had seeped out of him. Once Mr Fitzgerald had taken him in Ben had realised the anger he felt towards Lord Pottersdown was slowly draining away and, as he'd built himself into a success, he found he was thinking about the old Viscount less and less. It had only been Francesca who had haunted his thoughts, the girl he'd left behind.

Quickly he mounted the steps, trying to push away the entirely inappropriate memory of Francesca standing in his bedroom, looking him rebelliously in the eye and dropping the bedsheet she had wrapped around her body. That image would never leave him.

'Mr Crawford,' he said to the footman who opened the door. He was shown in to the drawing room where he'd visited previously and wasn't surprised to find the small room was already almost full to bursting.

'Mr Crawford,' Felicity gushed as she spotted him, 'What a delight to see you again. I was so happy when Francesca told me you would be at-

tending our humble dinner party this evening.'
Felicity paused, took his arm and lowered her
voice. 'Has she forgiven you yet?'

Ben remembered their morning spent in his
bed and grinned, 'I think she's getting there,'
he said.

'Good. I'd hate to see you out of favour because of me. Now, who should I introduce you
to?'

Ben surveyed the room, finding nine other
people besides Felicity and himself. Some he
knew, some he only recognised, but he had eyes
for only one. She was standing amid a small
group, listening intently to what one young
woman was saying, nodding her head in an
animated fashion.

'Will your parents be in attendance?' he
asked, noting their absence from the drawing
room.

'Father will, although I doubt he will appear
before dinner. Mother is indisposed.' She spoke
the words without any hint of frustration. Ben
had learned Lady Pottersdown hadn't been seen
at a social event since Francesca had married
and it seemed Felicity had just accepted her
mother's withdrawal from society graciously.
'Of course,' Felicity said, turning to Ben, 'you

must know my parents if you were acquainted with Francesca in childhood.'

'We have met,' Ben said, trying to keep any hint of emotion from his voice, 'but only once so I doubt they would remember me.'

It was a white lie. He had met Francesca's parents on more than one occasion, fleeting glimpses of annoyed faces as he was chased from the house by the footmen or reprimanded by Francesca's governesses for leading her astray.

'Good evening,' Lord Pottersdown said as he appeared in the doorway, face ruddied by too much drink both today and in the past few decades. Felicity had been wrong about him waiting to make an appearance until dinner was served. On his arm he felt Francesca's sister stiffen and wondered if the older man knew how much embarrassment and suffering he brought to his children, or if he just didn't care.

'Father,' Francesca said, breaking away from her little group with a smile of apology, 'I didn't think you were joining us until later.'

Everyone was focused on the interaction between Lord Pottersdown and his eldest daughter so Ben took the opportunity to look over the man who had condemned him to transportation for the sake of a couple of hundred pounds.

Lord Pottersdown looked much older than his fifty-odd years, his face lined and sallow in complexion with the bulbous nose that gave away his habit for over-imbibing. His mid-section had long ago run to fat and his clothes bulged across his stomach. Today there was a smile on his face, but an air of panic in his eyes.

Calm, Ben told himself. He had spent years working on the feelings of hatred and resentment he had towards those who had wronged him. When he'd first been taken in by Mr Fitzgerald he had been bitter and the feelings of hatred had eaten him up every day. Slowly, with a lot of love and patience, the older man had helped Ben to see that the only person these feelings were hurting was himself. Over time he'd shown Ben how to let go of the past and look to the future, to see everything he had been blessed with and even appreciate how his difficult interlude had shaped him into the man he was today.

Still, seeing Lord Pottersdown in the flesh again brought back some of feelings of anger and hatred.

'I must go and introduce myself,' Ben said, noting Felicity's surprise, but deciding to ignore it.

Quickly he moved over to where Francesca was unsuccessfully trying to manoeuvre her father from the room without making a scene. She glanced at him with a frown and seemed to try to signal with her eyes for him to keep away. Ben couldn't do that, something was pushing him to step closer, to finally look the man who'd caused him so much pain in the eye.

'Lord Pottersdown,' Ben said, 'what a lovely home you have.'

The Viscount and Francesca both looked around in mild surprise as if they'd never been paid such a compliment before.

'Thank you,' he said. His words weren't slurred, but there was a soft quality to the consonants that suggested Lord Pottersdown wasn't on his first drink of the evening.

'Crawford,' he said, offering his hand. He waited to see if there would be any recognition, but Lord Pottersdown's eyes remained vacant. Condemning someone to transportation wasn't enough to make an impression on the Viscount, it would seem.

'Father,' Francesca said, shooting Ben a concerned look, 'why don't you step through to the dining room? I'm sure dinner is just about to be announced.'

'In a moment, Francesca,' the older man said

with a dismissive wave of the hand, 'She does fuss,' he said, directing his words at Ben.

The arrival of another guest, a woman in her early forties who Ben did not know, stole Francesca's attention for a moment and Ben quickly guided Lord Pottersdown out of earshot before she could protest.

'I hear you are a man who likes a game of cards,' Ben said, wasting no time. 'Shall we have a game or two after dinner?'

He saw the older man hesitate and wondered if at last he had learnt his lesson, but after just a couple of seconds Lord Pottersdown was nodding his head, a gleam in his eye.

'I'm sure that can be arranged,' he said. 'Once the ladies retire, of course.'

Ben followed his gaze to where Francesca was deep in conversation with the new guest and he had to hide a smile. He could just imagine Francesca reprimanding her father for his reckless behaviour, even though it was almost unheard of for a daughter to speak to her father in such a manner.

'Wonderful,' Ben said, clapping the older man on the arm. 'I do enjoy a game of cards. Never have much luck, but it's the enjoyment that counts.'

Walking away, Ben fought hard not to grin.

He hadn't come to England to get his revenge on the Viscount, not like his friend Sam Robertson who had been almost completely consumed by the idea of revenge against the man who had wronged him. Nevertheless, he wasn't a saint and the opportunity to toy with the man for an hour or two was too good to pass up. Ben had no doubt he would beat the older man in the game of cards and of course there would be wagers, there always were. He planned to make Lord Pottersdown sweat for a while over the amount of money he owed after the card game. In the end he wouldn't actually make the man pay up—that would only serve to hurt Francesca in the long run—but a worrying couple of weeks was the least the man deserved.

Smiling nervously, Francesca glanced again at Ben. He was up to something—she was sure of it. After she'd invited him to the dinner party she'd realised what a foolish idea it had been—it would mean her father and Ben coming face to face. Never had she expected her father to remember the young boy he'd accused of stealing the family's valuables, but she did know Ben wouldn't have forgiven her father for the awful wrong he'd done him all those years ago.

Still, so far Ben was behaving impeccably. He was suave and confident at the dinner table full of people a good few social classes above him and acted as though he'd been born to live the easy life of a gentleman. Half the ladies in attendance were already looking at him with doe eyes and Francesca suspected he would woo the other half before the night was out.

'Gentlemen,' her father said, a very subtle slur to his words that probably no one else would pick up on, but Francesca had had years of experience detecting when her father had tipped over into an inebriated state, 'a glass of port, perhaps?'

Knowing this was her cue, Francesca reluctantly stood and gestured for the ladies to follow her into the drawing room.

As she closed the door behind her she lingered for a second and felt her heart sink when her father's voice drifted through, the suggestion of a card game coming only seconds after she'd left him with the male guests. Hoping Ben would have enough sense to put a stop to any game that left her father risking too much, she stepped away, plastering a cheerful smile on her face and summoning some small talk to distract herself.

* * *

'I say, that's rather a lot of money. Surely we should have an upper limit,' a weak-chinned man called Mr Rose said, eyeing Ben uneasily.

'Anyone can withdraw at any time,' Ben said, giving the other players his easy smile. 'There's no pressure to play if you can't meet the wager.'

Four of them sat around the table, with another of the gentlemen already having excused himself, stating he was terrible at cards and withdrawing to join the ladies.

'You know, I think I might just do that,' Mr Rose said after a moment's hesitation.

'And I, these stakes are too high for my meagre income,' a cheerful man by the name of Mr Wisern agreed, standing and executing a little bow before following Mr Rose from the room.

'How about you, Lord Pottersdown?' Ben asked mildly. 'Would you like to retreat, too?'

The Viscount licked his lips nervously and glanced at the cards in his hand. Ben already knew the answer. For the older man betting seemed to be a compulsion, just as drink was. He didn't know his limits, didn't know when to stop and admit defeat. It was no doubt the character flaw that had plunged Francesca's family into so much trouble and Lord Pottersdown wasn't about to change now.

'Perhaps just one or two more hands,' he said.

'Marvellous.' Ben raised the glass of port to his lips, taking the smallest sip. He could handle his alcohol, had drunk many a hardened criminal under the table back home in his youth, but now he was much more cautious. No matter how often you drank alcohol it still muddied your senses, dulling your thoughts and affecting your ability to make sensible decisions. Still, the act of lifting his glass to his lips had the desired effect. Lord Pottersdown unconsciously mirrored him, but instead of a tiny sip he took a few large gulps of the tawny port.

Quickly Ben got into the swing of the card game, letting Lord Pottersdown win a couple of hands to boost his confidence and make him sloppy. After a few minor losses Ben waited for a decent hand of cards. By this point he could read Lord Pottersdown's face and mannerisms easily and knew when the man was confident and when he had a poor hand and was bluffing.

Now there were only two of them they were playing piquet, a game Ben had grown up playing with his father and honed his instincts to perfection over the years in Australia.

'Shall we increase the wager?' Lord Pottersdown asked after winning a moderate sum.

'Why not?' Ben said, trying not to grin. He'd

been waiting for the older man to ask, not wanting to push through his wins until there was a substantial amount on the table. 'Shall we say five hundred pounds?'

He could tell it was more than Lord Pottersdown was expecting, but the Viscount clearly didn't want to lose face, and as with all reckless gamblers wherever they were in the world he thought his winning streak would continue and he'd have the chance to make some real money.

'Perhaps just for a game or two,' Lord Pottersdown said, licking his lips and glancing at the door as if expecting some disgruntled creditor to burst in and nab all his winnings from the table.

'Excellent.'

Ben dealt, watching Lord Pottersdown as he studied his cards, deciding which to discard and which to play.

Just as Lord Pottersdown laid down his first cards Francesca burst into the room. Ben didn't look up, knowing she would look either aghast or disapproving. Later he would explain, if she would let him, that he wasn't actually going to collect whatever debt her father ended up owing him, just make the old man sweat. It was the very least he deserved.

'Father,' she said, her tone clipped, and even

without looking up Ben could hear the high level of stress in her voice.

'Don't fuss, Francesca,' her father said. 'Go and rejoin the ladies. Mr Crawford and I will be through shortly.'

'You promised,' she said so quietly Ben could barely hear her. What he did note was the sound of complete desperation in her voice. 'Mr Crawford,' she said, turning to him, 'my father regrets that he will have to withdr—' She was cut off by an angry Lord Pottersdown.

'Quiet,' he ordered. 'Remember your place.'

Ben had known this moment would come and resolutely ignored the small voice telling him to stand and comfort the woman who he'd held so tenderly in his arms only a day and a half ago. Later he would explain, later he would kiss the small furrow between her perfectly shaped brows until it disappeared and she forgot all her worries, at least for a short time. But right now he had a card game to win and a viscount to destroy, at least for a few hours.

Glancing up, he saw the mixture of hurt and anger in her eyes. The hurt was aimed at him, the anger at her father, but he knew it wouldn't take much to sway it the other way.

She sat, folding her arms across her chest in a most unladylike gesture, and watched them, her eyes flitting from one side of the table to the other.

'Shall we continue?' Ben asked.

Lord Pottersdown nodded and the game proceeded. What happened next was like a carefully executed dance. Ben lulled the man into a false sense of security, quickly upped the wager and then proceeded to destroy him. After all of five minutes Lord Pottersdown was sitting with his head in his hands, one thousand pounds worse off, his normally ruddy face completely drained of any colour.

Francesca spared a disgusted glance for her father and stood. She crossed behind where Ben was standing and leaned in. 'Was that your plan all along?' she asked, her voice tight with pain and humiliation, 'Get close to me so you could destroy Father?' The words were said so quietly Lord Pottersdown couldn't hear, not that Ben thought he would take in a stampeding herd of elephants at this point.

He caught her wrist, holding firmly so she couldn't pull away, but ensuring he caused her no discomfort. 'I would never do anything to hurt you, Frannie,' he said.

Her eyes flared with anger, 'You suppose this doesn't hurt me?' she asked.

'Trust me,' he murmured. Quickly she pulled

away and strode from the room, her head held high, but Ben knew as soon as she was alone she would let her calm façade crack and the tears would start to flow.

He felt a stab of remorse, but reminded himself that he wasn't actually going to call in the debt. Apart from the worry Francesca would be no worse off and, if things went to plan, his little game with the Viscount would hopefully scare the man to stop gambling at least for a few months.

'Mr Crawford,' Lord Pottersdown said, 'I… er… I am a little low on funds at the moment. All to be resolved soon, of course…'

It would never be resolved.

'A debt is a debt,' Ben said, ensuring his voice was clipped and his manner abrupt.

'Of course, and I never renege on a debt,' Lord Pottersdown said quickly.

That was definitely a lie. A big one. The Viscount owed money all over town and had a reputation for trying to weasel his way out of any small debt he could.

'One thousand pounds, Lord Pottersdown, is not an insignificant amount.'

'No, no, no, no,' the Viscount said, seemingly unable to utter any other sounds.

'And I am not a patient man.'

'If you could just give me a few weeks.'

They both knew Lord Pottersdown would only be further in debt in a few weeks.

'Perhaps there is another solution,' Ben said, tapping his fingers on the table and conjuring up a pensive expression.

'Yes, anything,' the Viscount said eagerly.

'This house must be worth a fair few hundred pounds,' Ben said, looking up theatrically at the ceiling and around the walls.

'It's the family home,' Lord Pottersdown said.

Ben shrugged and fixed a hard stare on the Viscount. 'You have a debt to be settled and so far I haven't heard how you mean to pay it.'

'Surely as a gentleman…' Lord Pottersdown said.

'I suggest in future you find out a little more about whom you're playing against before you commit to such big wagers…' He paused and looked Lord Pottersdown directly in the eye. 'I am no gentleman.'

With his whole body sagging the Viscount began shaking his head, a pleading look in his eyes. 'It was only a game of cards.'

'A wager is a wager,' Ben said firmly. 'Of course I could let it be known about town that you have reneged outright on a debt. I doubt it would take long for the rest of your creditors to become nervous and come calling.'

'No,' Lord Pottersdown said quickly. Ben wondered just how extensive the man's borrowing was. The rumours had Lord Pottersdown barely surviving, but Ben thought the situation might be even more dire.

'The house then,' Ben said firmly.

'Where will my family live? My wife, my daughters?'

'I'm not a cruel man, Lord Pottersdown. They may remain living here until alternative accommodation is found.'

'Alternative accommodation?'

'I believe there are some cheaper rooms south of the river.'

'South of the river?' Lord Pottersdown spluttered, some of the colour returning to his face. 'I'm a *viscount*, a man from a long and noble line. I can't live *south of the river*.'

'You're a man so in debt you're selling your own daughter off to a scoundrel who has a reputation for beating his wives,' Ben said quietly. He stood. 'I shall return in a week's time with my solicitor. I suggest you have yours ready and waiting. Otherwise I shall ensure the rest of your debts are called in.'

Before Lord Pottersdown could say another

word Ben left the room. Of course he wouldn't call again—instead he'd let the man stew thinking he'd just lost the family home. No matter what the old scoundrel had done to him he wouldn't see Francesca and her sister homeless.

Chapter Fourteen

'How could you?' Francesca said as she caught up with him, grasping at his arm and pulling him to face her. She was livid, angry beyond anything she'd ever felt before, and all because of this man. Over the last few weeks Ben had got under her skin, burrowed deep and found a way into her heart. She cared for him, thought about him every moment of every day, and now she was confronted with the truth: he'd only ever been using her to get close to her father. To destroy him. To destroy their whole family.

'Hush,' Ben said, cupping her face in his hands and kissing her softly on the lips.

Francesca pulled away, aware that they were in the middle of a well-populated street and also that she shouldn't be kissing the enemy.

'Don't hush me. I trusted you. I…' she lowered her voice '… I gave myself to you.'

He smiled at her and she thought there was affection in his eyes, but knew that couldn't be true. You didn't destroy the life of someone you cared about.

'Frannie...' he said, but she pushed on.

'Was that your plan all along? To get your revenge on my father?' She felt the tears spill out on to her cheeks. 'I know he wronged you, Ben, I wished it could be different every day of the last eighteen years, but I thought you cared at least a little about me.'

'Stop this, Frannie,' he said, still remarkably calm amid all the accusations she was throwing his way.

'Was it *all* an act?' she asked, horrified at the pleading tone in her voice. When he'd kissed her and touched her it had felt so real, so wonderful. It would hurt so much to know that for him it had been nothing more than a step on his plan to get close to her.

'No,' he said. 'It wasn't an act.'

She searched his face and thought he was telling the truth, but didn't trust her judgement much.

'But you planned this all along? Got close to me to get to my father? Always knew you would make us homeless?'

'My beautiful girl,' Ben said, cupping her

face and shaking his head. 'Is that what you really think?'

She didn't know what to think. Seeing him standing here so calmly, so innocently, it was hard to believe he'd just condemned her family to losing their home and admitting to the world they were actually paupers.

'Come with me,' he said, taking her gently by the arm and leading her down the street. They were close to St James's Park, the gates just a little further down the street, and Francesca could see Ben was leading her that way. Despite what had happened earlier that evening she realised she trusted him enough to go into the park with him, even though it wasn't what young ladies did this late at night.

Once inside the park he sat her on a bench, took off his coat and draped it over her shoulders. She hadn't even noticed she was shivering after coming out without a coat.

'I hate your father, Frannie. The man ruined my life, condemned me to an eight-year sentence of transportation and hard labour for a crime I didn't commit and tore me from my family. I haven't seen my father for eighteen years.'

Still shaking with anger, she was surprised

when Ben caught her chin and tilted her head so she looked up at him.

'What your father did to me deserves punishment.'

'I know.' Deep down she knew Ben had every right to seek revenge on her father, but she'd been so convinced he cared for her, even just a little. So convinced that what they'd shared was real.

'You didn't have to pretend to like me to get close to my father,' she said, feeling more morose than angry now. 'He would have played cards with anyone.'

Francesca was looking down at her hands so was taken by surprise when Ben kissed her. His lips were warm and inviting and for a moment she wished she could just abandon herself to him and forget everything that made her life hard.

'Does this feel like pretence to you?' he asked, pulling away only slightly so his breath tickled her face as he spoke.

Instinctively she shook her head. It felt real and meaningful and wonderful.

'I like you, Frannie. And I'm attracted to you. Very much so—' Ben broke off with a short laugh '—probably too much. And I'm telling the truth when I say I don't want to hurt you.'

He paused again, ensuring she was looking at him, 'I'm not going to make you homeless. That was never my intention. I just wanted to put pressure on your father, to make him see there are consequences for his actions.'

'You won't go through with it?' she asked, feeling an instantaneous lightening in her heart.

'No, I won't go through with it. *He* deserves every punishment in hell,' Ben said, taking her hand, 'but you don't. In the end it would be you who would be hurt and I don't want that.'

Feeling the relief seeping through her body, she allowed herself to sag against him, his body warm and welcoming in the darkness.

'I thought…' she said, trailing off. He didn't need to know the details of all her insecurities.

'You thought I'd used you to get close to your father and that our time together was part of my revenge,' he summed up succinctly.

Even in the darkened park Francesca could see him shake his head ruefully. 'I have a bit of a reputation back home,' he said, planting a kiss on the top of her head. 'I'm known to be ruthless, a man who takes risks, a man not to be crossed in the course of my business. I'm very glad my business rivals cannot see me here.'

'Allowing my father to get away with his actions for my sake would go against the persona you've built for yourself?' Francesca asked.

'Oh, yes.'

'But you decided to anyway.'

'I couldn't help myself,' he said quietly, kissing her again, this time on her temple where her hairline ended.

'So what happened between us...' Francesca said, needing one final confirmation.

'Everything I did and everything I said was true,' he said sincerely.

Francesca felt her heart swell and knew she needed to be careful. She was beginning to care about Ben just a little too much. He'd made it perfectly clear he wasn't the sort of man to get tied down by emotions. Their dalliance together had been just that: a temporary, fleeting dalliance. The only person she would hurt if she allowed these feelings for Ben to continue would be herself.

Glancing at him in the darkness, she had a momentary flash of what her life might be like if she threw away everyone's expectations of her and ran off with this man. She could picture a life of freedom, a life of equality where she was treated as a human rather than a possession to be traded by the men around her. No doubt it would also be a life of passion.

Sighing, she pushed away the thought. Of course it could never happen—she had responsibilities, a duty to see her sister well provided for and her parents not sent to debtors' prison. And Ben had never offered anything more than a few intimate weeks. They were not of the same world; it could never work.

'Why the big sigh?' he asked as she leaned back against him, feeling his warmth engulfing her.

'No reason,' she said, trying to inject a brightness into her voice, but failing miserably.

'I have to go away in a couple of days,' Ben said quietly.

Francesca felt a tearing in her chest and wondered how those few little words could cause her so much pain. She barely knew the man sitting beside her, his departure shouldn't cause her so much upset.

'Back to Australia?' she asked morosely.

Ben laughed, 'Good Lord, no. I'm going to Essex, to see my family.'

She heard the mix of emotions in his voice, the excitement shadowed with something that sounded a little like apprehension.

'Your father is back from his trip?' she asked.

While they'd been lying in bed together a few days earlier Ben had told her of the bad timing of his arrival. A few days before his ship docked his father had been called to one of the estates he managed up north. Only now was he coming home, meaning their long-awaited reunion had been painfully delayed.

'He should return on Thursday,' Ben said, 'and he wrote he was most eager not to delay my visit any further.'

'Of course he's keen to see you,' Francesca said, picking up on the uncertainty in Ben's voice. The man next to her was strong emotionally. He'd been through so much at such a young age and come out with the ability still to care about his family and those around him. When he spoke of his father and brothers there was an uncharacteristic hesitation in his voice and Francesca knew it was not because he didn't want to see them again. Quite the opposite.

'I shall be gone for a few days,' Ben said. 'I'm not sure how many exactly. I suppose it will depend on how well the visit goes.'

'Your father will probably never want to let you leave.'

He shrugged and for a moment she was reminded of the young boy she'd once known. The image of him locked in a cell, awaiting trial for a crime he didn't commit, came to mind. He'd looked unsure and vulnerable then, too.

It wasn't a side to him she'd seen much since his return.

'I need to visit Elmington Manor,' Francesca said impulsively. 'I could accompany you on the journey if you would like.'

Elmington Manor was their moderately sized property in Essex, the same estate she and Ben had grown up running around and Ben's father had once managed. She did need to visit in the next few weeks, to take her old clothes out of storage ready for when her mourning period finished, but had planned on putting that task off for as long as possible. Now, it was a good excuse to travel to Essex with Ben. She thought he needed some moral support, a friend to reassure him that his family wasn't going to reject him after eighteen years. Not that he would ever ask for it.

She saw him hesitate, wondered if he would be too proud to accept her help. Most men wouldn't want to admit they were struggling emotionally with something like this.

'You're going anyway?' he asked.

'I need to sort out my clothes for when I come out of mourning,' she said.

'Then I would be very pleased to have your company.'

In the darkness she reached out and patted

the wood of the bench until her hand found his, then, lacing her fingers through his, she closed her eyes and smiled. Ben deserved a good relationship with his family and she would do everything in her power to make sure that's what he got.

Chapter Fifteen

The morning was crisp and clear as Ben waited on the outskirts of London at their agreed meeting point. He was on horseback, wrapped up in his thickest coat with his warmest gloves on his hands. Although he wouldn't ever admit to anyone in Australia that he missed his homeland, the cold, snowy winters in England were something he'd found himself dreaming about in the heat of the Australian summer.

In the distance he could see a carriage approaching and smiled ruefully. He knew Francesca would like nothing more than to be up on horseback riding alongside him, but she was tied by the expectations of society. A young woman did not ride from London to Essex on horseback when there was a carriage at her disposal. It wasn't the done thing, no matter how much she wanted to.

Shaking his head, he wondered what more he could do to help her break free of those restraints, to show her the world wouldn't end if she didn't conform to the expectations of a group of people she didn't much like anyway.

'Good morning,' he greeted Francesca as her carriage came to a stop beside him. The coachman looked pale and miserable to be out in such icy weather and was blowing on his hands impatiently.

'Good morning. Would you care to join me?' she asked, motioning to the seat opposite her in the carriage.

'I have a better idea,' he said. 'It's a beautiful morning, why don't you come and join me?'

'I don't have a mount.'

'This beast is strong enough to carry both of us for a while,' Ben said, enjoying the widening of Francesca's eyes as she realised what he was suggesting.

'You want me to come and ride with you?' she asked.

Suppressing a grin, Ben nodded. He loved the look of disbelief and mild indignation she got on her face when he suggested something that wasn't a societal norm.

'You never used to be scared of horses...' he taunted her.

'I'm not scared of the horse,' she said calmly, 'it's the man on its back I'm cautious of.'

'I promise to behave.'

'I don't think you know how to behave,' Francesca grumbled, but Ben saw her edging off her seat. He grinned, loving how easily he could read the woman in front of him. Deep down she wanted nothing more than to vault up behind him and feel the wind whipping at her face as they raced off ahead of the carriage. It was only years of conforming to what a well-brought-up young lady *should* do that was holding her back.

'Put up your hood and if anyone passes lower your head,' Ben said. 'Then no one will recognise you.' He could tell she was almost convinced. 'I'll let you sit in front,' he said eventually, knowing she wouldn't be able to resist that offer.

'Really?' Francesca asked, her eyes lighting up.

'If that would make you happy.'

Within a fraction of a second she was out of the carriage and inspecting his horse.

'How do you have a horse?' she asked, stroking the beautiful grey animal's nose with the affection of a girl who grew up in the countryside.

'Lady Winston, Fitzgerald's aunt whom we stayed with when I first arrived in London, she arranged for us to hire a mount each.'

'How generous,' Francesca murmured.

'She is. Outspoken and forthright, but unbelievably generous. Do you need a leg up?'

Placing her booted foot into his hand, Francesca pulled herself up on to the back of the horse, settling herself on its back. She was wearing a plain grey dress with a full skirt and her cloak over the top, not the most practical items for riding a horse, but Ben could see she would just about manage to sit sideways in front of him.

'Are you sure the horse will be able to manage both of us?' she asked.

Quickly he pulled himself up on to the horse's back, settling himself behind Francesca and looping an arm around her waist to support her.

'I've never ridden like this before,' she said, gripping the reins. From the tone of her voice he could tell she was smiling and wondered when making her smile had become quite so important to him.

He was barely listening to her words, distracted by the contour of her waist under his hand and the warmth of her body pressed against his.

'We shall meet you at the King's Head,' Francesca called to her coachman, who grumbled something inaudible in return.

With a squeal of delight she threw her head back as he spurred the horse on, and Ben made sure he allowed it to pick a nice steady speed that it would be able to maintain with an extra rider on its back.

Ben relaxed back, glad of the distraction of having Francesca with him. When she was in his arms he thought about things less, worried less. Carefully, ensuring he did not surprise her too much, he leaned forwards and placed a kiss on her cheek, feeling the fur from the inside of her new cloak tickle his lips.

'What was that for?' she asked, glancing round, but not able to quite meet his eye and keep her balance.

'For coming with me.'

Ben knew she'd seen the worry buried deep inside him, that she'd sensed his unease and nervousness at seeing his family again after so long and had offered to accompany him to distract him on the journey and offer what little support she could.

It was a kind gesture, one that showed their

friendship had blossomed again despite all that had gone before. Friendship…and something more.

Ben had thought the day they'd spent in bed together might slake his desire for Francesca, but in reality it had only heightened it. Before when he'd felt an attraction towards a woman a night or two in their arms had been enough to fulfil that so he could move on. Now, despite having had Francesca in his bed, he still thought about her almost every waking moment. And sleep didn't give him much respite either. The dreams…

'Tell me about your family now,' Francesca said, leaning back into him and warming his body with her own.

Ben took a moment to collect his thoughts. All he knew of his family had been from his father's letters, but seeing as they lived half a world apart he had been kept remarkably well-informed.

'Do you remember my brothers?' Ben asked.

There was a moment of hesitation before Francesca replied, as if she were trying hard to recall people from a long time ago.

'Thomas and William,' she said eventually.

'That's right.' Two boys who would have grown into men in the intervening years.

Thomas had been eight when Ben was arrested and Ben had fond memories of playing with his younger brother, but William had only been four. No doubt his youngest brother wouldn't remember him at all.

'They both work with Father and they still all live in Elswyre. Thomas was married, but his wife died in childbirth a couple of years ago. He has just the one son. William is still young and unattached as far as I'm aware.'

'And your father?'

This was one of the things Ben was most apprehensive about. Never in his letters had his father mentioned remarrying, but Ben wondered if that had been to spare his feelings when he was so far away. Their mother had died soon after William was born, wasting away for no apparent reason, going quickly from a healthy young woman to a shadow of her former self before passing away one night. His father had always blamed a weak chest, but in reality no one knew why Ben's mother had died. Ever since then their father had become everything to them. Through his own grief the older man had helped his children find their way in the world without their mother as well as taking on all the jobs his wife would ordinarily have done. To Ben he was a true hero, a man he'd looked up to and wanted to emulate. Part of his discomfort at the idea of finally going home centred around wondering if that had been a fantasy built up by a child or if it was the truth.

'I don't think he's ever remarried.'

'How extraordinary,' Francesca murmured.

It was extraordinary. He'd been a relatively young man with a good job and three children to look after. There wouldn't be many in his position who wouldn't find another wife to share the load.

'Enough,' Ben said, not wanting to think about how he might slot into a family he hadn't seen for eighteen years. 'Let's canter.'

In front of him he felt Francesca adjust her grip on the reins and lean forward ever so slightly before urging the horse on. As they picked up speed he heard her let out a little cry of pleasure and he noticed she didn't even tense as another carriage passed them on the road, the occupants looking out disapprovingly. If he could get Francesca to embrace her true nature, to realise she didn't always need to conform to society's expectations, before he left for Australia, then he would be happy.

Not happy, the little voice inside his head insisted. He tried to ignore it, focus instead on the woman in front of him and how her body felt pressed against his. He didn't want to have to examine how she made him feel emotionally. It was enough to admit that he still desired her, without acknowledging that he would find it hard to leave her behind. She'd burrowed her way under his skin and lodged herself treacherously close to his heart.

Silently he shook his head. He wasn't meant for a long-term relationship, he was better suited to short flings, dalliances where no one could get hurt. To commit for life to just one woman, that required a level of mutual trust he just didn't have.

It didn't matter anyway. In a few weeks Francesca would probably insist on marrying the odious Lord Huntley in some misguided attempt to save her sister. Even knowing her motivation, it hurt him more than he wanted to admit, the thought that she would choose Huntley over him.

Chapter Sixteen

Although it was only a little after three o'clock in the afternoon when they entered the village of Elswyre the sky had already lost its brightness and the sun was dropping ever lower.

'I'll escort you home first,' Ben said, knowing his voice was clipped and tense, but unable to help it. He felt nervous, more nervous than he had done for years, and he was torn between wanting to run to his father's house to reunite with his family and wanting to stay away in case it wasn't everything he'd hoped for.

They were sitting in the carriage, giving Ben's horse a rest after he'd carried them both for over twenty miles.

'There's no need,' Francesca said, patting him on the hand as if he were a small child, 'I have the carriage and the maid will be waiting for me.' She hesitated, as if unsure whether to continue. 'I could come with you,' she said eventually.

He frowned, the offer unexpected.

'Only if you want me to. I don't want to impose. I just thought it might be a little difficult, seeing your family again after so long and you might want someone by your side. I completely understand if you don't. I'm probably the last person you want for moral support.' Her words came out in a gush and for the first time in the last hour Ben found himself smiling.

'That's a very kind offer,' he said. He was just about to reject it, to send her on her way to Elmington Manor to begin the arduous task of sorting out her clothes for when she came out of mourning, but he found himself hesitating.

His family knew Francesca's father was responsible for Ben's conviction and subsequent transportation so she might not be the most welcome. Even so, he felt the warmth of her body by his side and knew he drew strength from her being there.

Silently he shook his head. He shouldn't need anyone to give him strength. He'd survived false imprisonment, two years on the filthy hulk ships, the perilous crossing to Australia and nearly six years of hard labour under the hot sun. From that dark time he'd risen and built an empire of some of the most successful and productive farms in Australia. Ben knew he was strong, knew he was a survivor, but right now he felt like a scared young lad.

'Thank you,' he said quietly, not able to admit how much he needed her in this moment.

They continued their journey through the village in silence, Francesca must have sensed his need to prepare for the reunion ahead and the familiar sights from his childhood were overwhelming. Not much had changed in nearly two decades. The high street still had the same small collection of shops, with only a couple of new shopfronts added. The village square looked identical to when Ben had last run around it with the other village children and the church still dominated Elswyre with its towering steeple and impressive stone exterior.

He leaned out of the window of the carriage, calling for the coachman to stop. The last bit of the journey he wished to do on foot.

Hopping down, he turned back to assist Francesca, wondering if he was making a mistake in allowing her to accompany him. It should be family time, all about the reunion, but he was unable to send her away. He wanted her reassuring presence by his side, her warmth, her kindness, her calming attitude.

They crossed the village square, going past the oldest houses in the village and turning off into a narrow street. His father's house, the house Ben had grown up in, was the second on the left.

It was quite an impressive size, especially for a working man. Years ago, even before Ben was born, his parents had inherited it from a wealthy aunt of his father's. It had been the reason they had moved to Elswyre and led to Ben's father taking the job as land steward for Lord Pottersdown.

He felt Francesca slip her hand into his and only then did he realise he'd frozen, stopped in the middle of the road, unable to take another step.

'He's your father, he loves you,' she murmured quietly, applying a little pressure to his hand to get him moving again.

Ben took another step, then stopped again as the door to the house was thrown open.

'Ben?' a clear voice called out.

It was unmistakably his father. Eighteen years and the man hardly looked any different. His once-dark hair was now filled with a smattering of grey and his face had acquired a few more lines, but apart from that it could have been exactly the man who'd hefted Ben up on to his shoulders during one of their long walks across the fields or told him a bedtime story while tucking him in at night.

'Father?' Ben said, hearing the layers of emotion in his voice. Beside him he felt Francesca step back discreetly, letting father and son have their moment.

With outstretched arms his father rushed towards him, pulling Ben towards his chest and embracing him for ten seconds before pulling away to study his son's face.

'My, you've changed,' his father said, 'although in some ways barely at all. It is good to have you home. I've been waiting for this day for eighteen years.'

The tears were flowing freely down his cheeks and Ben felt his own well up in his eyes. His father grasped his arm, leading him inside, seemingly unable to stop touching him as if scared Ben might disappear at any moment.

'Thomas,' Ben said, catching sight of his brother as he stepped into the hallway. 'And William.' He embraced the two men, memories of their childhood together flooding in and almost overwhelming him.

'Good to have you home, Brother,' Thomas said.

'We've been waiting for this day for a long time,' William added.

They were both big men, tall with broad shoulders and rich, dark hair and eyes just like their father. Ben favoured their mother more in looks with his green eyes, but the family resemblance was obvious.

'Come in, sit down, we have so much to catch up on,' Ben's father said, ushering them in to the comfortable room filled with armchairs and sofas at the front of the house.

Inside a little boy played on the floor, setting up line upon line of toy soldiers and moving them while babbling away happily to himself. Thomas's son, Ben supposed, the one his brother had sole care of since he'd lost his wife.

'My boy, Benjamin,' Thomas said quietly. 'We call him Benny.'

'I'm very pleased to meet you, Benny.' He felt a little stab of emotion at the thought of his brother wanting to remember him in this small way, giving his own son Ben's name.

The little boy grinned, then went happily back to playing his game.

Sitting down, Ben felt the familiarity of the house and for a moment he was back in those carefree days of his childhood where he was loved and cared for and thought everything in the world was good.

Realising he should introduce Francesca, he

glanced at his father. The man was reasonable and forgiving, but he didn't know how he would react to seeing Francesca after all this time.

'This is a friend, Father,' he said slowly.

'I know who she is.'

Ben glanced at Francesca, saw her cheeks redden, but she didn't back away and held the older man's gaze. Ben realised just how uncomfortable it must have been for her to suggest coming here with him today, but she'd done it anyway. For him.

The silence stretched out for nearly a minute, before Ben's father crossed to Francesca and took her hand.

'You're welcome in this house,' he said.

'Thank you,' Francesca said quietly. 'I'm sorry—'

Ben's father cut her off with a shake of his head. 'No need for that. You did everything you could, it wasn't your fault no one listened to you.' He glanced over at Ben with a hint of question in his eyes. 'And it would appear my son does not hold a grudge. We're happy to have you here.'

He motioned for Francesca to sit on the sofa next to Ben while a middle-aged woman bustled into the room, carrying a tray with a large teapot, cups and a cake ready for slicing.

'How are you, Father?' Ben asked. The older man looked well, his face was tanned and had a healthy glow, probably from all the hours spent outside.

'I'm well, Son. All the better for seeing you.'

'And your journey from the north?' Ben asked.

'As smooth as can be expected.' His father's voice was smooth and melodious and Ben felt the warmth inside him as it took him back to his childhood, the days where he was happy and carefree. 'But enough about me, I want to hear about you. What have you been doing since you've been back in England?'

Glancing at Francesca, he wondered how to answer that question. He could hardly tell his father he had been caught up pursuing a woman he had no right to be interested in. She was bound for marriage, albeit an inadvisable one, and he would one day soon return home to Australia.

'I travelled with George Fitzgerald and Sam Robertson,' Ben said, knowing his father would be aware of the two men from his letters to England that often spoke of the friends who were almost brothers. 'And while I awaited your return I stayed with them in London.'

Ben didn't miss the speculative glance his

father flashed at Francesca as he digested Ben's words.

'Tell us about Australia,' William said, his eyes wide and his tone enthusiastic.

'It's a wondrous country,' Ben said. 'Harsh and dangerous, but beautiful at the same time.'

'You've come to love it?' His father asked.

'Yes. I hated it for the first couple of years, until Mr Fitzgerald…' Ben trailed off, not sure how his father would react to hearing the name of the man who'd stepped up and taken Ben under his protection, becoming a second father in many ways.

'A man I will always be eternally grateful to,' he said quietly. 'I wished I could be there with you each and every day, but in my absence I'm just glad to know someone watched out for you, someone cared for you.'

'He did, Father. He was a good man.' Ben paused, remembering for a moment the man who had taken him and Robertson into his family. Only when he glanced at his brothers' eager faces did he continue with his descriptions of Australia. 'It seemed a dusty and cruel country when I first arrived and for many months I hated it. It was only when I'd served the first few years in Australia, when they deemed me trustworthy enough to work on the farms rather than do the hardest of the jobs—building roads—that I began to actually *see* my surroundings.'

'Is it very dangerous? All the strange creatures and wild natives?' Thomas asked, his honest and open face clouded with concern.

'There are some dangerous creatures. Snakes that will kill with a single bite. Spiders the size of a dinner plate, but we never had any trouble from the natives.'

'And you actually like it out there?' Thomas asked, incredulous.

'It's wild and untamed,' Ben said, trying to convey the allure of a land that was so vast and beautiful, but in a way completely different to the rolling green hills of England. 'The beaches are stretches of golden sand and inland the farmland is beautiful and bountiful. There are mountains and deserts and everything in between.'

'You'll go back?' his father asked quietly. There was a wealth of emotion hidden in that small question. Ben opened his mouth to answer, felt the words unable to come out. Beside him Francesca sought out his fingers with her own and squeezed, trying to reassure him. It was a tiny movement, their hands hidden under the layers of her skirt so no one else could see, but Ben felt the strength flowing from her into him.

'Of course you'll go back,' his father said, shaking his head. 'Your life is there, everything you've built for yourself.'

But not his family. And not Francesca.

Ben blinked at the thought. He'd never considered staying in England before, never even thought it was a possibility. For so long he'd been apprehensive about seeing his father again and meeting the brothers he hadn't seen since childhood, he hadn't thought much past it. This meeting was the culmination of his plans and now the future stretched out, empty and open, full of possibilities.

'I suppose I will have to,' Ben said quietly, glancing at Francesca.

That was one thing he should be certain of: his future wouldn't include Francesca. He might like her, care for her, spend his nights dreaming of having her soft body beside him, but he was not a man meant to settle down. Ever since his first dalliance with a woman he'd found it hard to imagine spending a lifetime with someone. Every time anyone even began to get close, he found he felt the beginnings of panic—the thought that if he started to care for someone, they might be wrenched away from him.

His friends always joked that one day he would fall head over heels in love and then the object of his affection would end their affair as he had with dozens of women before. Surreptitiously he glanced sideways at Francesca. Only now was he beginning to realise that it was Francesca, and the way they'd been pulled apart all those years ago, that had made him the way he was. Even if he didn't like to admit it, losing Francesca had shaped him into the man he was today—a man who knew he could never settle down out of fear of losing the one he loved.

Suppressing a grim chuckle, he shook his head. It didn't matter anyway; the object of his affection, the only woman who had ever come close to his heart, was steadfastly insisting on marrying a man who would make her miserable.

'Perhaps something might persuade you to stay,' Thomas said, casting a knowing glance at Ben and Francesca.

Ben shifted uncomfortably. His brother's remark was just a little too astute for comfort.

'I should leave you to your reunion,' Francesca said, her cheeks delightfully pink, but whether it was from the warmth of the roaring fire or her understanding of the knowing, but wrong, glances being exchanged across the room.

'Come to dinner,' Ben's father said, 'Our table is only humble, but you are most welcome at it. We eat at seven.'

'Thank you,' Francesca said quietly and Ben could see she was overwhelmed by the invitation from a man who should rightly hate her.

Standing, he escorted Francesca to the door, pausing as she pulled on her cloak and gloves.

'Enjoy them,' she said, standing on tiptoes and planting a kiss on his cheek. 'You deserve every moment of this.'

He watched her leave, realising that although he was back with the family he'd yearned for all those years he spent apart, he felt as if something were missing as she walked away.

Chapter Seventeen

'Tell me everything,' his father said as they strolled side by side around the village, their breath floating in an icy vapour and their posture stiff to try to combat the cold despite the thick coats they were wearing.

It was hard to know where to start. How did you compress eighteen years of life into a few short hours or days? Ben had written to his father over the years, long letters describing his situation, his successes and the people who surrounded him, but he knew it wasn't like hearing it first-hand.

'Tell me about your life now,' his father said, seeing Ben hesitate.

'I'm happy, Father,' Ben said, watching the older man nod in satisfaction. 'I'm my own master, I make my own decisions and my own mistakes. Australia is a curious land, over half the population are ex-convicts, but still it seems like a land of opportunity. Any man can rise up and become successful, no matter his past sins.'

'And your farms are thriving?'

'Very much so. Or at least they were when I left.' In total Ben owned seven farms, stretching out over a vast area in eastern Australia. The first he'd been given by Mr Fitzgerald the elder, a present when he'd turned eighteen, although legally he hadn't been able to take control of it until he'd served out his sentence two years later. That small parcel of land had flourished under his careful management and soon he had borrowed against it to buy more land. Ben took risks, but always calculated ones, and his strategy had paid off. He was now one of the wealthiest landowners in Australia and had a mixture of arable and cattle farms that provided him with an income that surpassed his wildest dreams.

'You have someone trusty looking after them?'

Ben thought of the man he'd left in charge, dependable, safe and certainly trustworthy. 'I do,' he said, but even he could hear the hesitation in his voice.

'You find it hard to let someone else look after things and make the decisions?' his father said with a knowing smile, 'You were the same as a lad.'

'I expect to make mistakes,' Ben said slowly, 'Everyone does. To plant a wrong crop one year, to move the cattle somewhere the water supply is dwindling, but they are *my* mistakes.'

'You find it hard to let go, to give up the responsibility…' his father paused and Ben felt his eyes on his face '…to trust?'

Hesitating only a second, Ben nodded. He'd forgotten how astute his father was, how well he read people and understood them with just a few hours in their company.

'And how about your personal life?' his father asked. 'Have you found someone special to share all this success with?'

An image of Francesca flashed across his mind, but quickly he suppressed it.

'No,' he said, trying to be abrupt and put an end to that line of conversation.

'That is a shame,' his father said, patting him affectionately on the arm, 'A companion, someone to share the highs and lows with, is the biggest blessing you can have in life. Apart from your children, of course, but one could argue it is difficult to beget one without the other.'

'You never remarried,' Ben said quietly. The question as to why had been on his mind for so long. It had been impossible to ask in a letter, but still he had a burning need to know why.

'I loved your mother with all my heart,' his father said. 'She lit up my world. I've never found anyone I care for the way I cared for her and it would be cruel to marry again and expect a woman to settle for anything less than the wholehearted love they deserve.'

'Were you ever tempted? When we were young?'

'To give you another mother of sorts?' his father clarified. 'No.' He laughed good naturedly. 'I supposed myself to be enough for you all.'

'You were.'

'But you do not have my excuse,' his father said, turning serious again. 'You have not loved and lost, so what is holding you back?'

Ben couldn't answer.

'Perhaps the one you want is somehow off limits to you?' his father prompted. 'Perhaps you've been holding back from loving anyone while you wait for the one your heart truly wants.'

'Father…'

'It's obvious to see, just as it was when you were a child.'

Again he opened his mouth to start denying

the attraction and feelings he had for Francesca, but his father stopped him.

'You loved her then, do you remember that?'

Ben shook his head. He'd thought of Francesca like a sister, like a best friend, nothing more. They'd only been children.

'Oh, it was an innocent sort of love, I have no doubt, but you loved her. Put her before yourself every time. I had visions of you two growing up and running off together, to escape her disapproving parents. But life worked out a little differently.'

'Just a little,' Ben murmured.

'I'm a hopeless romantic and I suppose I believe there is one true love for all of us out there,' his father said, stopping in front of the church. He motioned for Ben to go into the churchyard before him and then looped around in front, leading his son a few steps to the neatly kept grave. 'Your mother made me the happiest man alive. I would hate for you to miss out on that feeling.'

'She doesn't think of me that way,' Ben said, his mind filling up with images of Francesca's face lighting up when she saw him, her chin tilting for the illicit kisses, the light in her eyes as they discussed politics or agriculture or London gossip.

'Nonsense. I've only seen the two of you for a few minutes together and even I can see she's hopelessly in love with you.'

'A little infatuation, perhaps,' Ben conceded.

'Love,' his father insisted.

'She's practically engaged to another man.'

His father shrugged. 'Does she know a life with you is an option?'

With widened eyes Ben shook his head, trying not to let his complete surprise show on his face. It was funny how a parent, even one you hadn't seen for so many years, could pull down all the walls you'd built to protect yourself and render you speechless within a few minutes.

'She has some notion of saving her sister from a disastrous marriage by providing a decent dowry and stopping her father's creditors from destroying him completely.'

'She always did take on other people's problems,' his father murmured.

'So even if I did ask her to take a chance on me, she couldn't.'

'You could provide the dowry,' his father said quietly.

Ben blinked, wondering why he hadn't thought of that. It was simple, and infinitely better than Francesca being married to a man she hated for the rest of her life. Not that he was thinking of doing it so he could be with her...

'You have the funds.'

'She wouldn't...' Ben was unable to finish the sentence. The thought of being with Francesca was too good, too risky. What if he took away all the barriers and she still said no?

Still, the idea of waking up to Francesca in his bed every morning, taking her out on week-long trips to inspect his furthest farms, producing a brood of wild-haired children who looked just like their beautiful mother, that was tempting.

He watched as his father crouched down beside his mother's grave.

'She would have wanted you to find love.'

He remembered his mother, but not well. There were images of a beautiful woman who was always smiling, who took time from running the house to play and laugh with her children. He remembered cuddling up to her for bedtime stories and helping her knead bread in the kitchen.

Crouching beside his father, Ben laid a hand on the cool stone. His childhood seemed a whole lifetime ago, sometimes even a life that hadn't belonged to him.

They stayed in the graveyard for another few

minutes, Ben paying respect to his mother at the grave he thought he would never see.

'I'll let you be alone with her, follow on when you're ready,' his father said eventually.

As he watched his father walk away he sat down on the cold earth next to the gravestone and lowered his head.

'What about you, Mama?' he asked. 'What do you think I should do?'

Of course, there was no answer, no flash of divine inspiration. Instead Ben reached into the neck of his shirt and folded his fingers around the locket that rested against his chest. Francesca's locket—the one he'd been accused of stealing all those years ago. He'd worn it every day of his sentence. At first he told himself it was a reminder of how little things can change the direction of your life completely, but now he wasn't so sure. It had been a piece of the girl he'd loved, his only connection to her.

He smiled ruefully as he thought back to the day he'd been dragged from the county gaol to the magistrate's house before he was due in the courtroom for his short trial. Francesca's locket had been lying on the desk in the magistrate's study, glinting up at him. He'd slipped it into a pocket before he could even reason through his actions and kept it with him ever since.

His fingers brushed over the warm silver and he closed his eyes. There would be no answers here. This was a decision his mother couldn't help him with. Perhaps his father was right, perhaps he had been alone for too long. Perhaps he needed to stop being scared she would reject him due to their differences in class, or would somehow be taken away from him. Instead, perhaps he needed to find a way to make the woman he couldn't stop thinking about his.

Nervously Francesca knocked on the front door. She had spent the remainder of the afternoon with Ginny, the only housemaid left at Elmington Manor. Ginny was in her thirties, an age at which most housemaids had moved up or moved on, either to more senior household positions or to marriage, but neither seemed to appeal to the mousy woman and she stayed at Elmington Manor for a pittance of a wage and her room. Consequently the house was not in a great condition, but Francesca had cajoled the inherently lazy housemaid into opening up her bedroom, airing it off and flicking away the worst of the dust.

Tomorrow she would tackle the task of getting her old dresses, the ones in colours other than blacks and greys and mauves, out of storage.

Here, outside Ben's father's house, she felt nervous. Her stomach was roiling and her palms felt hot and sticky inside her gloves. It meant so much to her for Ben's family to like her, even when she knew she would probably never see them again. When they were younger Ben's parents had been kind and welcoming and level-headed, a lovely antidote to her chaotic family, and it would appear his father had not changed one bit.

'Lady Somersham,' Mr Crawford said as he opened the door, 'Welcome, come in.'

'Please call me Francesca,' she said.

'Ben is with his brothers,' Mr Crawford said, 'They're talking land management. Would you have a couple of minutes to spare for me before we find him?'

'Of course,' Francesca said, the nerves rearing again. She didn't know why Mr Crawford would want to talk to her in private, but she felt like a naughty child, probably because the last time she'd seen him before this afternoon she'd been ten years old and always getting into trouble with Ben.

'Come through to the garden.'

He led the way, taking her through the warm hall and out through the door in the kitchen to a garden that smelled of wet earth and herbs even at this time of year.

'How have you been, Francesca?' Mr Crawford asked, as he motioned for her to have a seat on a little bench that looked out over the grass.

'Well, thank you,' she answered, remembering all the times she'd come for lunch in this happy home as a child and all the times she'd wished it was her home.

'I'm not making small talk,' Mr Crawford said, and even in the darkness she could tell he was smiling. 'How have you really been?'

She hesitated. It wasn't the done thing to air all her woes to a man she hadn't seen for eighteen years, but Ben's father had a soothing way about him that made her want to spill every disaster and every uncertainty in her life.

'Ben said you were married,' Mr Crawford prompted, 'although he hinted it wasn't the happiest of unions.'

'Father arranged it,' Francesca said. She sighed and gave in to the urge to talk, no matter how improper it was. 'Lord Somersham was never violent, but when that is the best you can say about your late husband it is hardly a ringing endorsement, is it?'

'You were unhappy?'

She nodded. Although for years she'd tried

to pretend she was content, tried to accept this was what she had been born for, she had never been happy in her marriage.

'Yet you are considering marrying again, another man you do not care for.' He said the words so quietly it took Francesca a moment to absorb them.

'I must,' she said, 'My family…'

Patting her on the hand in a fatherly fashion, he shook his head. 'It is a poor state of affairs when a child has to be responsible for her parents. And the consequences of their actions.'

It was true, but there wasn't much she could so about it.

'If you were my daughter, your happiness would be paramount.'

Francesca laughed, trying to hide the bitter edge. So many times as a child she'd wished this man was her father instead of the drunken gambler that resided at Elmington Manor.

'I think you would be happier if you married Ben,' Mr Crawford said.

Francesca almost choked on the air she was breathing.

'Mr Crawford…' she said, but didn't know how to continue.

'You would,' he said with a shrug. 'You love

him. And love is a decent foundation to base a marriage on.'

'I barely know him,' she protested.

'Nonsense. You were inseparable for years.'

'Two decades ago.'

'People don't change.'

'Of course they do. I've changed.' She thought sadly back to the happy, carefree girl she'd been as a child and knew that person had been slowly eroded away until the woman she was today was all that was left.

'Not really,' Mr Crawford said and even in the darkness she could see him smile. 'Oh, maybe on the surface,' he conceded, 'but deep down, that core inner person, that will never change.'

They sat in silence for a few minutes and Francesca wondered at the warmth and love in the heart of this man. No wonder Ben had managed to survive such a terrible experience in his childhood. He had solid foundations built by his parents, foundations of love and self-belief and confidence in his decisions.

'Have a think about it,' Mr Crawford said. 'Consider whether you want to spend a life with a man you don't care for or take a chance on love.'

He stood before she could reply, turning and

walking back towards the house. Francesca felt the tears slipping down her cheeks. Whatever she'd expected to find here it wasn't this wonderful kindness. Mr Crawford had taken a precious few seconds away from his time with his son to talk to her about her future happiness. Her father wouldn't ever do such a thing—half the time she suspected he didn't even see her as a person, just a commodity to be traded—yet here was a man she had last seen eighteen years ago and he was trying to advocate for her future happiness.

Love. Was that what there was between her and Ben? Until now she'd been too scared to call it anything but affection, but perhaps it was love. She felt her whole being lift whenever Ben was close, thought about him constantly when they were apart and could only truly be happy when they were reunited again. Thinking back to the day they'd spent in his bed, she felt a now-familiar tingle of desire, but that wasn't all there was.

You've loved him for years, the little voice inside her head said. Surely it couldn't be true. She hadn't been able to forget Ben, but she'd always put that down to the terrible way they'd been torn apart.

'I see my father has been spreading his wisdom.' Ben's voice came from somewhere behind her.

'He is a very persuasive man,' Francesca murmured.

Ben sat on the bench next to her, looping an arm around her back and pulling her closer in a supremely intimate gesture.

'He thinks I am denying myself love and affection,' Ben said, grumbling in a way that told Francesca he probably agreed with his father, but didn't quite want to admit it. 'What did he want with you?'

'He was concerned about my future happiness,' Francesca said carefully. She wasn't ready to admit her feelings for Ben yet, not when she wasn't sure herself what they actually were.

'Then he has got some sense in him. *Everyone* is concerned about your future happiness.' He paused, then shook his head. 'I'm wrong. Everyone should be concerned about your future happiness, but your family seem incapable of thinking of anyone but themselves.'

They were harsh words, but Francesca couldn't protest, it was the truth.

'Except your sister. She's a decent human being and doesn't want you to sacrifice your happiness for hers.'

'What would you have me do?' Francesca

asked, a little sharper than she'd planned. 'If I didn't marry Lord Huntley, what would you have me do?'

'What would you want to do?' he asked, searching her face.

Run away with you. She couldn't say the words, even though she realised it was the truth.

Instead she shrugged, feeling his eyes on her and not knowing how to respond.

'We'd lose the house, the estate. Father's creditors would finally lose patience, I'm sure. I would have to find work, perhaps as a governess.'

She'd always wanted children, but after the unsuccessful years with Lord Somersham she doubted she would ever have any of her own. Perhaps being a governess wouldn't be too bad.

She saw a flash of disappointment flash across Ben's face and knew he despaired of her putting social appearances first, before anything that really mattered.

'You'd make a fine governess,' Ben said.

'And what about your relationship issues?' Francesca asked.

'I'm working on them.'

'Really?'

He chuckled. 'Well, I will certainly try to. A man doesn't like to be told he has flaws.'

'Do you think…?' She paused to take a deep breath. 'Do you think one day you might have a meaningful relationship?' she asked, knowing it was a deeply personal question.

'Who knows? I wouldn't like to promise anything I couldn't be sure to deliver.'

Francesca looked up sharply, unsure if what he was saying had a deeper meaning, whether he was talking about their situation, or if she was reading too much into his words.

'Come inside, let's have dinner. Perhaps tomorrow things will be clearer.'

Allowing him to take her arm as she got to her feet, Francesca felt a wave of sadness wash over her. Mr Crawford was right, she did yearn for a future with Ben, but there were too many obstacles, too many things keeping them apart. Added to that, he hadn't ever mentioned staying in England, not for her or anyone. Soon he would sail back to Australia and out of her life, and she couldn't build their relationship up into something it wasn't or it would be even worse when the time came for him to leave and for her to get on with her normal life.

Dinner was a cheery affair. Ben was sat in the place of honour at the head of the table, with Francesca on one side and his brother Thomas on the other. Further down the table his father and William sat, and even Thomas's young son Benny had been allowed to stay up as it was a special occasion.

For the first time in years he felt at peace, as if his homecoming had dampened down the turmoil that was always raging inside him.

'Ben came home covered in soot with dust all over his clothes.' His father was telling a story of one of Ben's exploits from his childhood, his face glowing with happiness.

'I remember that,' Francesca said slowly. 'You were convinced you could climb the chimney in the dining room at Elmington Manor, but the butler caught you before you were even half-way up and thrashed you with a carpet beater.'

'If I hadn't been caught, I would have been able to climb that chimney,' he said, grinning.

'Nonsense. It was too tall and even then you weren't *that* agile.'

'I was like a cat. Probably even more lithe than a cat.'

'I think you have a touch of selective memory,' Francesca murmured as his brothers laughed. 'You were always falling off things. *I* was the better climber.'

'You were not,' Ben said, gesturing with a

fork loaded with peas. 'The number of times I had to catch you or rescue you…'

'You're remembering it wrong. I always had to catch you.'

'I'd have squashed you.'

'You were quite a scrawny boy…'

'I don't know what you're talking about,' Ben said, grinning, 'I was a strapping lad, made of muscle.'

An unfamiliar sensation was washing over him and Ben realised it was contentment. Here, with Francesca by his side, surrounded by his family, he felt content. Perhaps he needed to consider what was important to him going forward. He might have built a life for himself in Australia, but was it the life he wanted?

'I want to propose a toast,' Mr Crawford said. 'To my boy, finally you're home. We've missed you more than you'll ever know.'

Ben looked around the table, seeing the happy, open faces and wondered whether he was being a fool even considering going back to Australia.

Perhaps his brothers would grow tired of him, resent the return of a man who'd they had thought long lost to the other side of the world, but there was no indication of anything like that yet. And his father was ecstatic to have his eldest son back home.

He had a lot of decisions to make and right now he didn't know where to start.

Chapter Eighteen

Feeling like a naughty child once again, Ben pulled back his arm and threw another pebble at Francesca's window. He hoped he had the right room—when he'd last been at Elmington Manor she had still had her bedroom in the nursery, but this was the only room on the first floor with a hint of a candle burning behind the curtains.

Another pebble left his hand and made a satisfying tapping sound against the window pane, this time resulting in movement in the room. The curtains twitched and he held his breath as Francesca looked out. Her hair was loose and untamed, the sleekness she had managed to maintain throughout the day long gone now, and she was dressed in a billowing cotton nightgown that made her look like someone from the last century.

Opening the window, she peered down at him.

'You could have knocked at the door,' Francesca said, an amused half-smile on her lips.

'And woken half the household?'

'There's only me and Ginny here, Father dismissed all the rest of the staff a couple of years ago.'

'Why use the front door when you can climb through a window?'

'What makes you think I'll let you through my window?'

'You can't resist my boyish charm or my devilish good looks.'

Francesca snorted, but motioned for him to come up anyway.

'I'm only letting you in because I want to see you climb up here.'

Although Ben had kept fit over the years, with his boxing and regular riding across the Australian countryside, scaling walls was not something he'd done for a very long time and it took a particular set of skills. Still, he wasn't about to admit defeat and go in through the front door.

Using the ground-floor window and a convenient metal pipe that ran down the edge of the building, he climbed, gripping on to Francesca's windowsill within a mere few seconds. Using all his strength, he pulled himself up, tumbling into the room with a loud crash. Francesca sat perched on the edge of her bed giggling.

'Easy,' Ben said, wiping the grime from his coat before shedding it and placing it over the back of a chair. It was much warmer inside than out and the effort of the climb had already warmed his muscles.

'I suppose it's not a chimney,' Francesca murmured.

'I'm happy to go downstairs right now and prove to you I can climb that chimney,' Ben said, starting for the door.

'You barely fit then and you're four times the size now.' She laughed. 'Although I wouldn't mind seeing you with your head stuck up the chimney.'

Ben turned and closed the window, latching it shut. The remains of a fire glowed in the grate and as he pulled the curtain he felt peculiarly warm and contented.

'I received a letter from the seventeen-eighties and they want their nightgown back,' Ben said.

Francesca looked down. 'I'll have you know this is the height of fashion.'

'The height of fashion from thirty years ago.'

'I wasn't expecting to receive any visitors,' she said primly, 'and it keeps me warm.'

'I could keep you warm,' he said, raising an eyebrow suggestively and making Francesca burst out laughing.

'Is that why you came? To defile an innocent and upstanding widow?'

'Do you know where I can find one of those?' he asked, taking a step closer.

'I was perfectly virtuous before you came back.'

'A man can't help being irresistible,' he said with a shrug, now close enough to loop his arms around her waist and pull her slender body towards him.

'You always were too confident for your own good.'

'There's no such thing,' he murmured, catching her earlobe between his teeth and feeling her body react in his arms.

Bunching the thick cotton in his hands he pulled the offending nightgown up and over Francesca's head, much more satisfied when he discarded it on the floor behind him and turned back to her now-naked body.

As her hands pulled first at his jacket and then his shirt he kissed her, stopping only when he needed to lift his garments over his head or step out of his trousers. Their bodies entwined they tumbled back on the bed.

Slowly Ben ran his hands over Francesca's body, feeling her rise up to meet his touch and hearing her moan with anticipation and pleasure. Everything about her felt right, she fit perfectly against him and Ben had never felt this level of desire with anyone else in his life.

With passion and tenderness, they made love. The moment Francesca cried out with pleasure she looked into his eyes and Ben felt something in his chest tighten.

Love, that was the word his father had used. Turning over and pulling Francesca into his arms, Ben felt her warmth and the reassuring beating of her heart in her chest.

'I come out of mourning in three days,' Francesca said quietly. It must be almost a year since Lord Somersham had died and Ben knew she couldn't stretch out her mourning period any longer. 'Father will accept Lord Huntley's proposal on my behalf.' They'd also now had all the eight days together they had promised one another. At the thought, Ben felt consumed by panic.

He didn't say anything. With Francesca in his arms he didn't want to think about losing her.

'Once I return to London…' She trailed off,

but Ben knew what she was saying. Once she returned to London she would not be able to see him again. An illicit liaison was one thing when she was merely a widow and had not yet promised herself to someone else, but Ben knew she would not break a vow to be faithful to another, no matter how much she wanted to.

'Don't marry him,' Ben said quietly.

'Ben, we've been through this a hundred times. I have to.'

'No, you don't.'

'My sister, my family.'

'I'll provide the dowry for your sister,' he said.

Francesca stiffened and then turned over to face him.

'I'll even sort something out for your odious father if it stops you from having to marry Huntley.'

'You don't mean that.'

'I do, Frannie. I can't stand the idea of you being unhappy for the rest of your life.'

'I couldn't let you do that.'

'Why not? I have plenty of money. I can't see a better cause to spend it on.'

'And in return?' she asked, her voice coming out as barely a whisper.

Ben closed his eyes for a moment. He wanted

to ask her to be his, to marry him and spend her life by his side. The words wouldn't quite come out, though. He felt selfish asking, as he knew he might not be able to give her what she deserved. He would be asking her to give up her status, her friends, her family. She would no longer be the widow of a viscount, but the wife of an ex-convict, albeit a wealthy one. He knew those things mattered to her, but he just didn't know how much.

Taking a deep breath, he pushed on.

'You would be free,' he said, stroking her cheek. 'You could choose to marry or not, choose the sort of life you lived.'

He watched as she swallowed, saw the nervousness on her face. 'A life with you?' she asked.

'Marry me,' he said, pushing away all his doubts. He wasn't great at taking risks, but how could he hold back from asking her when they both clearly wanted it so much?

She searched his eyes with her own and Ben felt a bubble of nerves as he realised she hadn't answered him yet.

'Are you sure?' she asked. 'I don't want you to ask just because you think otherwise I will throw my life away on Lord Huntley.'

Ben grinned. He was going about this all

wrong. No woman deserved to be proposed to like this. Sitting up, he turned Francesca to face him and took her hand in his own.

'I love you, Frannie,' he said. 'And I know you love me.'

'I always imagined my marriage proposal to be a little less arrogant...' Francesca said, trying to keep the smile from her face.

'Is that a yes?'

'Yes.'

Ben kissed her, feeling the soaring of his heart and wondering if this was what he'd wanted all along. Deep down he knew Francesca was one of the main reasons he'd returned to England, alongside seeing his family again, of course, but he'd told himself he had just wanted to see his friend, to make sure she was happy. Now he was beginning to wonder if he'd deluded himself all those years and if in fact he'd loved her all along.

'I feel like I'm in a dream,' Francesca murmured as she pulled away, looking into his eyes, 'and I don't want to wake up.'

'This is no dream, Frannie, this is the rest of our lives.'

Despite his words he agreed with her, this evening *did* have a dreamlike quality to it. He hadn't set out to propose to her, his words had been spontaneous even if the idea of spending the rest of his life with Francesca by his side had been circling in his head ever since his father had suggested Ben might be happier if he gave in to the feelings he had for her. In just a few short moments he'd completely changed the course of his life.

Never had he imagined sharing his life with anyone. Whenever he'd pictured his future it had always looked the same as the past few years: a successful business obtained through relentless hard work, pleasing but short-lived affairs, and keeping everyone at arm's length, deep down too scared they might be wrenched away from him.

'Is it possible to be this happy?' Francesca asked, her voice muffled as she spoke into his chest where she'd buried her face.

He knew the next few weeks would be difficult. Francesca would have to break the news to her family that she was not going to abide by their expectations and marry Lord Huntley. No doubt there would be harsh words and recriminations, but it would be worth it. Soon the drama would be behind them, Francesca would be free of her responsibility to her family and they would be husband and wife.

'Where will we live?' she asked.

'Do you mind?'

Slowly she shook her head. It would be a lot to ask to insist she leave her family and friends behind for an entirely new life in Australia, especially when Ben wasn't sure if he could do the same to his family once again. Perhaps they would be better settling in England, although then there would always be the pull of her father's antics and no getting away from the responsibility Francesca would feel towards her parents even after they'd done so little for her.

'There's no need to decide yet,' Ben said, stroking her hair. 'It is enough we know we'll be together. We can work out the details in time.'

'I shall have to tell Lord Huntley,' Francesca said, her fingers dancing across his abdomen distractedly.

'I'm more than happy to break the news,' Ben said with a grin. He would take satisfaction in informing the Viscount he had better start searching for a new wife.

'I'm sure you would be, but it should come from me.'

'Whatever you think best, although you don't owe that man anything.'

'I suppose not.'

They both fell silent. Ben's head was spinning with plans for the future. Right now he couldn't quite believe he'd actually asked Francesca to marry him, or that she'd said yes. His life was on such a different trajectory to what it had been even a few hours earlier and he felt like he needed some time to adjust. No doubt Francesca felt the same.

He sat up, but quickly Francesca's hands coaxed him back down.

'Stay,' she whispered. 'Who can protest if we're to be married?'

'It might give your maid a shock if she finds me here in the morning.'

Francesca grimaced. 'I doubt she'll be up before us. She's not used to having anyone residing at Elmington Manor, it's been so long since we opened the house up.'

With a satisfied smile on his face, Ben settled back down next to the woman he was going to marry.

Chapter Nineteen

It had been a week since Ben had proposed. A week of blissful happiness. They'd spent the time in Essex, long mornings in bed followed by leisurely afternoons riding out to visit Ben's family. Francesca could see the change in Ben and often wondered what had been the catalyst for it. There was no doubt that his reunion with his family, and with his father in particular, had changed him, but she also thought their own plans for the future might have played a role in the shift in his outlook.

From the little he'd told her and a substantial amount of reading in between the lines, Francesca had worked out that Ben had never allowed a woman to get close to him before. There had been affairs, and plenty of them if she read his expressions correctly, but no one he'd allowed close to his heart. She was in a privileged position and she was determined not to jeopardise his trust in her.

For her part Francesca swung between being wonderfully content to worrying about how she was going to break the news to her family and Lord Huntley. Of course they wouldn't approve. She was risking her future, all their futures, on a man who would never be accepted by society. It didn't matter that he hadn't committed the crime he'd been sentenced for, or that he was now a very successful and rich landowner, all that would matter to the people close to her was that he was not of their class.

Shaking her head, she reprimanded herself. Over the years, since making her debut in society and then marrying Lord Somersham, Francesca felt as though her true identity had been slowly eroded away. She'd been browbeaten into believing the trivial things in life were the most important. If you were told time and time again that it mattered what clothes you wore, who you were related to and were judged on how pretty your curtsy was, then you began to believe these inconsequential things were actually important. Since Ben had reappeared in her life she had felt some of the lies she'd been told over the years washing away and her true self re-emerging.

Still, it would take some time for all her so-ciety-induced behaviours to be modified and she still felt nervous about telling anyone of her decision to leave the world she'd always known and set up life with Ben instead.

Francesca was under no illusion that she would be required to leave everything she knew behind. Once she married Ben she wouldn't be accepted by the same social circle, she'd be excluded and shunned. It was a shallow and cruel reaction, and she shouldn't mind, but it was just like when the Patronesses had excluded her from getting a voucher for Almack's—she felt hurt and betrayed by the idea.

Perhaps it would be easier to start afresh in Australia. In Australia, Ben assured her, there wasn't the same prejudice. A man was admired for making his own way in the world, not for the family name he started with. They could build their lives together with no preconceptions, no expectations or interference from someone else.

She wasn't sure whether Ben was ready to leave his family again, though—after seeing them after so long—he'd started to cultivate a lovely relationship with his father and brothers. It would be extremely difficult to leave them behind, knowing he might not ever see them again.

Francesca's feelings on leaving her family behind were just as complicated. She'd miss her sister without a doubt, but her parents she had mixed emotions about. Her mother had been mentally absent for so long that Francesca had half-forgotten what it was like to have a proper conversation with the woman and her father was a selfish and impulsive man who'd put his own desires and urges above his family, almost rendering them destitute in the process.

Still, they were her family. She might hate how her father treated her, hate how he had been so selfish all those years ago to accuse Ben of theft when in reality he'd sold the family valuables to give him more funds for his gambling, but he was still her father. She could hate how he'd acted all these years, but she couldn't hate him.

Part of her wondered how it would feel to have parents invested in her happiness. For them to congratulate her on her impending union because they knew it would make her happy rather than thinking only of how it would affect them.

Francesca dawdled for another moment after the carriage had pulled up outside the front of their town house, fiddling with her skirts and summoning up the courage to go in and tell her parents her decision to marry Ben, not the man her father had chosen for her.

She wished she'd taken Ben up on his offer to accompany her, but when he'd suggested it she had told him it was best if she broke the news gently, on her own. Of course her father would be irate and her mother would probably tell her how selfish she was being, but it would be nothing that Francesca hadn't been dealing with her entire life. Throwing Ben's presence into the mix would make things worse.

Instead she'd made a detour on her journey, dropping Ben off at his rooms before returning here. They still hadn't finalised their plans as to where they would be living when they started their life together, but Ben had torn himself away from his family to give her the support she needed with hers.

Sighing, she resigned herself to an ugly few minutes once her parents found out her plans, summoned her courage and allowed the coachman to help her down from the carriage.

She was barely up the steps before the door had opened and her father loomed in the doorway.

'Get inside,' he said, his voice tight with anger.

Francesca swallowed, feeling the scratchy

dryness of her throat, and wondered if he knew already of her plans.

Roughly, he took her by the arm, his fingers digging in even through the thickness of the luxurious cloak Ben had bought her all those weeks ago. He manhandled her into his study, a room that was barely furnished, like so many in the house. There was an old desk and two chairs, nothing more, and Francesca was pushed forcefully to sit in one of the chairs.

'After everything I've done for you,' her father hissed, his face so close to hers that she could feel his breath on her cheeks. He'd been drinking, of course he had, but he wasn't yet inebriated. The anger was coming from a place of sobriety.

He pulled back, crossing the room to turn the key in the lock before slipping it into his pocket.

'Father,' Francesca said, trying to sound reasonable.

It was hard when she was cringing inside. When she was a child he'd beaten her a couple of times, when her minor misdemeanours had coincided with his episodes of particularly bad fortune, causing him to react poorly to any irritation, but he hadn't raised a hand to her since she'd become a young woman. Right now he looked as though he might murder her.

'Don't call me Father. You have no right. A *daughter* treats her father with respect. A *daughter* honours and obeys her father. A *daughter* does not scheme and collude with criminals behind her father's back to defraud him of what is rightfully his.'

Frowning as she tried to decipher his words, Francesca started to shake her head slowly.

'Don't shake your head and act all innocent,' he hissed. 'I know exactly what you've been up to. Using that criminal to defraud me out of my house. To take the roof over your own family's head for your own gain.'

Slowly understanding dawned. This wasn't about her engagement to Ben. It was about the wager he'd made with her father and the resulting agreement that he would take the house in lieu of payment.

'I knew nothing about the wager,' she said, 'but he won't go through with it.'

It was as if her words didn't even penetrate her father's mind. He curled up a lip in disgust, brought back a hand and slapped her squarely across the cheek. The sound of the blow reverberated in Francesca's ears and her head snapped back. Yelping involuntarily from the shock and the pain, Francesca recoiled. Never had she expected her father to act like this.

'And then I find my whore of a daughter is out prostituting herself to the very man who wants to ruin me.'

'Ben isn't going to ruin you, Father,' she said, her hand cupping her cheek. 'You did that to yourself a very long time ago.'

'So you don't deny it?'

Francesca tried to rein herself in, but something had been unleashed inside her. 'I don't deny I've spent the last week with a man I am not married to. I don't deny we've been intimate and I don't deny I've loved every minute of it.'

She saw her father raise his hand again and tried to stop herself from cowering away. These were only physical blows, she would recover, she told herself, but still she felt her arms raise up and her body jerk away.

'We're going to be married,' she blurted out, her eyes still closed in anticipation of the slap.

'No, you're not,' her father said. 'He's a dirty criminal. A thief, a liar, a cheat.'

Francesca laughed, seeing her father as he truly was for the first time; a man to be ridiculed.

'Don't laugh,' he said, raising his hand again. Francesca refused to cower and looked him directly in the eye.

'Eighteen years ago you ruined a young boy's

life and you have the audacity to call him a liar and a cheat.'

Her father laughed, a mirthless chuckle that scared her more than a raised hand could ever do. 'He was nothing, a nobody. A necessary sacrifice to save one of the greatest families in England.'

'He wasn't a nobody,' Francesca said, shaking her head in disgust. 'He had a family who loved him and a future that could have contained anything.'

'He was the son of a servant. A troublemaker. *A nobody.*'

Francesca looked at her father with disbelief. For her entire life she'd been making excuses for him, telling herself that he'd only done this or that because he didn't know any better. Now she could see she'd been wrong. Her father wasn't a bumbling fool, circumstances hadn't got the better of him, he was a cruel and petty man.

'I didn't recognise him at first,' her father said. 'Even when he came here and sat at my table I didn't recognise that runt of a child I sent to Australia.'

'Do you really have no remorse?' Francesca asked with disgust, but her father didn't seem to hear her.

'I invited him to my table, played cards with him and all he did was deceive me.'

'Hardly a crime, unlike what you did to him when he was a child.'

'Did he tell you he was planning on taking the house from me?'

Francesca nodded, not even bothering to try to explain again that Ben wouldn't have gone through with it. Her father wasn't listening, too caught up in his own monologue, too busy justifying his own heinous behaviour by condemning another.

'You probably laughed at me while you whored yourself to him,' her father said, picking up his glass and taking a gulp of the port that was filled almost to the brim. 'Well, I shall be the one laughing now.'

Feeling a spark of unease begin creeping through her body, Francesca tried to stand, but was jolted back down as her father pressed a forceful hand against her shoulder.

'What have you done?' she asked, her eyes flicking to the locked door.

Her father smiled, a malicious grin that showed his port-stained teeth and made Francesca feel sick inside.

'I hear the punishment for an ex-convict

found to be stealing again is much harsher. Perhaps even the noose.'

'No,' Francesca said. 'Please, Father, whatever it is you've done we can still put it right.'

'I'll not have that boy take my house from me,' her father said, 'or make a fool of me through my own daughter.'

She stood, lunging at her father, trying to grab the key to the door from the pocket he'd deposited it in, but despite the alcohol he'd imbibed already this morning her father was surprisingly quick.

'All these years,' Francesca said as he gripped her wrists, bruising the delicate skin with his fingers, 'I've made excuses for you, I've made allowances. All these years I've told myself you aren't evil, just desperate, but I can see now I was so wrong.'

Her father didn't deign to answer, instead gripping her by the shoulders and pushing her along in front of him. With the key she'd tried so desperately to get her hands on he opened the door, but before she could even think about escaping he pushed her roughly towards the stairs. When Francesca fought him every step of the way he picked her up, tossed her over his shoulder and started to ascend the stairs.

On the first floor he made a turn, bypassing her room and starting for the stairs that led up to the smaller rooms once used by the servants when they'd employed more than the bare minimum a house needed to get by. Out of the corner of her eye Francesca saw movement and raised her neck to see her mother's gaunt face peering out of the bedroom she hadn't emerged from for years.

'Mama,' she called. 'Help me!'

Francesca felt her heart break a little as her mother steadfastly refused to meet her eye, instead closing the door quietly on the situation in the hallway.

On the second floor her father, panting and gasping from the effort of carrying her when he did not normally engage in any physical activity, threw open one of the doors to an empty servant's bedroom and flung her unceremoniously inside. Before she had even had chance to get to her feet he had closed the door and locked it.

With a sinking heart Francesca rattled the handle. The door was solid and well made and unlikely to give way no matter what she did to it. Quickly she crossed to the window, wondering if that might provide her with an easy escape route.

It was locked and the glass thick, and the

window itself small. Hardly an ideal window to escape through. Slumping back against the wall, Francesca let her head drop into her hands and allowed the tears to fall. To think she'd been worried about leaving her family, she'd felt guilty about going back on the agreement her father had made with Lord Huntley to provide a little money in exchange for her hand in marriage. In accepting Ben's proposal she'd thought she was letting her family down.

All these years she'd made excuses for them. For her father who was selfish and cruel and her mother who hid herself away from the world, not rousing herself from her bedroom for anything at all.

She thought of Ben, the man who'd built a good life despite what her father had orchestrated against him. Now who knew what fresh lies her father had organised? It wasn't fair on him and it was all because of his acquaintance with her again.

Shaking her head, she told herself not to be ridiculous. It was her father's doing, not hers. She needed to learn when to accept responsibility for things and when to realise it was others at fault. It was her father who had done these things, both eighteen years ago and now.

Wiping away the tears, Francesca stood and

crossed to the window again. She couldn't change what her father had done, but she could work on a way of getting out of this situation and helping the man she loved.

Chapter Twenty

Ben ducked and weaved, landing a couple of punches on his opponent before backing away again. Today he felt light on his feet, as though he were flying through the air rather than walking on the ground, and his reaction time was nearly half what it normally was.

He dodged a couple of punches, landing one more on his opponent's chin before the man on the edge of the ring called time.

Ben shook hands with the other man, grabbed the cloth offered to mop his brow and crossed over to where George Fitzgerald had been watching him.

'I can't believe you're getting married, too,' Fitzgerald said, 'and to a lady. First Robertson and now you.'

Sam Robertson had set sail for Australia just before Ben had left for his trip to Essex with the beautiful Lady Georgina as his companion, despite her being due to walk down the aisle and wed a duke that very same day.

'There must be something in the air,' Ben said with a grin. 'It'll be you next.'

Fitzgerald grimaced. 'I hardly think so. How did it happen?'

Ben grinned, unable to stop himself. He still didn't really know how it had happened. One minute he'd been quite content conducting a passionate affair with his childhood friend and the next he'd decided he wanted to spend the rest of his life with her. Shaking his head, he knew that wasn't quite true. The feelings had been there for a while, he'd just needed some help to figure out exactly what they were.

'My father gave me some good advice,' he said slowly. 'He told me to look to what would make me happy and stop living in fear of having things taken away.'

'That is good advice,' Fitzgerald murmured, 'Especially for a man who doesn't trust anyone.' He looked unusually serious with a thoughtful frown on his face.

'Do you disapprove?' Ben asked. His friend's opinion was important to him. For so long Fitzgerald and Robertson had been like brothers to him, they'd been through so much together, and he wanted Fitzgerald to like Francesca.

'Good Lord, no,' Fitzgerald said. 'Any woman who can have you even think about settling down must be worth her weight in gold.' He paused, his expression turning serious. 'I just want you to be happy and it would seem Lady Somersham makes you happy.'

'She does,' Ben said quietly.

'I knew that was why you'd never forgotten her.'

'What do you mean?'

'You loved her all along,' Fitzgerald said simply.

Ben opened his mouth to protest, but slowly closed it again, considering his friend's words. For eighteen long years Francesca had haunted his thoughts. He'd assumed that was because of the dramatic way they'd been ripped apart without any natural closure to the relationship, but there might be some truth in Fitzgerald's words. Perhaps his love for her as a child was what had driven him back here.

'You are a romantic,' Ben said, shaking his head. It might be the truth, but he wasn't about to admit it. Eighteen years was a long time to be in love with someone without even knowing it yourself.

'So where will you live?' Fitzgerald asked. 'Here? Australia? Some neutral third country?'

Ben shrugged. 'We're not sure.'

'She's reluctant to leave her family?'

'Maybe. But I'm reluctant to leave mine.'

'The reunion was everything you hoped for?'

Ben nodded, remembering his father's happy face when he'd first set eyes on the son who'd been absent from his life for nearly two decades. He wasn't sure if he was ready to return to Australia yet, knowing that he might not ever be able to make the trip to England again.

'And your brothers were happy to see you?'

Ben had often wondered if his brothers would welcome him after so long. He'd read the story of the prodigal son in the Bible when he was a child—there could always be resentments from those who'd been at home all along when a brother returned. It was possible they wouldn't like him barging into the family, changing the dynamics.

'They were. There was no resentment, no hostility, just pure happiness that I'd made it home.'

'Take your time over the decision,' Fitzgerald said as they ascended the stairs from the boxing club. 'There's no need to rush. I'm sure you and Lady Somersham will be happy wherever you decide to be, but you don't want to regret your choice.'

Ben was just about to open his mouth to reply when a smartly dressed man crossed the street towards them. Behind him trailed four well-built young men. He'd seen enough of the world to know trouble when it approached.

'Do you know them?' Fitzgerald asked in his ear.

'No.'

'I'd say you've upset someone.'

Ben would have to agree. The sombre expressions of the men didn't hint at good news.

'Mr Benjamin Crawford?' the smartly dressed man asked, looking from Ben to Fitzgerald and then back again.

'That's me.'

'If you would come with me, sir, no fuss.'

Ben felt the hairs on the back of his neck stand on end at the sense of déjà vu. He might not know this man's name or where he came from, but he was certain he was a magistrate.

'Who are you?' Ben asked, trying to work out what he'd done and coming up with nothing.

'Mr Francis Poole, magistrate and Member of Parliament.'

'And why should I go with you?' Ben asked. He wasn't about to flee, there was no point. If he was accused of something, they wouldn't let him get away. The magistrate probably had a few more men stationed at various points nearby. Ben was fast on his feet, but he knew when he was outnumbered.

'You have been accused of a heinous crime,' Mr Poole said, his eyes scrutinising Ben, as if trying to work out if he were facing off with a dangerous man.

The pieces all started to fall into place. 'By Lord Pottersdown, no doubt,' he murmured to Fitzgerald.

'I have the authority to take you into my custody and search your premises.'

'What is it I'm supposed to have done this time?' Ben asked. He felt uneasy. It didn't matter if he was guilty or innocent, that didn't seem to concern the system of law in England overly. Once you had been falsely convicted of a crime you didn't commit and sentenced to hard labour and transportation you lost faith in the justice system.

'Theft,' the magistrate said, motioning for two of the brawny men he'd brought with him to approach Ben.

'Unlikely,' Fitzgerald said calmly. 'The old man is destitute and in debt, he doesn't have anything worth stealing.'

'A search of your rooms will either prove your innocence or condemn you,' Mr Poole said.

'Lord Pottersdown has a habit of planting evidence,' Ben said calmly. Inside he didn't feel calm. Part of him wanted to run, to flee and find the first ship to take him from this country, but he knew it would be pointless.

This time he had to stay and fight, to clear his name and put a stop to Lord Pottersdown's ridiculous attempts to blacken his name.

With a rush of concern he thought about Francesca. She'd returned home alone to tell her family she wasn't going to be marrying Lord Huntley and would instead marry Ben. No doubt the news wouldn't go down well and Ben wondered if he should be concerned for Francesca's safety. Surely her father wouldn't harm her. He hadn't before, but the old man was desperate, believing he was about to lose his house and have his debts come crashing down around his shoulders. Silently Ben cursed himself for making the Viscount believe he would take the town house from him—no doubt it was that deception that had triggered the old man to think about retaliation.

'Go and find Francesca,' Ben instructed Fitzgerald. 'Make sure she's safe.'

'And you?'

'This isn't my first time in custody,' Ben said grimly.

'Take care, I'll be back as soon as I can.' Fitzgerald paused, looking at the magistrate. 'Where will you be holding Mr Crawford?'

'The cells at Giltspur Street Compter.'

'That's ridiculous,' Fitzgerald protested. 'He's not a common criminal.'

Ben shook his head ruefully. Cells were much the same wherever you were held. Dark, filthy and full of hungry rodents. If he had anything to do with it, he wouldn't be staying long so it didn't much matter.

Lord Pottersdown might have got away with falsely accusing him once, but he'd been a child then, helpless and naïve. Now he was a man of the world with nearly twenty years of experience of dealing with the most hardened of criminals. This time he would fight every step of the way.

'I'll come with you,' Ben said, giving one of the brawny men a hard look until he stepped a little further away.

'Good. We don't want any trouble,' Mr Poole said.

'Have you been a magistrate long?' Ben asked.

'A few years.'

'Then you should know when a story is a load of twaddle,' Ben said, shaking his head.

'Lord Pottersdown is a respected man…'

'He's a desperate man with more debt than either you or I can begin to imagine and a vendetta against me.'

'A vendetta?' Mr Poole asked mildly.

'I'm going to marry his daughter and he does not approve, and there was a little matter of a gambling debt he was unable to pay.'

Ben did not think it would help his case if he mentioned the man had falsely accused him before. The magistrate probably wouldn't look too kindly on the information that his suspect was a convicted criminal. For theft.

'And his daughter would be…?'

'Lady Somersham.'

'And she'll confirm all of this for you, will she?'

'Yes.'

'Then it sounds like you have nothing to worry about, Mr Crawford. If you would just come with me while we sort everything out.'

Ben walked alongside the magistrate, the brawny enforcers keeping a few paces behind, but looking ready to pounce if Ben as much as put one foot wrong.

'Is this your address?' Mr Poole asked as they stopped outside the building that contained his humble set of rooms.

'It is.'

'Shall we go up together?' Mr Poole suggested reasonably.

Ben used his key in the door and allowed the magistrate to ascend the stairs first, before he followed, closely trailed by the silent guards.

Inside Ben's rooms looked just as he'd left them a few hours earlier to go to his boxing club. At first sight nothing had been disturbed and for a moment he was filled with a hopeful relief that Lord Pottersdown hadn't managed to actually plant anything to back up his story of theft.

'Do you mind?' Mr Poole asked, motioning to the rooms.

Ben shook his head. The question was just a courtesy from a polite man. Whatever his answer the magistrate would still search his rooms, still pull the clothes from the wardrobe and throw over the bedclothes. That was his job and responsibility.

While the other men searched Ben sat in his chair and watched. He cursed himself time and time again for goading Francesca's father, for poking him like a sleeping bear with the threat of losing his London home. It had been unnecessary and indulgent and now had sparked a chain of events that Ben had very little control over. He just hoped Francesca was safe and could come to his aid as soon as possible.

If they believe her, the little voice in his head said. Quickly he tried to silence it. Francesca was a grown woman now, a respected member of society, not a ten-year-old girl. The magistrate would have to believe her.

'Could you tell me what these are, sir?' the magistrate asked, holding up a bag in one hand, a bound stack of books in the other.

'I don't know,' Ben said slowly. They weren't his and they certainly hadn't come with the rooms.

'Lord Pottersdown reported three very valuable books missing alongside some assorted items from the house.'

'He's run out of jewellery to plant,' Ben murmured. It was a sorry state if all you could find to plant in a man's house was a few books and a couple of almost worthless trinkets. 'I did not take these items,' he said louder, for the benefit of the magistrate.

'How do you explain them coming to be in your rooms?'

'Perhaps my fiancée left them behind,' Ben

said, trying not to let the frustration become apparent in his voice.

'Take him to the cells' Mr Poole instructed one of the men who'd accompanied them. 'I want to go and talk to Lady Somersham and see if we can get this mess sorted.'

The cell was dank and filthy and smelled of urine and decay. He wasn't the only one in it, two huddled figures sat in one corner, whispering softly to one another. Another man was closer to Ben, his broad face suspicious and nervous.

'Good afternoon, gentlemen,' Ben said as he settled with his back against the wall. 'Lovely day to be spending in prison.'

Three sets of eyes regarded him, trying to work out if he was a threat or someone to be exploited.

The damp walls, repulsive smells and less than salubrious company took him back the early days of his incarceration. He'd been kept in the county gaol cell until he'd been convicted, which hadn't been too bad, but after that he'd spent nearly two years incarcerated on a hulk ship moored on the Thames, awaiting transportation. It had been one of the grimmest periods of his life and he refused to go back there.

He had to believe Francesca would come through for him, that she would confirm her father's nefarious plan to wrongfully accuse Ben again and he would be released. Still, it sat heavily on him that once again he was having to rely on someone else to get him out.

For a moment he closed his eyes and thought of his father. He'd be devastated by the news that Ben had been arrested again, but no doubt he would come and fight for his son. Ben knew he was blessed to have a family as supportive as his and, sitting in the darkness, he knew he could never leave them behind again. Once this was over he would start making plans for a new life with Francesca, but he would also see if he could incorporate his family into that life too.

'What did you do?' the suspicious man asked, sidling closer.

'Nothing,' Ben answered with a grimace. 'I'm innocent, of course.'

The man laughed, a cackle that turned into a cough. 'Aren't we all?'

Chapter Twenty-One

Francesca slumped down against the door and felt the tears begin to flow. Until now she'd refused to cry, wanting to instead conserve her energy for more useful pursuits. She'd been determined to escape and had spent the last six hours clawing at the door, the window, the skirting, anything that might allow her to be out of this awful room and find her way to the man she loved.

There was a pit of dread in her stomach. She knew her father had something awful planned for Ben and she knew that, when faced with the word of a viscount or the word of a convicted criminal, the law would always side with her father. Even if it was obvious he was a lying scoundrel. It was just the way the world worked.

Despite her very best efforts, and with cracked and bleeding fingers, she just hadn't been able to find a way out. The house might be needing a coat or two of paint, but it was irritatingly well built.

Francesca wiped the tears from her cheeks and listened at the door. Her best hope was to wait until Felicity came home from her shopping trip with her friends and then shout as loud as she could and hope her sister could let her out before their father stopped her.

There was nothing, no sounds downstairs, no footfalls coming up towards her. Just a silent house.

Wishing she had never come home, she pictured Ben's face, heard him whisper the reassurances she needed to hear. One day soon this would be over and they would be together again, ready to start their new life together.

Francesca turned back to the door and started pulling at the lock again, trying to work her fingers underneath it. In the hours she'd been in here it had only budged a very small amount, but she would keep going until she came up with another plan. For a moment she paused, pressing her ear to the door and wondering if she heard voices downstairs somewhere, but the noises were too faint. Deciding she had nothing to lose, she shouted anyway.

'Help,' she screamed as loudly as she could.

'Help me.' She repeated it a few more times before falling silent to listen. The walls and doors were thick, but surely if someone was there they would hear her screams.

Francesca waited for a minute, then tried again, hearing her voice cracking as she screamed and shouted, this time pounding on the door with both her fists.

'Help me. Let me out.'

Again she waited and listened, but the house was completely still and silent. Feeling the tears spill on to her cheeks once more, Francesca turned back to the lock.

She was still in shock, unable to believe her father had treated her so poorly. She'd known he was a selfish and small-minded man, but until now she'd always made excuses for his cruel deeds, telling herself he'd done things out of desperation or only when his judgement was clouded by alcohol. Now she could see him for what he really was—a cruel and vindictive man only interested in self-preservation. She felt embarrassed by how she'd made excuses for him over the years, even by how she hadn't acknowledged properly the heinous way he'd treated Ben all those years ago.

'I'm sorry, my love,' she said, knowing that now the scales had truly fallen from her eyes.

Never again would she put her father above the man she loved, or above anyone else for that matter. He deserved everything that happened to him, for no doubt the weight of his debts would come crashing down very soon. All she needed to do was make sure she and her sister weren't present when that happened.

Sparing a thought for her mother, Francesca felt the sadness mount. Although they lived in the same house and had done ever since the death of Francesca's husband, she'd seen her mother only a handful of times. Instead of being a source of wisdom and affection, her mother hid away in her bedroom, unwilling to engage in the world, standing by while her daughters struggled.

Still, she didn't know what her mother had endured over the years. Perhaps the self-imposed isolation was her only way of dealing with it.

Deciding that no matter what happened she would do her very best to get as far away from this house and her cruel father as possible, Francesca renewed her efforts to escape. Ben needed her and it was time to put him first. It was time to stop worrying about how society would judge her for her actions and do whatever it took to save the man she loved.

* * *

Ben sat across a rickety wooden table and looked the magistrate in the eye. Something was wrong. Right about now Francesca should be here, explaining the connection between them and clearing his name. Instead there was just the magistrate and two well-built men who looked as though they were hoping for trouble.

'I am charging you with theft,' Mr Poole said as soon as he'd made himself comfortable. 'You will appear in court within the next two weeks.'

Ben shook his head, his vision momentarily going blurry. There was a tightness in his chest and a momentary feeling of helplessness.

It only lasted a few seconds, then he rallied. He wasn't a boy this time, wasn't an innocent who could be pushed around and manipulated by the powerful men.

'Have you spoken to my fiancée?' he asked.

'Lady Somersham?'

'Yes.'

He expected the magistrate to shake his head, to make some excuse about not being able to find her. That was the only explanation for this turn of events.

'Lady Somersham denied any connection between the two of you. She informed me that you had been childhood friends before your conviction for theft eighteen years ago and, since returning to England, had persisted in making a nuisance of yourself.'

'No,' Ben whispered, feeling as though he'd been punched in the gut. 'That's not possible.'

'It seems you have been spinning quite a fantasy, Mr Crawford. You almost had me believing you.'

Ben barely heard the magistrate's words—his blood was pounding in his ears and a grey mist descended over his vision. It just wasn't possible. They were setting him up. He didn't know if the magistrate was working with Lord Pottersdown or if Francesca's father had found a way to deceive him, but he knew Francesca would never betray him, not like this. She'd fought for him when she was just ten years old, she would fight for him now.

'No,' he said again. 'No, no, no, no, no.' Each utterance was a little louder than the last until he was shouting the word. One of the men the magistrate had brought with him pushed Ben back into his seat roughly, before he'd even realised he was standing.

'I shall see you at your trial,' Mr Poole said, exiting the room quickly now he'd said all he had to say.

Ben barely felt the rough hands that pulled

him to his feet and dragged him back to the filthy cell. He didn't hear the rasping of the key in the lock or the receding footfalls of the guards. All he could think about was Francesca's beautiful face, how she sounded when she laughed, the unruly mass of hair as it cascaded down her back.

He wanted to hold her, to feel her in his arms one more time, to smell the sweet honey scent of her hair and to feel the softness of her skin under his fingers.

'Ben.' Fitzgerald's familiar voice roused him from the fitful sleep he'd sunk into. Through the small grate on the door he saw his friend and wondered how much he'd had to bribe the guards to let him in.

The sound of the key in the lock lifted Ben's spirits momentarily, but when Fitzgerald stepped in, rather than the guard to let Ben out, the hope dissipated pretty quickly. He was alternating between wild despair and forced optimism, but right now he knew he needed to get a grip on himself and take control of the situation.

'It's not looking good,' Fitzgerald murmured as he embraced his friend. 'We might need to get you out of here another way.'

'I'm worried about Francesca,' Ben said, pacing backwards and forward.

'You need to worry about yourself.'

Ben gave a dismissive wave of his hand. It was true things weren't looking good for him, but he was a survivor. One way or another he would get out of here and be a free man again.

Fitzgerald fell silent for a few minutes. 'I haven't been able to find her,' he said slowly. 'I didn't want to worry you.'

'The magistrate says he's spoken to her, that she's confirmed her father's story.'

'But you don't believe him.'

'Francesca would never betray me.'

'Then her father has probably locked her away somewhere,' Fitzgerald said. 'The magistrate will not be reasoned with. He says he has the testimony of Lord Pottersdown and Lady Somersham and they both confirm that you've been loitering and making threats. So either the magistrate is crooked, or has been tricked by the Viscount.'

Ben shook his head in disbelief.

'The items found in your rooms would not be enough to convict you alone,' Fitzgerald said, 'but with a statement from Lord Pottersdown I think it will convince a judge.'

'And the fair and unbiased justice system steals another ten years of my life.'

Fitzgerald cleared his throat and Ben registered the unease in his friend's eyes.

'The noose?' Ben asked, involuntarily touching his neck.

'Perhaps. It is a second offence and no doubt Lord Pottersdown would be calling for the harshest punishment. You know the importance of connections in a case like this. The magistrate will probably roll over and do whatever the Viscount asks.'

'That old bastard took eight years of my life, he's not going to get the rest of it.'

'I won't let that happen,' Fitzgerald said grimly. 'There are a couple of guards susceptible to a bribe. If we move fast, I think we could have you out of here tonight and on a ship for France at first light.'

'My cellmates inform me they don't check the cells between midnight and dawn,' Ben said.

'Then that will be the best time to move. Be ready.'

'I can't go without Francesca,' Ben said. He wouldn't leave her behind, wouldn't get on that ship without the woman he loved.

'You might have to,' Fitzgerald said grimly. 'I can always find her and send her on at a later date, but you will have people at your heels. You know how they don't like to lose a prisoner.'

'I can't go without her,' Ben repeated. He was imagining the worst, of Francesca scared and alone, locked in a dark room thinking that everyone had forgotten her. Once before he'd been forced to leave her in England—he wouldn't do it again.

'I'll see what I can do.'

'Thank you,' Ben said, embracing Fitzgerald.

'We'll get you out of here. In a couple of years' time we'll be sitting on the veranda at home laughing about this.'

Ben wasn't so sure. He had no doubt he would escape. The guards were underpaid and slow and Fitzgerald was a cunning man with a deep purse. Perhaps in a few years, once he and Francesca had managed to establish a life for themselves in Australia, he would feel less anger and hatred towards the man who was trying to steal his life for the second time, but he wasn't so sure.

'Keep your head down until tonight,' Fitzgerald said, banging on the door of the cell to let the guard know he was done.

As the heavy door closed behind his friend Ben slumped against the wall. He'd be leaving England once again as a criminal, even though neither time had he done anything wrong. Only on this occasion he'd also be an outlaw, a wanted man, no longer welcome in the country where his family resided.

It would devastate his father and Ben felt a new surge of anger at the thought of once again being wrenched away.

Chapter Twenty-Two

A soft noise from outside the door made Francesca sit up. She pressed her eye against the keyhole to see if it was someone who might help her in her attempt to escape or if it were her father. She'd been locked in the room for over eight hours and outside it was already dark. Perhaps her father had come to his senses and would let her out, let her leave to check Ben wasn't harmed by whatever scheme her father had planned.

'Felicity,' Francesca almost sobbed as her sister opened the door.

'Shh,' her sister warned, indicating the stairs. 'I had to wait for Father to fall asleep to get the key, but he's only dozing so keep quiet.'

Francesca embraced her sister.

'You need to go,' Felicity said, her face screwed up with worry. 'I'm not sure entirely what happened earlier, but Father had one of the maids dressed up and impersonating you to some man who'd called round. I only returned home when he was leaving, but it seemed very strange.'

'Impersonating me?' Francesca asked, wondering if her father had gone completely mad finally.

'I got the impression he was a magistrate,' Felicity said.

Understanding began to dawn. Although she didn't know the details of what her father had planned for Ben, she realised she'd been locked away so she couldn't let the truth out to the magistrate when he came calling. Her father's word would not be disputed and once again it would be enough to condemn Ben.

'Thank you,' Francesca said, giving her sister one last hug before she turned and hurried to the stairs.

'Good luck,' Felicity whispered.

Francesca dashed downstairs, grabbed her cloak, quietly opened the door and ran out into the street. She had a small amount of money on her, enough to find an empty hackney carriage and instruct the coachman to take her to Ben's lodgings. Throughout the journey she felt a mixture of nerves and anger. She didn't know what she would find, if anything, when she got there, but she had the feeling it wasn't going to be anything good. Her father had surpassed himself this time in his attempts to ruin as many people's lives as possible.

The rooms were dark with no sign of a candle burning behind the curtains, but Francesca hammered on the door all the same. It was opened almost immediately by a severe-looking woman who ushered Francesca inside and closed the door quietly behind her.

'What do you want?' the woman asked, looking Francesca up and down with irritation.

'I'm looking for Mr Crawford,' she said.

'You and half of the magistrates in London,' the woman grumbled. 'This is a respectable establishment with a good reputation, or it was before one of my rooms was ransacked and a guest dragged out in chains.'

Francesca knew the woman was exaggerating, but felt the panic well up inside her.

'Where have they taken him?' she asked.

'And he still owes this month's rent.'

'Where have they taken him?' Francesca repeated.

'Prison. To await trial, no doubt. Apparently he's a thief. Stole from some hoity-toity lord.'

'Which prison?' Francesca asked, her patience wearing thin.

'How am I supposed to know?'

Without another word Francesca turned and reached for the door handle.

'Giltspur Street Compter,' a soft voice called out as Francesca opened the door.

'Quiet,' the severe-looking woman said, shushing the young maid.

'Mr Crawford was a good man,' the maid said defiantly. 'He'll likely have been taken to the Giltspur Street Compter, that's the closest.'

'Thank you,' Francesca said, giving a nod of gratitude to the young maid.

'Good luck.'

She was out through the door and rushing back towards the carriage within seconds and instructed the coachman to take her to the prison.

Pacing up and down the small room, Francesca tried not to panic. The walls were dank and the smell from the cells wafted in through the open window when the wind blew in the right direction. When that happened she felt nauseous and wondered how the men coped being kept in such foul conditions.

She had arrived at the prison a little over half

an hour ago and demanded to see Ben. There had been a scuffle among the guards as they realised they were talking to a lady of wealth and influence, but eventually someone had agreed to fetch the prison warden who in turn had listened to her story and sent a guard to find the magistrate.

Now she waited, wondering how Ben was coping being locked up in a place like this again. He was a strong man, with reserves that even he wasn't aware of, but being falsely accused of a crime he didn't commit again, and being taken to a place like this, must be dredging up some painful memories.

'Good evening,' a tall thin man said as he entered the room. 'I'm Mr Poole.'

'Good evening, Mr Poole. I'm Lady Somersham.' She noted the look of confusion that crossed his face, but pressed on. 'I think there has been some mix up with Mr Crawford. I understand he has been accused of stealing from my father.'

'Forgive me, Lady Somersham, but I am finding it a little difficult to take this all in. I met a Lady Somersham, a Lady Francesca Somersham, at Lord Pottersdown's house earlier today.'

'You met an imposter,' Francesca said. She

wondered if he would believe her, wondered if he would dismiss her as the imposter instead, but was relieved to see understanding dawning on his face.

'An imposter?' he asked.

Francesca wondered who he had used. Perhaps Lilly the maid, who might be able to fit into Francesca's clothes, but her speech was pure working class.

'My father locked me in an empty servant's room this morning and kept me there ever since. I assume he paid someone to pretend to be me when you visited.'

'Is that so?' Mr Poole asked. 'And why would an upstanding gentleman like Lord Pottersdown do that?'

Francesca tried not to snort. Upstanding was not a word she'd used to describe her father for a very long time.

'Mr Crawford played a game of cards against my father. He won and my father could not honour the wager between them. Knowing of Mr Crawford's lower station in life, he thought to save himself the humiliation of losing his house to pay the debt by accusing Mr Crawford of stealing some items.'

'I'm finding it hard to believe…'

'That a man of his station would sink so

low?' Francesca asked, shaking her head. 'He has the most to lose.'

'I understand you have a close personal relationship with Mr Crawford.'

'I do. We are engaged to be married.'

'And do you know anything of Mr Crawford's villainous past?'

Francesca laughed grimly, 'Of course, if you could call it that. Again my father planted evidence and accused Mr Crawford of stealing from him, when in fact nothing had been taken.'

'There was evidence, I understand.'

'A locket. My locket. That I'd given him as a token of our friendship.'

Mr Poole leaned back in his chair and laced his fingers together as if contemplating the information Francesca had provided.

'You want me to believe that Mr Crawford has been set up, twice, to be accused of crimes he did not commit, by your own father.'

'It's the truth.'

Francesca could see some small part of the magistrate believed her. There must have been something he hadn't been happy with during his investigation, some doubt that niggled at him.

'I need to look into one or two things,' he said. 'Would you care to wait, Lady Somersham?'

'Of course.'

'I'll see about having some refreshment sent up.'

Mr Poole stood and made his way to the door, pausing before he opened it.

'You understand these are serious allegations against your father,' he said quietly.

'I understand.'

Francesca knew that, although bearing false testimony was a crime, her father would never have to stand up in court and answer for his actions. He was too well protected by his title and the family name.

She waited for well over an hour, wondering exactly what Mr Poole was doing with the time and hoping that he was astute enough to uncover the truth now he had more of the facts available to him. A guard with questionable personal hygiene brought her a dirty cup of water which Francesca smiled her thanks for, then left untouched on the small table. Even if it had been the finest wine she wouldn't have been able to touch it, her stomach was roiling inside her as she wondered what the next few hours would bring.

When the door opened again she felt a mixture of hope and dread as she saw Mr Poole enter.

'Thank you for your patience, Lady Somersham,' he said, 'I would like to extend my apologies for taking so long to verify your story. I hope you understand my need to check all the facts.'

'Of course,' Francesca murmured.

'I have spoken to your father…' Mr Poole grimaced '…or attempted to. He was a little the worse for wear.'

Francesca held her breath in the hope that in his drunken stupor her father had revealed the extent of his crimes against Ben.

'And I spoke to various members of your household. Their accounts have led me to believe that Mr Crawford was charged in error.'

Francesca felt the relief crash over her at his words.

'I have asked a guard to bring Mr Crawford up here and I will arrange the necessary documents for his release.'

'Thank you,' Francesca said quietly, knowing that Mr Poole had been more than conscientious. Many magistrates did not bother investigating the crimes they were supposed to look into, instead enjoying the privileges of the title without doing any real work. They were lucky that Mr Poole seemed to take his job seriously and wanted to see justice, not just make his own life easy.

'I am sorry for any inconvenience caused.'

'Thank you,' she repeated again.

Feeling her heart pound in her chest as the door opened, she watched as the warden entered the room and whispered in the magistrate's ear. She peered out into the darkness, half-expecting to see Ben in the shadows, waiting to be escorted into the room, but there were just two nervous-looking guards.

'What do you mean you can't find him?' the magistrate asked quietly, but not so quietly Francesca didn't hear every word.

'It would seem…er…that the prisoner has escaped.'

Francesca frowned. She was pretty certain they were talking about Ben.

'Where is Mr Crawford?' she asked in her haughtiest voice. Sometimes the years of mixing with only the most entitled people became useful, now she was a woman not to be refused an answer.

'Have you checked everywhere?' the magistrate asked.

'Yes, sir, everywhere. Twice.'

'Lady Somersham,' the magistrate said, 'it

would appear your fiancé has escaped from prison.'

'Shall I send out the hue and cry? Gather the guards for a manhunt?' the warden said, a gleam of excitement replacing the embarrassment that had been in his eyes.

Mr Poole considered for a moment.

'For an innocent man?' Francesca interjected quickly.

'A man who has escaped our custody,' the magistrate corrected her.

'A man you were just about to release,' she shot back.

'Stand your men down,' Mr Poole said after a long pause. 'Mr Crawford is no longer under arrest. Although I would like to speak to him,' he said, directing his last comment at Francesca. 'Please ask him to present himself so we can get this mattered cleared up for good.'

Francesca nodded, knowing persuading Ben to voluntarily step into a room with anyone official would be a hard task. He was probably booking a passage back to Australia right now, eager to leave the country that had nearly falsely convicted him for a second time.

'I will take my leave, gentlemen,' Francesca said, feeling a mounting panic. She didn't know where to find Ben, but she did know she only had a limited time. He would still think he was a wanted man, a man who had to flee the country immediately. She knew he wouldn't want to leave her behind, but he might not have a choice.

Chapter Twenty-Three

Ben paced across the drawing room, covering the space within five seconds before turning back and heading in the opposite direction.

'You boys and your dramas,' Lady Winston murmured from her position on the sofa.

After escaping the prison in the dead of night he'd been whisked away by Fitzgerald to his aunt's house, with his friend reasoning that the connection with Lady Winston would not be known by the warden or magistrate, and in any case they would think twice about storming into the house of a woman of his aunt's status.

'I need to go to her. I need to find her,' Ben said. Ever since his escape he hadn't been able to think of anything but Francesca.

'You need to lay low until the ship sails at dawn,' Fitzgerald said.

'The boy isn't going to go without his love,'

Lady Winston said, directing an admonishing glance at her nephew. 'So you might as well stop trying to persuade him and find Lady Somersham.'

'If they catch you…' Fitzgerald said.

'They won't catch me. They probably don't even know I've escaped. They had no reason to check the cells.'

'Where might she be?' Fitzgerald asked, bowing to the pressure to stop trying to persuade Ben to leave with or without Francesca.

'There hasn't been enough time for her father to take her to the country, so he's most likely got her locked up in his town house somewhere.'

'You want to pay him a visit?'

'I can't see any other way,' Ben said, knowing it might result in him being captured, but unable to think of another way to get Francesca.

'You're mad,' Fitzgerald murmured.

'Are you coming?'

'Of course I'm coming. I'm not going to let you roam the streets on your own, you lovesick fool.'

Lady Winston cackled and smacked her hand on the arm of the chair. 'Wonderful. You go get your girl. And don't get caught.'

Ben gave a nod, then strode from the room,

not needing to turn to know Fitzgerald was right there beside him.

Lord Pottersdown's town house was only a few streets away, but they took the carriage all the same just in case they needed to make a speedy exit. Ben sat flicking the curtain back and peering out of the window, all the time hoping to catch a glimpse of Francesca, even though he knew she had no reason to be wandering the streets.

'So I take it you'll be returning to Australia, then?' Fitzgerald asked as they weaved through the empty streets.

'My hand has been forced,' Ben murmured. He hadn't been able to decide where he had wanted to build his life with Francesca. In Australia he had his home, his farms, his livelihood and his friends, but in England he had his family. Now it looked as though that decision had been taken from him. Even if he somehow managed to clear his name, he wouldn't be able to stay here. Twice he'd been arrested for crimes he didn't commit. He wouldn't ever be able to live a life here without always looking over his shoulder, without wondering when he might next be hauled in by a magistrate.

'Perhaps it is for the best,' Fitzgerald said. 'A new start for you and Francesca.'

Ben nodded. It might be easier for Francesca away from the eyes of society. They could be together without the judgement of the people she had spent her life socialising with. This way they would be free to build their life together without worrying what anyone else thought.

Before Ben could answer, they pulled up outside Lord Pottersdown's town house and both men looked out uneasily.

'How are we going to do this?' Fitzgerald asked.

'Storm the house, find Francesca, get her out and make a dash for the docks.'

'You make it sound so simple.'

Ben shrugged. He didn't know what they would do if Francesca wasn't being kept somewhere in the house.

'Let's go.'

They jumped down from the carriage and approached the door, Fitzgerald knocking and Ben standing to one side so he wouldn't immediately be seen by whoever answered the door.

A maid opened the door, peering out through a little crack, and giving Fitzgerald a suspicious look.

'Mr George Fitzgerald,' he said, holding out a card, 'Sorry about the late hour, but I had a message from Lord Pottersdown.'

The maid opened the door a little wider to accept the card and at that moment Ben stepped forward, planting his foot in the way of the door so it couldn't be closed.

'Good evening,' he said, slipping inside before the maid even had chance to blink.

'Quiet,' a woman's voice hissed from the end of the hallway. For a moment Ben thought it might be Francesca and his heart soared, but then he realised the silhouette was too petite, the voice not quite the right tone.

'Where's Francesca?' he demanded, watching as Felicity hurried forward and closed the door behind them, dismissing the maid with a scowl.

'Isn't she with you?' she asked, sending a bolt of dread through Ben's stomach. 'Father locked her up in one of the upstairs rooms. I let her out when he passed out a couple of hours ago. She left to go and tell the magistrate the charges against you were false.'

There was a loud snore from one of the downstairs rooms and they all jumped, but the snores continued and Ben cautiously stepped forward to peer in the room. Lord Pottersdown was fast asleep, his head lolling back at an uncomfortable angle. Quietly Ben closed the door, holding the handle to minimise the click.

'I need to find her,' Ben said, feeling increasingly desperate with each passing minute.

'Did they release you before she arrived?' Felicity asked.

'They didn't release him,' Fitzgerald explained, watching Ben closely as he prowled up and down the hallway.

'You escaped?'

'I've had dealings with the English justice system before,' Ben said. 'I wasn't going to put my faith in it a second time.' He paused, then made a decision. 'We need to trace the route between here and the prison. Francesca has to be somewhere on it.'

'I hope you find her,' Felicity said, a sad little smile on her face. Ben realised that the woman in front of him knew she might never see her sister again, but she still wanted him to succeed none the less. 'I'll stay here and keep Father distracted if he wakes up.'

'Thank you.'

Francesca felt as though time was running out. She'd first checked Ben's rooms, but of course he hadn't been foolish enough to return there after his escape from prison. Next she'd headed for Lady Winston's town house, knowing Ben might have sought refuge with the aunt of his friend. Lady Winston had flung open the door herself when Francesca had knocked and quickly sent her on, telling her that Ben had gone to find her at her father's house. Now she was nearly back to where she had started, but was dreading what she might find if her father had woken to find Ben barging into the house.

Just as she rounded the corner into her street, she saw a familiar silhouette bounding down the steps in front of her father's house. Inside her chest her heart skipped a beat and she felt a rush of relief suffusing through her.

'Ben,' she called, not caring it was the middle of the night and they might wake the neighbours.

She watched as he turned and looked at her, watched as the smile of relief lit up his face. Francesca broke out into a run, her feet sliding across the damp paving stones, and flung herself into the arms of the man she loved.

'Frannie,' he murmured into her hair, kissing her again and again wherever his lips could find skin.

'I thought I'd lost you,' she said. 'Again.'

'Never.'

'I was so scared. I can't believe what Father did to you.' Even as she said the words she realised it wasn't true. For so long she'd been making excuses for her father, but the reality was he was a cruel and heartless man who only cared for his own needs. 'How did you get out of prison? I went there and they checked the cells and you weren't anywhere to be found.'

'I escaped,' he said. 'I wasn't going to wait for the law to condemn me again.'

'I'm so sorry I couldn't come sooner. Father locked me up in one of the upstairs rooms. Felicity released me, but only once Father had passed out. I came to find you as soon as I was able.'

'I know,' he murmured, bending down and cutting off her sentence with a long kiss. She felt all the panic and stress of the last twelve hours begin to melt away. 'We will have time to pick apart what happened once we're on the ship, but right now I'm a wanted man. We should leave.'

Francesca shook her head, smiling at the man she loved. 'It's all explained,' she said quietly, taking his hand in hers. 'I told the magistrate everything—how Father lied and planted the items you were meant to have stolen, how he owed you a lot of money with the gambling debt. He believed me and has decided not to pursue any of the charges against you.'

Ben looked at her with astonishment for a moment.

'They're not chasing you. The magistrate asked if I would bring you to him to sort out the formalities, but you're a free man.'

With one hand, he stroked her cheek, 'I love you, Frannie,' he said softly, 'But I think you've been duped. Magistrates don't just drop charges on a woman's word.'

'He listened to me, looked into the things I was saying and he believed me.'

'I can't risk it,' Ben said, glancing at Fitzgerald. Francesca saw his friend shake his head out of the corner of his eye. 'There is a ship sailing in two hours. We'll be in France before they even have chance to mount a proper search for me.'

'There isn't going to be a search,' Francesca said. 'We can stay here, there's no need to flee.'

Ben shrugged, 'Perhaps not. Perhaps you found the one magistrate in England who believes in the law and doing the right thing, but I'm not prepared to risk my life on it. If they catch me, Frannie, it might be the noose.'

She fell silent. She understood his concerns. Eighteen years ago he'd been innocent as well, but that hadn't saved him from an eight year sentence, transportation to one of the harshest countries on earth and the end of his life in England. Still, they didn't have to leave everything behind this time. The magistrate had *assured* her he would drop the charges against Ben. They could stay in England at least for a while, work out how they wanted to live their lives.

'Come on,' he said, gripping her hand.

'I can't just leave,' she said.

'Of course you can.'

'My family…'

He looked at her with disbelief. 'The family that locked you up and tried to have me hanged for theft?'

'I can't excuse my father,' she said, 'but I can't just leave them like this, without saying goodbye, without making sure they will survive.'

'I'm leaving, Frannie. I'm sailing for France and then on to Australia.'

She shook her head. Part of her wanted to take his hand and go with him without any further protest, but she knew there was no need to run.

'We can stay here, make a life for ourselves,' she said. It wasn't that she was averse to the idea of living in Australia—it was just everything she knew was here. In England she knew how to live, how to socialise. Surely she would flounder elsewhere?

'Are you still worrying what people will think of you?' Ben asked with exasperation in his voice. 'If you leave, are you worried that your family will sink under their debts and the family name be dragged through the mud?'

'Of course I'm worried about my family,' she said, a little sharper than she'd intended.

'But are you worried about your family, or are you worried about how it will look when the scandal breaks? Damn it, Frannie, none of that matters.'

She shook her head. She knew none of that mattered, but she still couldn't quite bring herself to leave everything behind.

'Perhaps it's me you're ashamed of,' he said quietly. 'If you marry me you won't have a title, you'll just be the wife of an ex-convict.'

'I don't care about the title,' she said. 'And you are a finer man than any duke or earl.'

'Think about what you want,' he said, some of the harshness fading from his voice. 'Do you want status and a place in society, or do you want a simple life with a man who loves you?'

Ben watched as she turned away, walking back towards the house, and he felt his heart break in two. He had never thought she would actually choose to stay in England. He understood it would be difficult for her to leave her family, he'd had first-hand experience of having to do just that, but he thought she would do it for him.

'We have to go,' Fitzgerald said quietly. 'The ship…'

Ben nodded, but didn't move. He couldn't leave without her. Once they'd been ripped apart and it had been the hardest time of his life. Eighteen years he'd tried to live without her and hadn't succeeded, and, now he knew her intimately, he couldn't imagine his life without her.

'Frannie,' he called out, his voice sounding pleading even to his own ears. She was already up the steps and inside the house.

'You can't miss that ship,' Fitzgerald said, manoeuvring Ben closer to the carriage.

He pictured her face, the way her eyes lit up when she smiled, the softness of her lips and the unruly hair that tumbled around her shoulders. Even though it hurt so much to see her walk away, he *had* to try one last time to persuade her to come with him.

Quickly he darted forward, bounding up the steps and striding in through the door. Inside he came to an abrupt halt. Francesca was standing there embracing her sister, both women crying softly.

'Go, you fool,' Felicity said, giving Francesca an encouraging smile.

'Frannie,' Ben asked, hardly daring to hope. 'I thought…?'

'I lost you once,' she said, her face serious. 'I'm never losing you again.'

He reached forward for her, pulling her close to his chest and kissing her deeply. Ben felt like singing, like shouting with joy from the rooftops.

'I might not agree with how you want to leave the country,' Francesca said, 'but I will go to the ends of the earth with you rather than have to spend time without you ever again.'

'And your family?'

'Leave them to me,' Felicity said grimly.

'Felicity…'

'You need to stop worrying about me,' Felicity said to her sister. 'I'm not a child any more.'

'You can't stay here…'

'I'm not planning to, not long term. I have arranged a position as a governess. In Devon.'

Ben felt his eyebrows raise in surprise. It was a bold move for the daughter of a viscount.

'And in the meantime?' Francesca asked.

'I've been placating Father for a long time,'

Felicity said. 'I'm sure I can sidestep his rage for a few more weeks.'

'Perhaps I could suggest an alternative,' Fitzgerald said. 'My aunt is always bemoaning the lack of company. I'm sure she would be pleased to have you stay until things are a little more settled.'

Felicity only took a moment to consider, nodding her head to the suggestion and seeming not to mind she would be leaving with only the clothes on her back for now.

'Good, that's sorted. Now we need to get you to that ship.'

Ben gripped Francesca's hand. He felt a surge of hope for the future. This wasn't quite how he imagined leaving England, but what really mattered was the time he'd spent here. The wonderful days with his family, getting to know them again and realising how much they cared, how much they had always cared. Perhaps one day he might return—if Francesca was right about the magistrate believing her, then in a few years they might be able to come back for another visit. Or maybe he would persuade his family to make the trip to Australia.

Then there was the woman standing beside him. Francesca. His Frannie. He would traverse the world a thousand times to find her.

He waited as she glanced back over her shoulder, expecting to see sadness in her eyes as she turned around, but instead there was a glimmer of anticipation.

'I love you, Frannie,' Ben murmured, realising that he had everything he wanted standing right beside him. Wherever they were in the world it didn't matter, as long as they had each other. 'We will build a new life together,' he murmured. 'A family of our own.'

Epilogue

Ben stood hand in hand with Francesca, watching the big ship come in to the bay. Three days they'd made the journey down to the port area, knowing it would be soon that the ship carrying Ben's family would arrive, but not knowing the exact date. Today they'd been in luck, with the tall masts in view even as the sun rose over the shimmering sea.

'I can't believe we're all going to be together,' Ben said, shading his eyes as he watched the ship's slow progress.

It was like a dream come true. For three months he and Francesca had been back in Australia. He'd loved showing her the land he now thought of as home, the rich fields, the vast expanses of farmland, and further afield the hazy blue mountains and beaches framed by long stretches of golden sand. They were happy here. Francesca had slipped easily into the role of an Australian landowner's wife and most days would ride out with him to solve the problems in the furthest corners of his land and to keep the farms ticking over. He could see she didn't miss the world of London society, the balls and the expectations to always be presented perfectly with impeccable manners. Here things were different. You were respected for your hard work and self-made success, not a title inherited from a grandfather.

'I wonder how they found the voyage?' Francesca murmured, watching the ship as it neared. Now they could see the tiny figures racing about the deck as the sailors prepared the vessel to dock.

He and Francesca had made that same voyage, setting out a year ago. The long months on board had flown by, a much different experience than the first time he'd sailed from England to Australia when each day on the transport ship had seemed like an eternity. With Francesca by his side the voyage across the world had been enjoyable.

'Come with me,' Ben said, taking her hand. It would still be over an hour until the ship had safely anchored and the unloading of the passengers would begin. Although he was eager to see his father and brothers, Ben had a different motive for bringing Francesca out here today.

They wandered through the streets of the settlement. It had changed in the time Ben had been away, becoming more organised, more permanent. It was as though the people of Australia realised they were here to stay and were finally building something more solid than the camps that had welcomed them when he and Sam Robertson had first arrived nearly twenty years ago. Despite this it was still small, still a town you could walk through without needing to stop and take refreshments even in the heat of the summer. They climbed a small hill and once they were at the top Ben pointed to the land in the distance.

'See that there,' he said, indicating the wild area between the settlement and the hazy blue mountains in the distance. 'I've put in an offer for five thousand acres.'

'Five thousand…' She shook her head with a small smile on her face. Even after the months she'd spent in Australia she still seemed surprised at the vast areas of land available to be farmed.

'I thought I would gift it to my father and brothers, let them have some land of their own to manage.'

'That's very generous,' Francesca said.

It was the least he could do. Ben still couldn't believe his father and both his brothers had given up their lives in England to come join them out here in Australia. In fact, they'd jumped at the chance. Ben had sold Australia as a land of opportunity and he knew his brothers were eager to see what they could make of themselves in this fledging country. His father was just pleased to have all the family together for the future.

'When Mr Fitzgerald gave me my first parcel of land on my eighteenth birthday it was a wonderful feeling. Like someone believed in me. He wasn't asking me to work for him, to report to him, he was trusting me to make a success on my own.'

'And you want to give that to your brothers.'

Ben nodded. He turned slightly so they were looking at a stretch of land to the west.

'That area there is for sale, too, although I'll have to get in before Robertson claims it,' Ben said. The land in question was a strip between where his farms started and his friend's land ended. They both would enjoy being direct neighbours, whoever owned the land. 'I thought I might put in a bid for it. For the future.' He looked pointedly down at Francesca's midsection and she bit her lip.

Slowly her belly was beginning to swell. When she'd first tentatively mentioned she thought she might be pregnant neither had dared to hope. Francesca had been married for such a long time to Lord Somersham with no sign of a pregnancy, she'd long ago resigned herself to the fact that she couldn't have children. They'd discussed it before their wedding and Ben had assured her he did not mind. That had been the truth—he'd rather have Francesca even with no hope of children than a future without the woman he loved. However, when she'd missed her monthly courses not just once, but three times, and when she'd started finding certain smells utterly nauseating, Ben had begun to hope.

Just last week a doctor had confirmed the pregnancy, putting her about four months along.

'I still can't believe it,' Francesca said, her face lighting up as she thought of their unborn child. Only a few months ago Robertson and his new wife, Georgina, had given birth to a beautiful baby girl. Francesca visited at least once a week and Ben had seen the longing in her eyes every time she came home. Now, they were going to be blessed themselves.

'Is this how you ever envisaged your life?' Ben asked.

Francesca shook her head. 'A little over a year ago I was resigned to a miserable marriage to Lord Huntley and a life of dull domesticity.'

'Do you ever regret it?' He often wondered. For him he had just returned to his old life, with the added bonus of the woman he loved by his side. Francesca had given up so much more.

She turned to him and stepped closer, reaching out for his hand.

'Not for even a single second.'

Ben grinned. Only a certain type of woman would be suited to the rough and adventurous life Australia offered, but Francesca had loved every minute of it. He felt like the most blessed man in the world. He had a collection of successful farms, his family arriving to start their lives out here and the woman he loved to share each wonderful moment with. And soon they would have the only thing they'd never even hoped to wish for, a child to complete their family.

'Good. The voyage is too far to take you back to England.'

Playfully Francesca punched him on the arm, giggling as he caught her wrists and swung her round to kiss him. Then, arm in arm, they started off back down the hill to watch the progress of the ship bringing Ben's family as it made its way into Sydney Cove.

* * * * *

MILLS & BOON

Coming next month

THE BROODING DUKE OF DANFORTH
Christine Merrill

'You spent more time talking to my father than you ever did to me. The day of the wedding arrived and I realised that I had not seen you since the day you made the offer. But my father had spoken to you at least a dozen times.'

'We share a club,' Benedict said absently.

'And we were to share a bed,' she snapped.

For the first time since Abigail had met him, the façade of perpetual ennui disappeared and she saw real emotion on his face. His eyes darkened to the deep green of the sea in a storm and his lips parted in a smile that had nothing to do with mirth. Then, he moved closer until she could feel the heat of his body through the air between them. 'Yes, Miss Prescott, after our wedding, I would have taken you to my bed. But a meeting of bodies is one thing and a meeting of minds is quite another. I had hoped that, after some time together, the latter would develop from the former.'

'And I hoped quite the opposite,' she said, surprised. 'It cannot be possible to enjoy the marital act with a complete stranger.'

In response, he laughed. And something deep inside her trembled in answer to the sound. 'Would you care to wager on the fact?'

'It is likely different for men,' she added, taking a

steadying breath to counter the odd sensations that the question evoked.

'In a way, perhaps.' He placed a hand on the wall beside her head and leaned even closer, until she felt his breath at each word. 'In my experience, it matters little whether the woman is a friend or a stranger. But for a woman?'

His voice grew soft until it was barely more than a whisper. And against all modesty, she leaned closer to him, so she would not miss a word.

'The pleasure of the act has much to do with the skill of the partner. I can assure you, Miss Prescott, you would have had nothing to worry about.'

Then he reached for her. And without another thought she closed her eyes and waited for his kiss.

Continue reading
THE BROODING DUKE OF DANFORTH
Christine Merrill

Available next month
www.millsandboon.co.uk

COMING SOON!

We really hope you enjoyed reading this book. If you're looking for more romance, be sure to head to the shops when new books are available on

Thursday 30th May

LET'S TALK
Romance

For exclusive extracts, competitions
and special offers, find us online:

- facebook.com/millsandboon
- @MillsandBoon
- @MillsandBoonUK

Get in touch on 01413 063232

For all the latest titles coming soon, visit
millsandboon.co.uk/nextmonth